UNDER DARKNESS
(A SCI-FI THRILLER)
(2nd Edition)

by Jasper T. Scott

JasperTscott.com
@JasperTscott

Cover Art by Tom Edwards
TomEdwardsDesign.com

AUTHOR'S CONTENT RATING: 14A

Language: Moderate
Sexual Content: Mild
Violence: Moderate

Author's Guarantee: If you find anything you consider inappropriate for this rating, please e-mail me at JasperTscott@gmail.com and I will either remove the content or change the rating accordingly.

ACKNOWLEDGMENTS

When I started this career, I started out with a team of one—me. The sheer lack of polish showed, and I had to publish seven different editions to subsequently erase all of the typos and other problems. Today, I'm proud to say I have a team of dozens, of whom at least twenty provide meaningful feedback for each and every novel I write. Needless to say, they save me a lot of embarrassment! My editors, Aaron Sikes and Dave Cantrell are the ones who catch the bulk of my mistakes, and I owe them a big thank you as usual. Another thank you goes to Ian Jedlica, my proofreader, who has eyes like a hawk! And then there are all those advance readers who wade through my rough drafts to find the diamonds within. A big thank you goes to B. Allen Thobois, Dara McLain, Dave Topan, Davis Shellabarger, George Dixon, Gerald Geddings, Harry Huyler, Jackie Gartside, John Williams, Karol Ross, Kenny Harvey, Mary Kastle, Michael Madsen, Paul Burch, Raymond Burt, Rose Getch, and William Schmidt. You are my heroes.

Finally, many thanks to the Muse.

To those who dare,
And to those who dream.
To everyone who's stronger than they seem.
—Jasper Scott

*"Believe in me / I know you've waited for so long /
Believe in me / Sometimes the weak become the strong."*
—STAIND, Believe

DRAMATIS PERSONAE

Main Characters

Bill Steele
Beth Steele
Don Hale
Doctor Ashley Carter
Corporal Gibson
Commander Wilde

Secondary Characters

<u>Navy and Marines</u>
Captain Arthur Reed
Commander Michael Morris
Corporal Lee
Lieutenant Spooner
Private Dekker "Deks"
Private Clarke
Private Kelly

<u>Tourists</u>
James
Kayla
Alison

Michael
Melanie
Paul
Allen
Avery Walsh

<u>Hotel Staff</u>
Jenna Jones
Hanna Kahele
Akela Smith
Toby White
Eric Monte
Sean

Minor Characters

Sarah Hale
Principal Kalani
Director Coben
Sergeant Colton
Admiral Harris
Lieutenant Peterson
Chief Petty Officer Miller
Corpsman Diaz
Corpsman Reese

PART 1 - THE ECLIPSE

CHAPTER 1

A dripping, red-faced, blond-haired tourist in a green Hawaiian shirt stormed through the lobby like a crusader.

Bill Steele saw him coming, and interrupted his conversation with his resort manager, Eric Monte, to head off the angry tourist before he could reach the front desk.

"Aloha. May I help you with something?" Bill asked.

"Yes. My wife and our sons just came back from the beach covered in sand and salt water. When we got back to our room and turned on the shower, the water was shit brown, and smelled like it, too. My wife would be down here screaming at you, but she's covered in shit-water and crying in the tub."

A phone rang in the background, and Bill heard Sean, the day clerk, answer it. "Aloha! Koa Kai Resort, front desk speaking. How can I help you? ... You want to cancel your reservation? No, no charge. What name is it under? Uh-huh. Yep, I've got it. All... Wait! Before you go, I'm supposed to ask why you want to cancel your stay with us... Ah, right, I get you... uh huh."

"Hello!" Angry Tourist waved his hand in front of Bill's face, drawing his attention away from Sean's bumbling phone call. "Are you even listening to me?"

Bill blinked and nodded. "Of course, sir. I am very sorry for your inconvenience."

"Inconvenience!" Angry Tourist thundered. His cheeks bulged, and his sunburned face turned an even deeper shade of red.

Bill struggled to remember the man's name, but there wasn't enough space in his addled brain to remember all of his guests' names. "I assure you we're working as fast as we can to resolve the problem. In the meantime, I'll have bottled water sent up to your room that your wife can use to bathe."

"That's a good start," the man grunted. "But not good enough. I want a full refund for today and every day that we have to spend without water. Do you understand me?"

Bill smiled tightly. "I'll speak to the manager and see what we can do for you, sir."

"The *manager?*" A squiggly vein popped out on Angry Tourist's forehead. "You're not the manager? Then who the hell am I speaking with?"

"The owner."

"And you can't authorize a refund for your own hotel?"

"I didn't say that."

"So what's the problem?"

"No problem, sir."

"My name is James! James Lucas! Not sir!"

"Of course, Mr. Lucas. I promise we'll have the water back soon, and ameliorative measures will be taken to compensate you for your trouble."

"Yeah, you'd better compensate the hell out of me. You don't want to see what kind of review you're going to get if you don't."

"I understand your frustration, Mr. Lucas. Please return to your room, and I'll send someone up with three gallons of clean, bottled water for your wife."

"What about me? And our kids?"

"Five gallons. I'm afraid that's the best I can do."

James Lucas nodded once, his eyes dark and promising mayhem. "Fine, the kids and I will shower in the pool. Hope you like it sandy."

With that, he turned and marched toward the elevators, tracking sand through the lobby, his sandals squelching as he went.

Bill let out a tension-filled breath, but before he

could even fill his lungs with another, one of the elevators dinged open, and a family of five came marching out. The wife was wearing designer sunglasses. She took the lead, aiming straight for him and the front desk.

Bill turned and fled behind the desk. He found Eric on one of the phone lines to the no-show plumbers, and Sean on the other line—hopefully not with another cancellation.

With both of them occupied, he was the resort's only line of defense. Bill turned back around and smiled, bracing for another round of complaints. This was not what he'd had in mind when he'd decided to trade his car dealership and the hustle and bustle of LA for the slower pace of a tropical island paradise. It was supposed to have been an endless vacation, sipping cocktails on the beach while his manager took care of the resort.

Sean lowered the receiver to his shoulder and caught Bill's eye with a wave. "Mr. Steele?"

Bill faced his day-clerk, a square-jawed, blonde and tanned version of Michelangelo's David who spent all his free hours watching the sunset from a surfboard. He would have fit in perfectly in LA, minus the lack of ambition and self-direction which seemed to plague all of Bill's employees.

"Yes, Sean?"

"It's Mr. Kalani from Kauai High."

"Principal Kalani?" Bill echoed.

"Yes, sir."

"Well, what is it?"

"It's your daughter. She got into a fight at school. She's been suspended."

Bill blinked. "What do you mean she got in a fight? You mean like a fist fight?"

Sean shrugged. "I guess. They need you to pick her up."

Bill resisted the urge to scream. "Tell him I'll be right there."

"Yes, sir."

Someone harrumphed, and Bill faced the front desk to see the elevator woman with the designer sunglasses—a tall, rail-thin specimen in a pure white dress that contrasted sharply with her short black hair, but blended perfectly with her flawless milk-white skin. That complexion told him she'd only come here to indulge her family while she spent her days at the spa. Her husband and three kids hung back in their swimming trunks and sandals, wearing beach towels for shirts.

"May I help you, ma'am?" Bill tried.

"No wonder this resort is falling apart. You can't even manage your own family."

"I apologize for any inconvenience you've suffered due to the current lack of running water, ma'am, but my family is not a subject for

— 12 —

discussion, and frankly, I'm surprised to hear a mother of three talk that way: businesses are *managed,* but families are *raised.*" The woman's jaw dropped, and a small smile sprang to her husband's face. "Please feel free to address any concerns you may have with my manager—" Bill turned to find the man in question standing behind him.

"I've got this," Eric said while straightening his glasses. "Go get Beth."

"Thank you," Bill replied. He ran around the reception desk—

And almost knocked over a porter pushing a luggage cart full of bottled water. "Sorry," he mouthed and slowed to a brisk walk, heading for the sliding glass doors at the entrance of the lobby. Just before he reached the doors, the elevator dinged and a pair of Chinese tourists came out of the elevator, pulling luggage behind them.

"Hey, hold up," he said, but neither of them turned at the sound of his voice, so he switched to Mandarin. *"Wait. Where you go?"* he said. Before buying the Koa Kai, he'd taken Mandarin classes for a year to prep for joining an old college friend as co-owner of a hotel in Shanghai, but that hadn't panned out, and now all he was left with was the experience.

The tourist stopped and glanced over his

shoulder, his eyebrows elevating in surprise. He replied in the same language just as Bill caught up to him at the front doors.

"We go to Marriot next door. Water working at Marriot."

"Stay. Water back soon!" Bill replied, pushing his rudimentary grasp of the language to the limit.

"No stay. Wife not happy," the man replied, shaking his head. *"Sorry."* With that, he continued on his way, striding out the doors and through the parking lot to catch up with his wife. She was already waiting by the trunk of their car. Attracting the world's rich upper crust had its drawbacks. They expected a flawless experience, not showers belching mud, and toilets that wouldn't flush.

With a sigh, Bill stepped out into the hot summer air, fragrant with the smell of baking sand and salty ocean. Palm trees rustled and children squealed distantly, waves swished to shore...

Bill sucked in a deep breath, trying to remember how he'd felt the first time he'd come to this resort—like a heavy weight had left his chest, and he could actually breathe for the first time in years. Bill's lips quirked into a bitter smile. It hadn't taken long to return to breathlessness.

* * *

Warm air honeyed with Hawaiian blossoms billowed through the open windows of Bill's

Cadillac XTS. Sunlight gleamed like diamonds in the gaps between the dense greenery on either side of the road, and the wind of the car's passing echoed off the vegetation, stirring long grass to life with a persistent swishing sound that drowned out the quiet whisper of the Caddy's hybrid engine. Route 50, or Kaumualii Highway, as the locals called it, was a scenic three-lane road that hardly merited being called a highway. For starters, *three* lanes didn't make sense no matter where you were from, much less to Bill's LA-branded brain.

All of his friends had warned him that island life would take some getting used to, but he hadn't been in the mood to listen to them after his divorce left him homeless and broken-hearted. In an unexpected coup, he'd gotten to keep custody of his daughter. She'd chosen to move with him to Kauai after her mother decided to re-marry just two months after the divorce. Beth obviously held that against her mother, or else she really didn't like her stepfather, Colton. Either way, Bill should have thought twice about letting her join him here. She'd always been closer to her mother. He'd just been the workaholic stranger who paid all the bills—the guy smiling like an idiot in all the photos pinned to the fridge. Raising a teenage daughter by himself at the same time as owning and managing a four-star vacation resort was proving more complicated than he'd ever imagined possible.

Bill let out a long, slow breath. Managing. That shouldn't have been his job. Eric Monte had given Bill a false sense of security with his glasses, middle-aged spread, and pasty white skin, all of which told Bill that he'd never set foot (let alone belly) on a surfboard in his entire life. At the time Eric had seemed like a good choice for the Koa Kai's third replacement head manager, but stiff competition, high running costs, and rising vacancy rates throughout the islands had left him on a tight budget. A more experienced manager would have cost more but would have also remembered to get the plumbers back in the slow season after they'd done their temporary patch job on that burst pipe in February. Now the repair job was twice as big, there was sediment in all the water feeds, and they had ninety rooms full of angry guests all plotting to write bad reviews that would scare off future clientele. It didn't help that the Marriot was right next door with a better beach, more rooms, better pools, bigger grounds, and the same nightly rates. Add to all of that his wild teenage daughter who seemed to think that life consisted of surfing and partying on the beach with boys, and it was no wonder he was buying Pepto-Bismol buy the case.

The drive went by in a blur of lush greenery

and blue skies. Twenty minutes later he pulled into the parking lot at Kauai High. Inside, he asked the receptionist about his daughter. She smiled sympathetically and escorted him down the hall to the nurse's office. He opened the door to see Beth lying on an examination table, her left eye bruised and swollen.

Bill's anger vanished under a rug of parental concern, and he rushed to his daughter's side. "Are you okay?" he asked.

Beth sat up with a wince, and gingerly pressed a pack of ice to her eye. "I'm fine." She tucked a feathery lock of brown hair behind one ear to keep it out of the way.

"What happened?" Realizing something was missing, Bill spun in a quick circle. "Where's the other girl?"

"It wasn't a girl," Beth said quietly.

Horror stabbed through Bill. "You mean a *boy* did this?"

The school nurse sidled up to them. "I'm afraid so."

"What happened? Where is he!" Bill roared.

"Please calm down, Mr. Steele. He's in the hospital. Beth broke his nose."

Bill rounded on her. "You did *what?*"

Beth's lips twitched, but she said nothing.

"How did this happen?" Bill demanded of the

nurse.

"I don't have all the details, but I do know that your daughter started it. The principal wants to see you both before you leave the campus."

Bill rounded on Beth, blinking furiously. "Well? Are you going to explain yourself, or do I have to assume the worst?"

"Matt told Toby that he saw me kissing another boy at the bonfire last night, which was a total lie, and—"

"Wait." Bill held up a hand and massaged a sudden headache away from his eyeballs with the other. "This is about a boy? Please tell me you're joking. You have a new boyfriend every other week!"

Beth's lower jaw zigzagged as she ground her teeth, and her brown eyes blazed like hot coals—a look her mother had patented ages ago. "Toby and I have been together since the beginning of the year!"

Bill waved his hand at her. "I don't want to hear it."

"You never want to hear anything! You never listen!"

"Let's go, Beth." Bill snapped his fingers. "Now."

Beth scowled at him as she swung her legs over the side of the table and hopped down.

The nurse glanced at Bill. "The principal's office is down the hall and to the—"

"I know the way," Bill replied, taking Beth by the arm and dragging her out of the nurse's office at a brisk pace.

* * *

"Ouch, you're hurting me!" Beth said.

Her dad blew out a sigh and released her arm as they strode down the hall to the principal's office. As soon as they arrived, the secretary escorted them in.

"Please sit," Principal Kalani said, gesturing to the chairs in front of his big desk with a massive arm and comically small, thick-fingered hand. Kalani was a blob—so fat he made his desk look small, with no neck, a round face, and deep-set black eyes that reminded Beth of raisins.

Kalani regarded them in silence for a long moment, a deeply-disappointed look etched onto his taut, tanned face.

"According to witnesses," Kalani began, looking at Bill, "Your daughter, Beth, and Matt Cole were seen arguing outside the cafeteria just after lunch. Beth then kicked Matt Cole in the groin, and after he recovered, he punched her in the face. At that point she jumped on his back, using her nails to scratch at his face and eyes while she screamed obscenities in his ear, calling into focus his alleged sexual orientation." Kalani stopped to glare at Beth with his raisin eyes.

"Is that true, Beth?" Bill asked.

"He's in love with his best friend!" she blurted out.

Bill sighed. "Please go on, Mr. Kalani."

"They fell down together, and Matt broke his nose on the pavement. Beth claims that it was an accident, but Matt says she deliberately smashed his face into the ground. Fortunately for your daughter, witness accounts are conflicting, so she won't be expelled. She is, however, suspended until next week."

"Aren't they doing midterms this week?" Bill asked. "She can't afford to miss those."

"She should have thought of that before assaulting a fellow student. I'm sorry, but Beth started it, and I have to tell Matt's parents something. The other students need to see that there are consequences. Beth is very lucky she's not being expelled."

"What about him? He punched my daughter in the face!"

"After she provoked him," Mr. Kalani said.

Bill stood up, his face turning red. "So instead of kicking her out, you're going to make her fail the tenth grade? How is that any better?"

"She still has plenty of time to make up her

grades, and some of her teachers may be willing to provide make-up tests."

"She's skating by as it is!"

"Expulsion is still an option, Mr. Steele. If you believe that would be a more suitable outcome..."

Bill smiled thinly at the principal. "No, thank you. Now if you'll excuse us, I have another crisis to deal with back at the resort."

Mr. Kalani smiled tightly back and gestured to the door with one of his small, fat-rounded hands. "Good luck."

CHAPTER 2

"You're grounded," Bill said once they were both sitting in his car. "No parties, no surfing, and no lounging by the pool. If I even see you looking at a swimsuit, you'll be on the next plane to LA to live with your mother. Oh, and no TV either."

"*What?*" Beth shrieked. "You can't do that! What am I supposed to do all week?"

Bill arched an eyebrow at his daughter as he pressed the button to start his car. "Homework?"

"I don't have any; I'm suspended, remember?"

"Then read a book. There are plenty in the lobby."

The car ride home was long and quiet, which was just fine with Bill. He needed time alone with his thoughts. With these recent troubles he was seriously beginning to think Beth *should* go back and live with her mother in LA. He'd miss her like crazy, but the resort demanded his full attention, and she was almost never around anyway. He could count the number of hours they spent together in a week on one hand and still have three or four fingers left over.

When they got back to the resort, Beth grabbed her backpack from the backseat and went straight to the elevators without having to be told, while Bill went to check in with his manager. The lobby was crowded with irritated guests, and the pool and poolside bar were equally full. Bill shuddered to think of what all those drinks were doing to toilets and urinals that couldn't be flushed.

"Tell me there's good news," Bill said as he walked behind the reception desk.

"The plumbers arrived," Eric said. "But then they left to get supplies."

Bill buried his face in his hands. "How long have they been gone?"

"Half an hour?"

"Is that a question?"

"No, sir."

"I want them back here *now*."

"Yes, Mr. Steele."

"And where's Sean?" Bill cast about, looking for the day clerk. The reception area was empty.

"He went to get more water for the guests."

"We're out already? What about the restaurant?"

"We've been using it to flush toilets, and—"

"*Bottled* water to flush toilets? Are you

insane?"

"They were starting to stink."

"So get ocean water!"

"But the sand would clog the pipes."

"Ocean water *without* sand in it, Eric! You just have to wade out a few extra feet to fill a bucket with clean water!"

Eric's lips curled and his nose wrinkled. "Me, sir?"

There was a reason Eric was so pale. The ocean and all the *creatures* that lived in the reefs terrified him. "Not *you*," Bill said. "Get the waiters to do it, or the porters, or some of the cleaning staff."

"But they'll wet their uniforms."

Bill used his index finger to prod Eric in the chest. "That's the least of our problems. Figure it out, or you're fired, do you understand me?"

"Yes, sir."

Storming off in no particular direction, Bill's feet seemed to move of their own accord. He needed a moment to clear his head, somewhere away from his floundering business and the domestic problems with his daughter. His feet carried him past the pool full of splashing, squealing children. Adults lay tanning in the sun with their noses buried in books or chatting loudly at the cabana bar. The resort with all its noisy tourists faded into the background as he followed the footpath to the beach.

He reached the Surf and Snorkel hut with its surf and boogie boards resting against the wall and noticed that Toby, the surf instructor, was nowhere to be seen. *Typical,* Bill thought. He would have fired him ages ago, but the seventeen-year-old high-school dropout wasn't as stupid as he looked. Dating the boss's daughter was a rare form of job security. When they'd first started dating, Bill had assumed it wouldn't last; Beth would catch Toby flirting with one of the tourists and that would be that, but Toby had been on his best behavior ever since they'd met.

Kicking up sand in his brown leather boat shoes, Bill stared fixedly at the sparkling cerulean water. It drew him in like a riptide. He kicked off his shoes and pulled off his socks as he reached the smooth, darkened slope of wet sand leading to the water's edge. In seconds his ankles were covered by the warm, lapping waves. Gentle currents pushed and pulled, making him sway, dragging the sand out from under his feet and tickling his toes.

Dark bands of coral wove through the greens and blues of clear, shallow water. Snorkeling was a popular activity on resort beaches with their glassy water and colorful fish darting through the reefs. Bill imagined floating out there, face-down and staring at the fish, his ears wrapped in the blessed silence of the water, nothing but the rhythmic sounds of his breathing and heartbeat to impose on his senses.

Investing in this resort had been a mistake. He should have just used his millions to live at one as a guest, or to become a beach bum like Toby, but with a mansion in Princeville. *That* would have been the endless vacation he'd pictured. Screw purpose and having a reason to get out of bed in the morning. What he really wanted was to sleep in every day with room service after a long day at the beach. But in that alternate life his daughter wouldn't be with him, and maybe he'd have taken up surfing and become good buddies with Toby, the moron.

Bill sighed. But who was he kidding? He wouldn't last more than a week with nothing to do. The problems with the resort would pass.

A dark shadow passed over the ocean, rolling in swiftly to sweep away his bright, sun-soaked fantasies.

Bill's brow furrowed, and he glanced up, searching for the dark cloud that he imagined to be passing in front of the sun, but there weren't any clouds in the sky, and the sun winked out before he could even find it. "What the hell?" Bill muttered as the shadow swept over him and twilight fell, leaving him blinking stupidly and waving his hands in front of his face to make sure he could still see them.

Sudden blindness. Was that a thing? Maybe he was having a stroke. But then he heard and vaguely saw the snorkelers in the water splashing frantically as if they'd all suddenly forgotten how to swim. Sunbathers on the shore sat up, screaming and pointing at the sky. The darkness deepened from twilight until it was as thick and black as crude oil, and coating everything in sight. *An eclipse?* he wondered. Why hadn't he heard anything about it on the news?

Then he spotted a familiar crescent hovering above the horizon, shimmering silver on the water. Terror coiled in the pit of Bill's stomach, and acid bubbled into the back of his throat.

Whatever this was, it wasn't an eclipse.

CHAPTER 3

Bill ran back up the beach barefoot and spraying sand, having forgotten all about his shoes. He heard his guests screaming and yelling long before he reached the pool. Everyone was out of the water and staring up at the sky. Hurrying by them, Bill heard some babbling about the end of the world, others sobbing or screaming. One man was taking advantage of the bartender's inattention to pour himself shots. "To the end of the world!" he said, raising the first of several glasses, and downing it in one gulp.

Bill recognized that man as the husband of the rail-thin matriarch who'd tried to lecture him about running a family.

The matriarch stepped in front of him with hands planted on her waist. "Mr. Steele! Why weren't we told there would be an eclipse today?"

Bill tried to dart around her, but she side-stepped to block him once more. "Well?"

"This is *not* an eclipse, ma'am."

"*Not* an eclipse? Then what on Earth is it?"

A rising orange hue suffused the black sky, followed by a thunderous *boom* and rapid-fire echoes of it, drawing screams from the pool goers and drowning out any possibility of an answer.

Someone shouted, "They're here!"

Bill looked up and shaded his eyes against the glare of at least a dozen streaks of light, each of them limned and wreathed in fire as they rocketed down over the island. A meteor shower?

"They're here!" someone shouted. "We're not alone!"

Those objects weren't burning up in the atmosphere, and one of them looked to be headed straight for them.

"Everyone get inside!" Bill said. Chaos erupted as people pushed and shoved to be the first ones up the path from the pool. Visions of a tsunami wiping out his hotel flashed through Bill's head as he followed his screaming guests up to the lobby.

Crowding through the sliding glass doors with the others, Bill scanned the luxurious chambers, searching for Eric. He found his manager at the computer station, surrounded by a knot of cleaning staff, porters, and waiters from the restaurant. Bill ran over there with several of his guests. Everyone crowded around a single monitor, watching a live news report from KITV Island News.

"This just in," the anchorwoman said. "The entire island of Kauai has suddenly and inexplicably plunged into darkness in the middle of the day. Meteors are raining down all over the island, and planes flying into Lihue Airport have reported a dark shadow spreading across the water as far as fifty miles from the shore. Eyewitnesses say they watched the sun vanish as if a curtain were being drawn across the sky.

"We're going live to the scene now with Curtis Chapman in Lihue. Curtis?" The scene cut to show a man with thinning brown hair standing on a hill, his comb-over threatening to take flight in a stiff breeze. Spotlights blazed, revealing every wrinkle on Curtis's tanned, leathery face. In the background, a flaming meteor streaked down, heading straight for the city lights below. He held a microphone with the KITV Island News logo on it and stood there blinking at the camera, waiting for an unseen cue to speak.

"Hello, Katy," Curtis said. "As you can see behind me, right now one of the meteors is falling directly over Lihue. It's hard to tell how much of a threat it represents at this point, but as we pan the camera—" The camera began to slide away from him. "—you can see other meteors raining down all over the island and dozens more appearing with every passing minute. To the southwest, you can see several of them headed for the city of Koloa, and several more for Hanapepe and Waimea."

"Koloa—that's us, right?" one of the tourists standing behind Bill asked.

He turned to regard the man. It was Angry Tourist, James Lucas, the one who'd been complaining about the shit water and demanding a refund. "Yes, that's us," Bill said.

Their gazes met, and Bill saw that James' eyes were glassy from one too many cocktails.

"What could possibly blot out the sun?" someone asked.

"They said it's spreading," another added.

"What is? *What* is spreading?" a woman asked in a terrified voice. She stood close to James, clutching his arm while two young children hugged her legs.

"Shhh! Everyone be quiet, and maybe we'll find out!" Eric said.

"The first wave of meteors are touching down now!" Curtis said from the computer's speakers.

Bill expected muffled explosions to crackle out and light up the night in the valley behind Curtis, but that didn't happen. In fact, nothing happened other than the meteors disappearing and more raining down.

"That's strange..." Curtis said. "The impacts

appear to be causing only minor damage as if these meteors are either very light or somehow slowing themselves as they fall."

"Thrusters," James suggested.

"So they're not meteors?" his wife asked.

"No, they're landing craft. It's aliens."

Worried murmurs spread through the crowd, a crowd which was growing fast as elevators dinged open, bringing more guests down to the lobby with every passing minute. Bill traded worried looks with Eric and then turned to address his guests. "Calm down, everyone! We don't know what we're dealing with. If this were an invasion, don't you think someone would know something about it? NASA would have seen them coming."

"You don't know that!" someone yelled.

"We're all going to die!" another person wailed.

"Maybe it's some kind of sunspot activity," Eric suggested.

"Sunspots? Are you crazy?" James bellowed. "Sunspots don't block out whole sections of the sky and rain meteors that magically *slow down* before they hit the ground!"

"So it *is* aliens," one of the waiters said.

Worried murmurs grew to a frenzy, and Bill began to fear that the crowd would tear his hotel apart. Bill pushed past James and jumped up on an empty desk beside Eric. He raised his hands for attention. "Everyone listen to me!" No one did. "Settle down!" Still no sign of calm.

Bill whistled as loud as he could between his fingers, and a brittle silence fell. All eyes turned to him, and suddenly they could hear the news again, but Curtis Chapman's terrified speculations weren't helping.

"Eric, shut that off!" The manager did as asked, and Bill went on, "Thank you. The safest place for any of you to be right now is in your rooms. Whatever this is, the authorities and the military can handle it. We're in one of the most heavily militarized states in the entire country, so if aliens really are invading, you can bet there's an entire fleet sailing toward us right now. In the meantime, all we can do is sit tight and stay calm. Draw your blinds and turn off your lights. We're going to do the same thing here in the lobby and everywhere else in the resort to draw as little attention to ourselves as possible."

"What do they want?" someone asked.

"We still don't know that we're dealing with a *they*," Bill chided. "There could be a perfectly natural explanation for what's happening right now."

"Like what?" James demanded.

"Like... a large asteroid skimming through the

upper atmosphere and eclipsing the sun. Pieces would break off and rain down just as we're seeing with these meteors."

"That's a transitory event," James replied. He pointed to the darkness outside. "The sun would be back by now."

Just then, the night peeled away with a bright flash of light.

Heads turned, eyes wide and hopeful, but it wasn't the sun. It was a meteor streaking down on a tail of fire. It landed in the ocean with a muffled roar.

Guests screamed and scattered, tripping over each other as they ran for the stairs and elevators. Bill froze, staring across the pool in horror, waiting for a tsunami to come and wake him from this nightmare. His thoughts turned to Beth in their suite on the third floor of the resort, and he hoped to God that would be high enough.

"Dad?" a familiar voice cut through his daze, and he saw Beth striding in from the direction of the pool with Toby, the MIA surf instructor. "What's happening?"

CHAPTER 4

Bill jumped off the desk, grabbed Beth by the arm and ran for the stairs. "Let's go!" he shouted.

"Ouch!" Beth complained.

"Hey, Mr. Steele, let her go, *brah*."

"Shut up, Toby!" Bill tossed a worried look over his shoulder as he ran, but the dark wall of water he expected to see bursting through the lobby windows never came. Not wanting to risk it, he didn't slow down. Phones rang insistently at the reception desk, but no one was there to answer them. Sean had probably been on his way back with the water when the darkness fell. They reached the stairs behind the last of the screaming guests from the lobby. Bill took the stairs two at a time, dragging his daughter up.

"*Braddah*, this is *lolo!*" Toby said as they reached the second floor.

Beth stopped resisting, and Bill let her go. They continued up the stairs to the third floor and then started running down the inner hall to their suite at the end. A small crowd of guests was running up ahead, periodically stopping to swipe their key cards and slam their doors.

Arriving at their room, Bill stopped and swiped his own key card. A solid beep sounded in time to a *thunk,* and a green light snapped on above the lock. Turning the handle and pushing the door open, he ushered Toby and his daughter through, and then followed them in and locked the deadbolt. He drew the chain across the door for added security. Bill strode through a brief foyer, past a kitchen table, and into the living room. Toby and Beth were already seated on the couch, Toby reaching for the remote. Bill went straight up to the ocean-facing balcony with its sliding glass doors and drew heavy blackout curtains across the glass. That done, he turned to face his daughter. He could see that she was wearing a bright red bikini under her crop top and denim mini shorts, but now wasn't the time to discuss it.

Toby turned up the volume on the TV, and Curtis Chapman's terrified voice returned, but faintly and coming in and out. Bill watched the camera bobbing to keep up with Chapman as he ran down a darkened path. The reporter periodically glanced back at the camera to make frantic exclamations.

"I'm sorry, we didn't catch that, Curtis," the

anchorwoman back at the station said, her brow furrowing from her corner of the screen. "Did you say something is chasing you?"

Before Curtis could reply, the cameraman tripped and fell, and the camera went flying. Bill could have sworn he heard screaming in the background as the camera tumbled down the hill, but then the signal died, and the colored bars of a test pattern appeared. A split second later, the anchorwoman's troubled face took over the entire screen.

"We umm... appear to be having some technical difficulties right now, but we'll be back on the scene in just a minute. While we're waiting, I'm told that NASA has an update for us, so we're going to go to the mainland now to speak with—"

The TV winked off with the lights and utter darkness swept over them.

* * *

"Dad..." Beth whimpered.

"It's okay," Bill whispered. "I'm here. Everything is going to be okay."

"Shit! Shit! Shit!" Toby said.

"Shut up," Bill hissed. "I'm going to go get a flashlight."

Beth's cell phone came out. The screen lit her face blue-white; then a dazzling white light snapped on at the back, and the shadows in the

— 37 —

living room retreated. "Here, use mine," she said, passing the phone to him.

Bill smiled and nodded, accepting the phone and using it to light the way to the pantry closet where he kept batteries, spare light bulbs, and flashlights below the canned goods.

Beth and Toby followed closely, whispering urgently. Toby cried out and cursed as he ran into something, and Bill smiled.

Reaching the pantry closet opposite the kitchen, Bill bent down and retrieved a pair of flashlights from the bottom shelf. Taking one for himself and flicking it on, he handed the other to Toby and passed Beth's cell phone back to her.

Three clear white beams lit the hallway, bouncing off walls and floor and lighting each other's faces.

"What are we going to do?" Beth asked.

"*We* aren't going to do anything," Bill said. "You're staying right here."

"Brah, *you* shouldn't go anywhere, either."

"I have a hotel full of guests in the dark with no water, all terrified out of their minds. The least I can do is pass out flashlights."

"You don't want to be alone out there, man," Toby said. "*Da kine* on the TV said something about *da kine* chasin' him."

Bill frowned. *Da kine* was local pidgin for

whatchamacallit, or basically anything that you couldn't or didn't want to name.

Bill clapped a hand on Toby's shoulder and squeezed *hard.* "Don't worry, Toby, I won't be alone. You're coming with me."

CHAPTER 5

"Don't go," Beth said, her heart skipping erratically in her chest. She couldn't believe this was happening.

"You'll be fine," her dad said, rattling the door chain as he slid it off.

"Yeah, brah, let's just hang here and wait for the power to come back. People got their cell phones for flashlights." Toby nodded to Beth, and she squeezed his hand. She appreciated the effort, but she knew her dad. Once he got an idea in his head...

His eyes pinched, the crows' feet around them scrunching up like accordions. Her dad was only forty-three, but he'd managed to add a couple of years over the past eighteen months with the Hawaiian sun.

"I'd also like to see what happened to the power," Bill said. "It might just be a surge that tripped the breakers."

Beth chewed her lower lip. "We don't know

what's out there."

Bill smiled tightly and shook his head. "I don't buy that this is aliens."

"You gotta wake up, man!" Toby said. This is E-effin-T. Their mothership's blockin' the sun, just like in *Independent Day*."

"It's Mr. Steele or Boss, not *man*, or *brah*. And I think you mean *Independence* Day."

"Sure, Boss."

Bill's eyes flashed, but he shook his head. "As for whatever is blocking the sun, it could be an orbital test of some new technology. A low-flying satellite with a solar sail, for example."

"You don't really believe that," Beth said. "You're just trying to make me feel better."

"We'll be back soon. Keep the door locked."

"But—"

Bill opened the door to a darkened hallway and dragged Toby out with him. Their flashlights bobbed on the opposite wall. Beth felt warm, humid air swirl in, driven by a whistling breeze from exterior openings at the near and far ends of the hall.

Beth clutched the door handle and began to ease the door shut. Her father flashed a reassuring grin and nodded. Toby looked much less sure of himself, his flashlight sweeping in broad arcs as he checked the walls and floor for monsters.

"Lock the door," Bill whispered.

Beth closed it with a click and flicked the deadbolt on; then she slid the brass chain back into place and quickly spun around to make sure nothing crept up behind her. Of course, nothing was there, but that didn't stop her palms from sweating or her heart from thundering in her chest.

"Come on, Beth, get yourself together," she whispered. "You're safe here. You're on the third floor, and there's no way in besides the front door."

Creeping back to the living room couch, Beth swept her phone light around in jittery arcs. Shadows danced in the kitchen as the beam shone over the bar counter beside the kitchen table. Something could easily hide behind the counter. The darkened hall to the bedrooms was another source of anxiety. Her dad's bedroom had its own balcony. Was the sliding door locked? She doubted it. Why bother when they were three floors up? Beth swept her phone into line with the blackout curtains drawn across the living room balcony. Her dad had shut the blinds, but had he also locked the doors? She couldn't remember; she'd been focused on the TV at the time. The TV anchor's bemused voice echoed through Beth's head—*did you say something is chasing you?*

Beth hurried up to the living room balcony on

shaking legs, reached blindly past the curtains, and yanked the locking lever down. She felt the mechanism hook into place, and then tested the door, trying to slide it open. It moved a centimeter before catching on the lock and holding fast.

A shaky sigh escaped her lips, and Beth turned around. The hallway yawned before her, its contents unknown, impossible to see from this angle. The kitchen and all its shadows lay to one side, perfect for an ambush if something were waiting for her there. She froze, her heart pounding and breathing reduced to shallow gasps. She wanted to crawl into her bed and hide.

"Enough," Beth whispered to herself. "You're sixteen, not six."

Emboldened by her declaration, she took long strides toward the hall. At the opening, she shone her phone light down to the end. Shadows scurried away like cockroaches. Her dad's door lay open at the end, pale moonlight pooling on the tiles. The eclipse made Beth feel like she'd jumped into a time machine and somehow skipped the whole afternoon. Whatever was blocking the sun it had somehow left the moon free to shine, even though it was only—Beth checked the time on her phone— two thirty in the afternoon. Wasn't the Moon only supposed to come up at night? Maybe she should have paid more attention in science class.

Beside her dad's door, the folding louvered doors that concealed the washer and dryer stack were folded in the middle and slightly ajar.

Adrenaline sparked in Beth's fingertips. Remembering that her fears were childish and had no actual basis, she smiled and shook her head, striding confidently down the hall. She shone her light into the kitchen as she went by, but saw nothing hiding behind the kitchen counter. Next up was the bathroom, and likewise, nothing was hiding behind the sliding glass door of the shower. She didn't even bother to open the door to her room and check inside. Her pace slowed only when she reached the end of the hall. She grabbed the handle of the louvered doors and planted her foot against them while scanning her father's room. His bed was made and gleaming with moonlight. The sliding glass doors to his balcony were cracked *open.* A gentle breeze whistled through the gap, almost inaudible over the drumbeat of her heart. Beth's guts clenched. Her dad must have accidentally left the doors ajar. Eyes flicking to the louvered doors she was holding, Beth gave them a quick shove.

But the doors bounced back. She blinked in terror, acid dread bubbling up and stabbing like a hot knife in her chest. Something blocked the door.

Beth tried again, harder this time. The door

almost folded straight, but then it sprang back and scrolled halfway open.

Beth screamed and stumbled away, tripping over her own feet. She fell hard, instinctively throwing up the hand holding her phone up to shield her face, while her other went back to cushion her fall.

Something dark leapt down from the top shelf and landed at her feet with an airy *whup*. She screamed as she kicked the creature away, but it kept coming at her. Scrambling backward, she aimed her phone at it to get a good look— it was just a pillow.

Beth laughed until her breath came in halting gasps. "Some monster you are." Pushing off the floor, a sharp pain erupted in her wrist, and then another from her tailbone. Beth winced and let out a shuddery breath. She picked up the pillow and stuffed it into the top shelf above the dryer. Now the louvered doors closed and clicked into place. Shining her phone light back into her dad's room, she headed for the open doors to his balcony. Hairs prickled along the nape of her neck as she realized that she hadn't checked her dad's en suite bathroom.

But she forced her fears down, remembering the pillow scare. At the balcony, Beth hesitated with her sweaty palm greasing the cool metal handle of the sliding glass door.

Not knowing what was out there only amplified her fears. Steeling herself, she yanked the door open and stepped out into the warm, steamy air. The smell of salty ocean mingled with fresh vegetation and fragrant flowers. At the open end of the U-shaped Koa Kai complex, the dark, rippled ocean shone with a narrow river of silver from the still-rising moon. A wide band of stars sparkled along the horizon, up to an invisible barrier at about forty-five degrees. The sky was pure black above that.

Waves whispered to shore amidst the distant, muffled roar of machinery. Probably the generators from the Marriott next door. Beth couldn't see any lights over the moonlit rooftops of adjacent buildings in the Koa Kai, but she suspected they'd find the Marriott basking in its own lights if they wandered over there.

Her eyes dipped down to see the courtyard below cloaked in oily shadows. The pool formed a black stain. Only the faintest glimmer of moonlight sparkled on its surface. Beth shone her light down, but the beam dispersed long before it illuminated anything. She turned her ear to the ground and listened—

The breeze rustled palm fronds, generators droned from the Marriott, and waves swished across wet sand.

Her dad was right. Aliens weren't invading. She began to feel stupid for being so scared. On the water she was fearless, she would tackle any wave, no matter how high—just like she'd tackled Toby's friend, Matt, and smashed his nose on the pavement. It wasn't like her to be afraid.

Beth turned and walked back through the sliding doors. As she slid them shut, a new sound slithered in—a *splash.*

Fresh terror electrified Beth's veins. That sound had come from the pool. Surely none of the guests had gone out for a swim in utter darkness, with the sky falling all around them. But what else could it be? A stray dog? A bird?

Beth slid the door open another foot and popped her head out. More splashing... followed by voices. A man and a woman.

Beth let out her breath in a rush, then shut and locked the door with a snort. "It takes all kinds of crazy to make a world," she muttered as she drew the curtains across the glass. Somehow knowing there were people out there in the pool made her feel better. If aliens hadn't gotten them, they definitely wouldn't get her. But somehow this didn't seem like an extraterrestrial threat anymore. Her dad's explanation of some new technology seemed a lot more likely—some kind of solar shield from an experimental satellite.

Except that didn't explain the meteors.

Beth swept the divergent thought aside with a frown as she headed back to the living room to wait for her dad and Toby. There had to be a reasonable explanation for all of this. Just as she was flopping into the couch, a woman's muffled scream yanked Beth's eyes to the curtained balcony.

CHAPTER 6

"Shhh, someone's going to hear us!" Melanie said.

Paul ran one hand down her naked backside, the other up her front, straying briefly between her legs, then up to cup her bare breasts. "Let them hear. They're all hiding in their rooms," he said, pressing her back against the edge of the pool.

"Maybe we should be, too," Melanie replied, sounding suddenly scared and sober. After the sun had magically disappeared and the meteors began raining down, they'd emptied the mini bar together. Dutch courage. Paul now had enough of it coursing through his veins to make him feel invincible. The resort lost power halfway through their binge, leaving them to grope each other in the dark, something they would have been doing with or without the mysterious eclipse and blackout—what else were honeymoons for?

Then in their drunken state, they'd stripped off their remaining clothes and dashed out the doors of their ground floor garden suite to the pool.

Paul trailed kisses down his wife's throat and pressed himself more insistently against her.

"Paul..."

"Mmmmm," he mumbled while nipping at her earlobe.

"Let's go back inside. I thought I heard something in the bushes."

He stopped and humored her by scanning their surroundings. The pool shimmered with a narrow band of moonlight peeking through the fronds of a palm tree, but everything else was too black to see. The horizon was a dark screen against soaring black trunks of palm trees and the sheer black walls of the surrounding buildings. Crickets hummed, and some kind of machinery roared faintly; the pool sloshed with echoes of their movements, but Paul didn't hear any bushes rustling.

"It's just your imagination, Mel."

"What if it isn't? What if aliens are blocking the sun with a spaceship and those meteors were landing craft?"

Paul snorted. "This is some freaky shit, that's for sure, but it's not ET. Hundred to one we're dealing with some super-secret Russian satellite— or maybe Chinese. Remember when they'd put that artificial moon in the sky? Everyone thought they were crazy, and then they did it. And then it crashed." Paul chuckled darkly.

"Shhhh!" Melanie urged.

"There's nothing out here." As he said that, he snaked a hand around under the water and pinched his wife's butt.

She jumped and screamed in terror. Then, realizing it was him, she splashed water in his face. "That's not funny, Paul!" She began wading away from him, heading for the nearest gleaming silver ladder.

"Hey, where are you going?"

"Back to our room."

"Mel, come on! I was just screwing around."

"Well, now you're going to have to do that by yourself. You can join me when you're ready to apologize." Melanie yanked herself halfway out of the pool, and Paul got a tantalizing look at her naked backside in the moonlight. A split second later she went streaking back to their suite.

With his alcohol-numbed brain too slow to react immediately, Paul stared blankly after his wife's vanishing form until he heard the glass door to their room slide shut behind her. Frustrated by her sudden departure, Paul decided to stay in the pool for a while. Let her worry.

Flipping over, he floated up on his back and began swimming leisurely to the other side. There weren't any stars above, which he thought was strange—or maybe not so strange; whatever had blocked the sun was obviously blocking them too.

A lone meteor fell flaming from the sky, heading inland to the mountains in the center of the island. The shower was over.

Paul's knuckles grazed the edge of the pool, and he grabbed it to stop himself before his head could collide with the wall. Maybe the backstroke wasn't such a good idea.

He flipped over to grab the edge of the pool with both hands, and floated there, eyes peeking over the rim to the distant sheen of the ocean. He listened to the gentle waves from his own movements lapping at the side of the pool and *glugging* in and out of the pool skimmer's trap door. A gentle breeze clattered through the palm trees, crickets sang, and the ocean rumbled with a suddenly larger set of waves—probably echoes from the meteor that had landed in the water earlier.

The water grew calm now that Paul had stopped moving, the air became still, and then even the crickets fell silent.

Feeling suddenly exposed, Paul shivered and turned around. Maybe it was time to go back inside. He didn't want Mel to worry too much.

Before he could push off the wall and swim to

the other side, something broke the still water with a muted splash. The other side of the pool was too dark to see except for moonlit ripples marching out to greet Paul. Behind their leading edge, bigger ripples curved in a bow wave around a partially submerged body as it swam toward him.

Paul smiled slowly. Melanie had come back to scare him—tit for tat. Good. Maybe after she got even, they could get back to enjoying their honeymoon.

"I see you," he said. "You're not going to get me like that, Mel. You've got to have the element of surprise."

The bow wave disappeared as Mel stopped swimming—or swam down deeper to avoid detection. He cast about, groping blindly under the water to catch her before she could catch him.

The waves of her approach reached him without her, rocking him gently against the wall. Long seconds passed, and the rippled surface of the pool grew still once more. Doubt furrowed Paul's brow, scratching through the patina of his drunken bravado. "Okay, you got me, Mel. You can come up for air now."

But still, nothing happened.

"Mel...?"

* * *

Beth stood on the living room balcony, peering

down to the roiling water of the pool. "Hello? Are you ok—" Violent splashing and a muffled cry interrupted her.

Beth's pulse beat like a drum in her ears. The splashing ceased and the pool grew still.

"Hello?" Beth tried again, but this time the darkness swallowed her voice without a peep.

An overwhelming urge to run built up inside of her until she was bouncing on her toes. What had she seen? Who had been in the pool a minute ago? And why weren't they answering?

Beth's imagination painted a pale, glistening silhouette swimming to the side of the pool, then climbing out, and padding off into the bushes on four legs.

Four legs. Not two. A shiver shook Beth's body. She wasn't imagining things. Squinting into the jagged shadows of foliage around the pool, she tried to get a better look, but whatever it was, it was gone, and she had a bad feeling that whoever had been in the pool, they were gone now, too.

Unable to stand it anymore, Beth turned and ran back inside. Her legs and hands shaking violently, she flicked the lock down and jumped into the far corner of the couch. Beth pulled her knees up to her chest and hugged them with a pillow, watching the sliding glass doors with wide, unblinking eyes.

CHAPTER 7

Bill flipped the master circuit breaker with a noisy *snap*. "Nothing," he sighed. Not that he'd expected otherwise. None of the individual breakers had been tripped, so flicking them all off and then on again wasn't likely to help. Not only that, but Bill could clearly hear the generators at the Marriott droning away. The Koa Kai wasn't the only place without power.

"Now what?" Toby asked.

"Now, we go to storage and get flashlights for the guests."

Toby nodded quickly. "Where's that?"

Bill frowned. "You've been working here for more than a year, and you don't know where storage is?"

"Man, I just teach the *haole* how to catch a wave. I don't know where you stow your shit."

"Just follow me," Bill grumbled, leading the way out of the electrical room with his flashlight. They emerged on the covered terrace running along the back of the main building. Bill shut the metal doors to the electrical room and headed toward the storage rooms.

Toby kept pace beside him, determined not to get left alone. "Man, we need to get back inside," he whispered.

A muffled voice drifted through the flowering hedge beside them. Bill stopped to listen. It was a man, his voice coming from the direction of the pool. Bill couldn't believe someone had gone out for a swim in the middle of all this.

"*Lolo buggah,*" Toby muttered—*crazy fool,* Bill translated.

Silence fell.

"Come on," Bill said, catching Toby's elbow with his free hand to drag him along. Before they took more than two steps, a loud splash issued from the pool, followed by a scream and more splashing.

Bill stopped cold, his ears straining, palms sweating, and heart rattling against his sternum. His thoughts raced, struggling to catch up.

Silence condensed around them like a thick fog, stifling the sounds just as abruptly as they had begun.

Toby began tugging insistently, trying to flee. "*LESGO,*" he whispered sharply.

Bill resisted the urge to shine his flashlight in

the direction of the pool and call out to whoever was down there.

Instead, he flicked off his flashlight, and Toby quickly did the same. Bill hurried down the terrace to the Koa Kai's only restaurant. Weaving through a maze of tables and chairs, Bill led them to the nearest set of doors and yanked one of them open. Toby squeezed by him in his hurry to get inside. Breathing hard, both of them spun around to peer through the doors and windows of the restaurant.

"What the *eff* was that?" Toby whispered. The kid had no problem swearing, but a handful of words apparently violated the sacred code of his conservative Hawaiian upbringing.

"Maybe nothing," Bill suggested as he flicked his flashlight back on and shone the beam through the glass. Fully half of the light bloomed on the surface, bouncing back to illuminate his own reflection. "It's probably just some of the guests fooling around in the pool."

"No, brah, *something* is out there. Do you have any guns?"

Seeing nothing outside, Bill turned to face Toby with a frown. "Guns? No. Why would I have guns at a resort?"

"You gotta have something! Some kinda weapon, brah! Knives from the kitchen, at least!"

"Through there," Bill replied, nodding to the

shadowy door that led there.

Toby sighed. "Better than nothing. We better go get 'em."

"You do that," Bill replied. "I'm going to go back to the lobby."

"That's lolo, braddah! We split up now, we gonna be *make die dead.*"

Bill frowned. "Speak English, damn it."

"Okay, you're crazy, and you gonna get us killed."

"The thing is, Toby, if there is something out there, and it isn't human, butcher knives aren't going to help, and it's probably heard us already."

"So lock the doors, man."

"I don't have the key, and besides, we left the doors in the lobby open when we went out, remember? Someone has to shut them."

Toby gaped at him. "Shit."

"Yeah, shit."

"All the more reason to get weapons! Knives are better than nothin, brah. Come on."

"Maybe." Bill gave in with a nod. "All right, let's see what we can find."

CHAPTER 8

They hurried through the restaurant to the kitchen's swinging door. Tables were strewn with plates of unfinished food, chairs pushed out, others knocked over and lying on the ground. They reached the kitchen door and pushed through into a warm, fragrant space, gleaming with stainless steel, and crowded with pots and pans full of food that sat cooling on the burners. Partially diced veggies lay abandoned on cutting boards, sharp knives gleaming beside them. Toby snatched the nearest one and held it up like a prized trophy. Then he pinned his flashlight under one arm and grabbed the handle of a frying pan. Flipping the food out on the stove, he handed it to Bill, who stared dubiously at the pan before swinging it around experimentally and drawing whooshing sounds from the air.

"Where is everyone?" Toby asked, casting about quickly.

"They saw that meteor land in the ocean. My

guess is they fled up the stairs and elevators with all of the guests," Bill explained. "They're probably hiding with them in their rooms."

"So we're alone down here?" Toby asked in fading whisper.

"Yeah, I'd bet on that."

"Then we gotta go!"

"Actually, I want to go take a look out by the pool."

Toby's cheeks bulged with an incredulous reply, but Bill held up a hand to stop him before it could burst from his lips.

"You can wait here if you want. I need to know what we're dealing with. If anything."

"I'm out. I'll see you at da room, brah."

Bill nodded. "Fine."

Toby followed him out of the kitchen, and then promptly darted left, heading for the doors that separated the restaurant from the lobby. Bill watched him go with a frown. He'd evidently forgotten about the lobby doors that they'd left open.

They reached their respective exits at the same time. Bill stepped out into the premature night while Toby ran into the lobby. Sweeping his flashlight around the restaurant's *lanai,* Bill found more half-finished meals and overturned chairs. Shadows slithered through it all, but there wasn't anything lying in wait for him there, so he moved on, heading through a gap in the railing around the lanai and down a narrow, flower-lined path to the pool.

Crickets and a gentle breeze tickling through the palms overhead were the only sounds. Now strangely absent was the droning roar of the Marriott's generators.

"Hello?" Bill called out as he neared the pool, more to scare something off than to actually get an answer.

The bobbing beam of his flashlight revealed wet, gleaming puddles around the pool. Relief flooded through Bill, easing some of the tension in his chest. He'd been right. The commotion they'd heard had been some of the guests fooling around in the pool.

But as he drew near to the pool, Bill saw that some of those puddles were too thick to be water; then he saw red smears around them, and his stride faltered. Sweeping his flashlight around, the beam flashed over the pool. The water was dark and cloudy with blood. Soggy chunks of meat floated around the ragged, three-limbed body of a naked man. His missing arm was nowhere in sight.

Bill whirled around, frantically scanning the darkness with his flashlight. Shadows danced around bushes and trees. A watery, bloody trail led from one corner of the pool straight to the open doors of the lobby.

Somewhere a door slid open, and Bill jumped with fright.

"Hello?" a woman asked in a trembling voice. "Paul?"

Bill swept his flashlight toward the sound of that voice and found a pretty young woman standing on the balcony of one of the garden suites, wearing nothing but a skimpy nightgown. Long brown hair cascaded over her shoulders.

"Paul, is that you?"

She wouldn't be able to see him through the glare of his flashlight. Bill hoped Paul wasn't the dead man in the pool. He was about to call out to her, to warn her to go inside and lock her door, when he heard a twig snap from the direction of the beach.

Spinning around, Bill shined his flashlight in the direction of the sound. The beam illuminated a dense clump of red and pink ginger plants. "Go away!" he screamed.

"Who are you talking to?" the woman asked.

Something pale and glistening seemed to flow away from the green stalks of the ginger plants, down a grassy slope and out of sight.

"Hello! Have you seen my husband? He was in the pool! Is he there with you?"

Bill stared hard into the foliage, eyes burning with the need to blink. "Get inside!" he said.

"What? Why?"

They didn't have time to stand around and argue. Snapping out of it, Bill sprinted around the pool, leaping over loungers to avoid the slick puddles of bloody water on the tiled surround. His still-bare feet hit the grass. The woman's eyes grew round as he approached, and she scrambled back inside. The glass door slid shut in front of him just as he collided with it, his frying pan smacked the glass with a *thunk*, and a long, jagged crack appeared. The woman screamed and backed away.

He tried yanking the door open, but it was locked. "Let me in, damn it!" Bill said, banging on the door with his flashlight. Hairs stood up on the back of his neck, and he whirled around, terror clawing inside of him at the thought of what might have followed him from the pool. Leaning against the sliding door, he shone his flashlight back the way he'd come and flicked the beam back and forth over grass, flowers, bushes, and pool loungers.

"Whatever you are, you don't want to mess with me!" Bill said in a loud voice.

A metal railing shivered directly overhead, and Bill glanced up to see a dark shape clinging to the balcony above him. His heart seized in his chest, and his flashlight tracked swiftly up...

CHAPTER 9

The door behind Bill slid open, and he fell inside with a painful jolt that sent shooting pains ricocheting up his spine. His frying pan smacked the tiles, followed by the back of his head. The door slid shut just as quickly as it had opened, and then something heavy bounced off it with a loud *thump* and a shrill squeal like nails on a chalkboard.

Bill sat up quickly, his head still spinning, and shone his flashlight through the cracked glass of the sliding door. There was nothing there.

"Did you see it?" Bill asked, glancing up at the pretty young woman who had let him in.

She quickly shook her head, her blue eyes wide and staring. "No, did you see my husband?"

"Was he the one skinny-dipping in the pool?"

"You did see him! Where is he?"

Bill eased himself off the floor and regarded the woman before him. She had a young, pretty face, long dark hair, and glassy, hopeful blue eyes. He vaguely recognized her. She was the better half of one of the two honeymooner couples currently checked in at his resort. Her name came drifting back to mind. Bill was ashamed to admit that it was easier to remember the names of pretty female guests. "Melanie, right?"

"Yes," she said. "Please, I have to know. Did you see Paul? Was the pool empty?"

Bill grimaced, remembering the cloudy crimson water and the remains of the naked man floating there. He looked like he'd had a run-in with a shark. "I'm very sorry, but he's dead."

"What? No..." she whimpered. Her voice caught and broke, and she crumpled to the floor, looking suddenly small and child-like. She looked up with tears streaming from her eyes. "How?"

Bill hesitated. She didn't need to know the details. "I don't know."

"But then... how can you be sure that he's dead?"

"Trust me. He is." Bill dropped to his haunches and set the frying pan down gently so he could place a hand on the woman's shoulder. "I'm very sorry, Melanie."

"But... it's just a satellite! Paul said that it was just—" She sobbed into her hands.

"That's what I thought, too..." Bill said, trailing off as his attention switched from the newly-wedded widow to the cracked glass of the patio door. He got up and walked over to examine it. There was a big, greasy smudge just above knee height, and a set of four, long scratches beside it. *Claw marks?* Tracing those furrows with his fingertips, Bill frowned. None of this made any sense.

Even if aliens were invading, why blot out the sun? And why send down primitive monsters with claws and teeth for weapons instead of an army with guns? And why on *Earth,* would they choose to invade Kauai? Surely there were hundreds of better, more strategic targets.

"He can't be dead," Melanie said in a dull voice.

Bill turned to see her staring fixedly out the door, her sobs spent for the moment. Her cheeks gleamed in the reflected glow of his flashlight. She looked like she'd reached the first stage of grief: denial, but he didn't have time for her to go through the others. He needed to go up and check on his daughter.

"Listen, stay here, okay?" he said, hurrying by her on his way to the front door of the suite. "Keep the door locked, and don't go out for any reason."

Just as he reached the door, something cold touched his arm. He flinched and recoiled from it, stumbling into the closet beside the door and throwing up his hands to defend himself.

It was just Melanie. She'd followed him to the door.

"Shit!" he hissed.

"Where are you going?"

"To get my daughter and go for help."

"I'm going with you," she said.

"It's safer here," he insisted.

"The door is broken," she said, thrusting out a hand to indicate the cracked glass of the sliding patio door. "And that thing out there knows we're here. It could come back."

Bill hesitated. "Fine." He nodded to the kitchenette. "Get yourself a knife or something."

Melanie darted into the kitchen and pulled a butcher knife from the wooden knife block on the counter. "What about you?" she asked. "Where's that skillet?"

Bill snorted. He'd be damned if he was going to die clutching a frying pan. Besides, if they were dealing with some kind of unintelligent or semi-intelligent monster, they might be able to scare it more easily than they could hurt it. Ducking into the kitchen, Bill rifled through one of the drawers until he found a barbecue lighter with a long stem. Then he went to check under the sink for the complimentary cleaning supplies he knew should be there. But the cabinet was empty. "Damn it, it's not here!"

"Looking for this?" Melanie asked, holding out a can of Lysol.

"Yeah." He took it with a tight smile and stuffed the lighter in his pocket before walking back to the front door. Gripping his flashlight under one arm, he grabbed the door handle. "Ready?" he asked.

"Let's go," Melanie replied, holding her knife above her shoulder, ready to stab.

Just before Bill could yank the door open, someone pounded on it urgently. "Who's there?" he asked.

No answer.

He checked the peephole, but of course, he couldn't see anything in the darkened hallway. "Identify yourself," he demanded.

The knocking returned, but softer, more distant. A door clicked open somewhere further down the hall.

"Hello?" a man asked. "Hey, is anyone there?"

Bill's eye widened behind the peephole.

"Who is it?" a woman added.

"Just some stupid kid playing a prank," the man replied.

The door clicked shut, and just a few seconds after that, the screaming began.

CHAPTER 10

Beth sat on her bed under the covers with her knees drawn up to her chest, sweeping her flashlight obsessively between the window and the door. She'd heard the screams from the people in the pool; first the woman, then the man. And she'd heard other noises, too... pleading, shouting, and thumping sounds coming through the walls from neighboring rooms.

Where were her dad and Toby? They'd been gone too long. What if something had happened to them and they weren't coming back? What if—

A muffled banging interrupted her thoughts. It sounded like someone was knocking at the door...

Bang, bang, bang!

Beth froze, terrified to leave the safety of her room. What if it was her dad and Toby? But her dad had a key so he could let himself in.

Then she remembered drawing the brass chain across the door. They weren't getting in like that.

"Shit!" Beth muttered and flung the covers

aside. Jumping out of bed, she stormed up to her door, unlocked it, and pulled it open.

The door thundered with another round of knocking. "Hang on, I'm coming!" Beth said irritably. Her legs shaking, she swept her fear under a carpet of anger. They were going to get an earful for leaving her alone so long.

Beth breezed through the living room, past the dining table to the front door, but instead of seeing it cracked open with the chain pulled taut as she'd expected, she saw that the door was still shut. Her dad had a key, so whoever was knocking, it wasn't him.

Maybe it was Toby. Had they been separated? Icy dread gripped her with the thought that something might have happened to her dad.

"Please be okay, please be okay," she whispered.

Reaching the door, she said, "Hello? Who's there?" and then placed her ear against the door to listen for a reply.

"Come get some!" a loud voice said, followed by a loud *bang,* and then two more. Gunshots. A deep, trilling roar answered, like a bear with a stutter, followed by a scrabbling of claws on tiles, and heavy footsteps approaching fast.

"Hello?" Beth called through her door. "Is someone out there?"

The footsteps stopped.

Knock, knock, knock! The door shook, and Beth jumped.

"Open the door! Quick!"

"Who is it?"

"Does it matter? Hurry, before that thing comes back!"

Beth slid off the chain and pulled open the door. A big man with a flashlight and an unkempt blond beard stumbled in and slammed the door behind him. He flicked the deadbolt into place and stood with his back against the door, as if the lock might not hold.

Beth stared at the stranger. He wore a blue cap with a red C on it, and a gray Hawaiian shirt covered in blood. She felt like she'd seen him drinking beers by the pool sometime over the past few days. Beth's gaze slipped down the man's blood-soaked shirt to the gun in his hand.

"What's going on? Where did you get that?"

"I brought it with me," he said. "Damn good thing I did, too, or we'd be fish in a fucking barrel right now."

Suddenly wary of this stranger more than whatever was outside, Beth backed up a couple of steps. "You can't bring a gun on a plane..."

"I didn't have to. I live here."

"You live here? Then why come here for a

vacation?"

"A man can't take a vacation close to home?" He snorted and shook his head. "What's your name?"

"Beth."

"I'm Don. Now, listen up, we have to get out of here."

"No, my dad will be back soon. I have to wait for him."

Don fixed her with an uncertain look. "He went out?"

Beth nodded. "With my boyfriend."

"Well, I hate to pop your bubble, kid, but they're dead."

"What?" Tears sprang to Beth's eyes. "You saw them?"

Don shrugged. "Maybe, maybe not, but I found over a dozen people up here all slashed to pieces."

"By what?" Beth shrieked.

"I didn't get more than a glance before it took off. Slick, transparent skin. A little smaller than you—fast and smart, but naked as a baby. No armor or weapons. Not exactly what you see in the movies when aliens invade."

"So it is aliens," Beth said, feeling suddenly cold all over.

"I can't imagine what else," Don replied.

"Animals don't knock on people's doors to get them to open up. Besides, something has to be blocking the sun, right?"

"And the stars," Beth said.

Don grimaced. "I didn't notice that. You couldn't see *any* stars?"

Beth hesitated. "There were a few, but only out toward the horizon."

"Then whatever is hovering over us is either low to the ground or just that damn big. Either way, we're at ground zero here, which means the safest thing for us to do is run. Are you coming with me?"

Beth shook her head. "I have to wait for my dad."

Don's permanently furrowed brow tightened. "You're not safe here, kid. Those things can get up to the balcony and force the locks. What do you think I'm doing out of my room?"

Beth whirled around to check that nothing was out on the balcony trying to break in.

"Still think you'd rather stay here?"

"Maybe. How do I know I can trust you?"

"What?"

Beth crossed her arms, doing her best to look brave. "For all I know *you* killed the people up here, not an alien. You brought a gun to a hotel. Who does that? A serial killer, maybe."

Don's lips curved into a wry grin. "Or someone who's used to sleeping with a gun beside his pillow. Look, kid, I was in the army for eight years. Afghanistan." He slowly shook his head. "Some people have a favorite blanket or a pillow that makes them feel safe. I've got my gun."

Beth frowned. "If I go with you, where are we going?"

"Nawiliwili Harbor. I have a boat there. It's not much, but it'll get us to Oahu, at least."

Beth knew the harbor well. It was in the town of Lihue, within walking distance of her school. "You have a car to get us there?" she asked.

"A truck."

Beth felt crazy for even thinking about leaving her room with a stranger, but staying here alone with monsters trying to break in seemed even less appealing. "We'll look for my dad on the way out?"

Don looked hesitant. "So long as you don't go around shouting his name and drawing attention to us."

Her palms sweating and skin itching, Beth nodded quickly. "Okay, let's go."

CHAPTER 11

Captain Arthur Reed stood on the bridge of his ship, the *USS Port Royal,* watching his helmsman take them ever deeper into the inexplicable darkness that had fallen over the island of Kauai. NASA's report stated that an unidentified, square-bottomed metallic object measuring nearly eight hundred kilometers on each side had dropped into low Earth orbit just over four hundred kilometers from the surface at 1421 local time, which was—Reed checked his watch—only fifty-seven minutes ago. From there it had executed maneuvers to put itself directly over Kauai, causing a complete eclipse of the sun over nearly ninety degrees of the sky.

But what Reed really wanted to know was why no one had seen it coming. You don't just *miss* an alien spaceship the size of Texas. NASA claimed that it must have some kind of cloaking technology to elude detection. But that sounded like ass-covering to Reed. Someone had screwed up.

Regardless, the very presence of the object in question left no question as to its origins. As for the 'meteors' that had rained down all over the island after the spaceship's arrival, best guess was that they were some kind of landing craft. God only knew what had come out of them, but whatever it was, Reed *knew* that it wasn't friendly. The electromagnetic pulse that had detonated above the island soon after the aliens' dropships began vanishing over the horizon only confirmed it as far as he was concerned.

Unfortunately, the powers that be had decided to pussyfoot around. They believed that launching a preemptive strike against an interstellar spaceship would be both futile and foolish. Reed didn't agree. If it were up to him, and he had access to the nuclear football, he wouldn't hesitate to order an all-out attack.

Unfortunately, he was not the President, and he was bound by a chain of command that would promptly put him out of a job and into prison if he stepped out of line. He had explicit orders not to engage the visitors under any circumstances. His mission was to approach the island, drop anchor at a respectful distance, and send out the recon teams. Those recon teams were in turn bound by the same orders to avoid engagement at all costs, and to use non-lethal force until, and only if, American lives were threatened.

But Captain Reed didn't like the idea of how the history books would portray him if he got his men killed by sending them into an alien beachhead unprepared. As per their orders, his Marines would go out packing stun grenades, shotguns loaded with XREP cartridges, and even grenade launchers sporting the military's latest 40mm HEMI projectiles, but they would also go packing all the deadlier counterparts of those weapons. The team leaders knew that live rounds were a last resort, but if all else failed, Reed didn't expect his men to roll over and die. Besides, he seriously doubted that the non-lethals would do anything.

For starters, the aliens probably wore suits of high-tech armor that would repel all but the heaviest rounds, and even if their armor wasn't that sophisticated, they might not be vulnerable to the same types of stimuli as humans. Electrical-based taser systems like XREP and HEMI might be useless, and stun grenades would only be useful against beings with eyes and ears. What if they had completely different senses?

There were far too many unknowns, so Captain Reef had ordered the missile cruiser's inflatable CRRCs to be loaded up with enough firepower to arm a third world coup, and frankly, he hoped the Marines in those boats would get the chance to use it.

Glancing up, Captain Reef scowled at the empty black square in the sky. If those alien *buggahs*, as the locals would say, had chosen to squat their collective asses over New York or Washington, no one would be tip-toeing around, afraid to hurt their feelings with an armed response. No, they were only cautious because the aliens hadn't sent landers down anywhere else besides Kauai. Having apparently lost their minds, his superiors assumed this meant that aliens had traveled halfway across the galaxy for the express purpose of claiming just one small island.

Well, I call bullshit, Reed thought. This was some kind of field test for them. *They want to see how we respond. Test our mettle.*

"Helm, mark your head," Reed said.

"Mark my head, aye, two seven three, sir."

"Keep her so."

"Aye, keeping her so."

Reed nodded to his executive officer. "Commander Morris, what's our ETA?"

"One hour, seven minutes, sir."

"Too long. Lee helm, set speed to flank."

"Aye, setting speed to flank, sir," the officer at the lee helm replied.

"XO, get me an update from Lieutenant

Spooner. I want our recon teams ready to launch the minute we drop anchor."

"Aye, captain, I'll check their status."

CHAPTER 12

Bill heard a door click open, and then the knocking returned. When no one answered, the sound moved on further down the hall. Something was out there, knocking on doors to trick people into opening them—and then creeping in and killing them.

"We have to do something," Bill said.

"Maybe we should stay," Melanie replied.

He rounded on her and pointed at the cracked glass of the patio door. "You said it yourself. Something could break in here any minute. I'm not going to die hiding in here like a coward. If something's going to rip my guts out, better that happen while I'm out trying to save lives. Now, are you coming with me or not?"

Another scream sounded, and Bill's hand tightened on the door handle. "Do it for your husband," he said and thrust his flashlight into her chest. "I'm going to need both of my hands free," he explained.

Before Melanie could even nod her consent, he yanked the door open and leapt into the hallway, brandishing his barbecue lighter and can of Lysol. A shaky beam of light followed him out, revealing blood-smeared floors and something crouching in the shadows of an open doorway near the edge of the flashlight's range.

"Shit," Bill muttered. "I think it's eating someone! Come on!" He started down the hall at a run, not waiting to see if Melanie followed. "Hey!" he yelled. The creature in the open doorway looked up, and Bill caught a glint of large black eyes—four of them in a row where a forehead should be. The creature's head and body glistened as if wet; it had translucent, hairless skin, and no clothing or armor of any kind.

The monster's jaws popped open as Bill approached and jagged, glass-colored teeth appeared. The aperture of the black eyes narrowed as translucent skin squeezed into wrinkled cones around them; Bill wondered if that was how the creature focused its eyes.

It drew itself up onto hind legs, brushing the ceiling with its head. Bill stopped and gaped at the monster. It had four long legs. The front set branched at the knees into two pairs of additional limbs with broad hands and three fingers. Gleaming, glass-like claws tipped each finger. The creature held one of those branching forelimbs out, reaching for him, and Bill saw that the primary limb ended in a sturdy, hoof-like pad, while the smaller, skinnier set unfolded to a length of at least six feet each.

Bill felt like he was trapped in a childhood nightmare, the monster under his bed had come to life, and his feet froze as if they were stuck in molasses.

"What do you want?" he asked. The creature cocked its head at him, and then let out a stuttering roar that left his ears ringing and filled the air with a rotten stench. A long black tongue snaked out between glass-like teeth as if to taste his fear—

And then it lunged. Bill let out a guttural scream and used his lighter to turn a can of Lysol into a pitiful flame-thrower with barely two feet of range.

CHAPTER 13

James Lucas had told his wife and kids to hide in one of the bedrooms of their 2nd-floor suite—the one without the balcony—while he and the resort manager, Eric Monte, stayed in the living room to guard the entrance with makeshift weapons. James held a wooden leg in each of his meaty fists, while Eric Monte brandished a paring knife and a barbecue skewer from the kitchen.

Eric's phone sat on the kitchen counter illuminating the entry area with diffuse light reflected from the ceiling. James stood just behind the door with his ear pressed to it. He and Eric had both heard people screaming outside and on the floor below; they'd also heard what sounded like gunshots on the floor above, but maybe they'd been mistaken. How would a tourist manage to smuggle a gun in their luggage?

James' thoughts were interrupted by faint, thumping footsteps and a dragging sound. He frowned and placed a chair leg to his lips like a giant finger.

Eric's eyes widened, and he grew very still. The footsteps soon faded into the distance. James resisted the urge to ease the door open for a look at whatever was out there, but he knew better than that. Besides, it was too dark in the hallway to see anything. Instead, he waited through long, sweaty seconds. Seconds turned to minutes, and the footsteps didn't return.

"What was it?" Eric whispered.

James just shook his head. *How the hell should I know?* So far his vacation had been nothing but one disaster after the next. First, his wife, Kayla, had gotten stung by a jellyfish and he'd had to pee on her, then Alison caught the flu, followed by her brother, Michael, after that, the water outage, and now...

Now they were at ground zero of something straight out of the movies. Aliens. To tell the naked truth he'd never believed in all of that *Enquirer* bullshit, but this was the real deal, and it was scary as all hell. What did they want? Why had they blotted out the sun? Why Kauai? Who were they? What did they even look like?

The questions were endless, and the only answers he had were the screams that came echoing through the walls. It seemed the invaders had come for the express purpose of killing and terrifying tourists, but that made absolutely zero sense.

This was supposed to have been his family's last happy memory before James told Kayla the truth and everything went to hell. It wasn't supposed to go to hell before he could spill the beans.

He hadn't planned to cheat on his wife, but working eighty-hour weeks at his law firm to distinguish himself as a candidate for partner had meant that he spent far more time with his fellow associates, and paralegals like Amy, than with his wife. Throw in an office party six months later to congratulate him for being made partner, and suddenly all of his unfulfilled desires and fantasies boiled over. Amy's eyes had been filled with stars, or maybe dollar signs, and his with lust for a woman twenty years younger than his wife. All it had taken was a cheap bottle of champagne to stir the pot. And now... now he was in the middle of a nightmare that made all of that look about the size of an ant from space—which was probably exactly how these aliens saw humans.

Fuck this, James thought. *I'm not going to die like a rat in this hole.* "We have to get out of here," he said in a bold voice.

"You want to go... *out?*" Eric sounded incredulous. "Those *things* are out there. We're safer where we are."

"I bet that's what all the others thought, too," James replied. "Those creatures are getting them out of their rooms somehow."

"You have children, Mr. Lucas."

"Which is why I need to get them out of here!"

"Help will be on the way. We just need to be patient," Eric said.

"How the hell do you know? Even if help does come, there are a million other places they might go first."

"Even if we do go out—then what?" Eric asked.

"Those things landed all over the island, right? There were maybe a few dozen landers. One of them came down in the ocean right in front of *us.* That's why they're here now. But if we could get away and go somewhere else, somewhere they didn't land, or better yet get to the harbor, steal a boat and get the hell away from Kauai..." James began nodding along with the wisdom of his plan. "We just have to get to the parking lot, to our rental car, and from there to the nearest harbor."

Eric looked skeptical, but James could see the wheels turning inside his head. "You're parked out front?"

"Right out front," James said. "We just have to get down the hall, down one flight of stairs and out those sliding glass doors at the entrance."

"What if we run into one of those creatures along the way?"

James knocked his chair legs together lightly. "You let me worry about that."

Eric frowned. "I don't know..."

"You can stay if you want, but we're leaving." James sucked in a deep breath, his chest puffing up with macho self-assurance. Now all he had to do was convince his wife.

* * *

The monster hesitated at the sight of the flames billowing from Bill's hand, and Bill screamed at the top of his lungs, hoping to scare the creature off. Four black eyes squinted inside clenching, wrinkled cones of translucent flesh. A black tongue licked the air, and folding forelimbs bent at the joints, rearing back, fingertips rubbing together like a praying mantis's legs. The monster tossed its head back and made a shrill trilling noise in the back of its throat. To Bill's horror, he heard an echo of that sound somewhere behind him, approaching fast.

He glanced over his shoulder, but couldn't see anything in the darkened hall. Melanie stood frozen just outside the door to her room, the flashlight he'd given her shining in his direction. The second monster trilled again, and there came a galloping sound. Melanie whirled around, and the flashlight swept away with her, leaving Bill in darkness, staring up at a fire-lit monster. The flames were guttering as if the can of disinfectant was running out of juice. *No...*

Bill began backing away, but the monster advanced at the same pace. Glancing back once more, he saw Melanie's flashlight reveal a second translucent monster racing toward them on four legs. She screamed and ran back into her room. The hallway plunged into utter darkness; Bill heard the door slam, then lock, and his heart spasmed painfully. His breath hitched in his throat, and an awful sinking feeling crawled into his stomach.

"Get away!" he said as his Lysol flame-thrower sputtered and darkness swelled. A bony arm came arcing out to reach him, snaking around the sputtering fire. Bill gritted his teeth and swept the flames over that arm before it could reach him. The monster squealed like a piglet and withdrew—only to seize him from the other side with one of its other limbs. Sharp claws slashed through his shirt and bit into his shoulder; he cried out as hot blood coursed down his arm. Somehow he managed to keep his grip on the can of Lysol, but he couldn't reach the arm that had grabbed him. All he could do was keep those glassy teeth away.

"Somebody help!" Bill cried.

A low, stuttering growl started up, right beside his ear, and more claws bit into him around his ribs. A giant hand seized the back of his head and pulled it back. He struggled pitifully, provoking fresh agony from all the places where alien claws had skewered him. Another alien arm swept up in front of him. The hoof-like pad of the central leg appeared, gleaming in the sputtering flames still spewing from his makeshift weapon. He saw tree-ring-like patterns on the bottom of the hoof, and... some kind of orifice. It was a puckered mouth, he realized, just as it dilated open. He struggled to sweep his glorified candle into line and burn the gaping throat, but the flames had died down to barely six inches. All Bill could do was watch as that sucking mouth gaped wide and drifted toward him. He writhed and screamed, afraid to even guess what would happen next.

CHAPTER 14

Beth heard the screams as soon as she and Don reached the first-floor landing.

"That sounded like my Dad!" she whispered sharply.

Don reluctantly stopped and turned as he reached the sliding glass doors of the front entrance. "Kid, we can't."

Beth set her jaw. "Maybe *you* can't." She turned toward the sound of her dad's screams and ran, lighting the way with her phone. She ran past the elevators and the stairs, through the lobby, and opened the door to Building C. A long, shadowy hallway stretched before her, and the screams snapped into louder, sharper focus. Gritting her teeth, Beth ran as fast as she could, never for a moment wondering what she would do when she arrived.

A dim flicker of flames illuminated large, hulking shadows clutching someone on all sides. Beth recognized her dad's loose-fitting white cotton shirt and brown shorts.

"Dad!" she cried.

Rumbling growls sounded as she approached, but her dad gave no reply. Skidding to a stop just five feet from them, Beth's eyes flicked over the translucent creatures holding her father. Their heads turned, and four black eyes squinted at her in the light of her phone's flash. One of them peeled away from her dad, the other she saw had completely covered his face.

"Let him go!"

The one that had peeled away began advancing on her with four arms raised and poised to strike. A mouth full of jagged, glassy teeth yawned open, and a big black tongue darted out. Beth backed away quickly, shining her light into the monster's eyes, hoping to blind it. She was gratified to see the knots of wrinkled flesh around those eyes tighten until they were just four gleaming pinpricks inside the creature's massive head. It growled at her, and she gave a shaky smile.

"You like that four eyes?"

It stopped advancing and shrank back a few feet, hind legs bending to lunge. She saw those legs snap straight a second later. The monster growled as its jaws opened wide enough to swallow her whole.

"Get down!" someone knocked her over, and two gunshots followed, deafening her. Beth landed hard and stared up at Don. He held his handgun in one hand, his flashlight in the other. The monster squealed and withdrew, blood gushing like water from a pair of ragged holes in its torso. It dropped to all fours, extra limbs folding up, and shrank like a balloon with a leak until it couldn't have been any larger than she was.

"Get!" Don said but held his fire. "You want more?" he roared, shaking his gun with a metallic rattle. "I've got plenty where that came from!"

The creature shook its head and shoulders like a wet dog, and then bounded down the corridor, quickly fading from sight. The one holding Beth's father withdrew from him, but slowly and reluctantly. Horror stabbed in Beth's gut as his face appeared, glistening with blood.

"Get away from him!" Beth screamed.

Don's gun went off again. The monster squealed and released Bill, letting him fall with a sickening thud. Then the alien dropped to all fours and dashed away in the same direction as the first.

Beth hurried to her dad's side and knelt beside him. "Dad!" She cradled his head in her lap, scanning him for injuries. His eyes were shut, and she wasn't sure if he was breathing, but besides a few bleeding welts on his cheeks, there was no sign of any damage.

"Dad?" she tried again, and this time lightly slapped his cheek. His eyes fluttered open, and he gasped, sucking in a sudden breath. Tears sprang to Beth's eyes, and she smiled.

"We have to get out of here," Don said. "Before those things come back."

"Can you walk, Dad?"

"I'm fine," he said, jumping to his feet and hauling her up after him. Don turned and started jogging back the way they'd come. They ran after him, but her father darted abruptly to one side and knocked loudly on one of the doors.

"Melanie!" he said. "It's me, Bill. The resort owner."

"Are they gone?" a trembling voice asked.

Don stopped and turn to them, waving them over with the hand holding his gun. "Come on!" he yelled.

The door cracked open, a golden chain gleaming in the light of Beth's phone. A pretty woman appeared in the gap, her cheeks streaked with tears.

A hand flew to her mouth when she saw Bill. "What happened to you?!"

"I'm fine," he said. "My daughter rescued me, but we have to go before they come back."

The door clicked shut in their faces.

A galloping sound began, faint, but quickly drawing near.

"Shit," Don hissed. "We have to go, now!"

The chain rattled, and the door swung open. Melanie stumbled out, holding a flashlight. The galloping sound was louder now.

"Wha—" the woman turned toward the noise.

"Let's go!" Bill said and tried to haul her toward Don by her arm, but she struggled, afraid to leave the safety of her room. Beth ran up ahead of them and then turned to walk backward and shine her phone into the shadows behind them. A pair of glistening monsters were crawling toward them at a frightening pace, four legs bent at the knees and splayed out from their bodies like spiders.

"They're coming!" Beth screamed.

"Run, damn it!" Don said.

Bill tugged on Melanie's arm, but she wouldn't budge from the doorway, so he gave up and let her go.

The young woman's door slammed and locked, and the three of them ran as fast as they could to get back to the lobby, not even daring to look back.

They crashed into the swinging door at the end of the corridor, bursting out beside the stairs. Don promptly turned and planted his shoulder against the door. "Help me!" he said.

Beth went to brace the door with him, but her dad came and nudged her aside. "I've got it," he said, and Beth stepped back. The galloping noise became a crescendo, and she held her breath.

The door thumped with violent impacts; both Don and Bill lost precious inches as the door cracked open. Pale, translucent fingers appeared in the gap. Curving three-inch claws like shards of glass scraped and scrabbled, digging out giant splinters from the wooden door frame.

Stuttering roars shivered through the air, vibrating through Beth. The men fought to hold their ground, but their feet were slipping on the tiled floor. They struggled, panting and cursing, losing precious centimeters. The door was inching open with every passing second.

A stampede of footsteps sounded in the stairwell behind them. Beth spun around, remembering the galloping sound that preceded the aliens, and she screamed at the top of her lungs.

CHAPTER 15

Just before they reached the bottom of the first flight of stairs, James heard a girl scream; the sound came from the lobby. Up ahead Eric Monte suddenly stopped, and James almost knocked him over.

"That sounded like Beth," Eric whispered.

"Who?" James asked.

"The owner's daughter," Eric replied.

"Maybe we should go back," James' wife, Kayla, said.

"Daddy..." Michael whimpered, and wrapped his arms in a vice around one of James' legs. He was only six years old.

"Shhh," James said, placing a big hand on his son's head, and cocking one ear toward the sound. The screaming stopped, replaced by men's voices echoing from the stairwell. "They're in trouble, but I don't think they're under attack."

"How do you know?" Kayla asked.

"Because the girl stopped screaming and the

others are *talking,* not choking on their own blood."

"James!" Kayla chided sharply.

"Shhh!" he snapped.

"I'm not going down there," Eric said.

"Did I ask you to?" James replied. He snatched the man's phone away. "Everyone stay here and be quiet."

"But—" Michael latched onto his leg again.

"Kay, get him off me."

She pried their son's hands away, and he screamed.

"Damn it all to hell! Now the whole world knows we're here. Everyone follow me."

James hit the landing, hurried around the bend, and down the last flight of stairs to the lobby. A teenage girl appeared under the beam of his stolen phone, peering up at him with wide eyes and a furrowed brow.

"Hey, what's going on down there?" James called out.

"We need help holding the door!" a man called back before the girl could reply.

James hurried down the stairs, following the voices around the corner to a wooden door with two men in blood-soaked shirts bracing it against scrabbling, jelly-fish colored hands with circular palms and three long fingers on each.

"Shit!" James said and body-checked the door

with all of his considerable weight.

Something squealed on the other side, and the jelly-fish hands withdrew, allowing the door to bang shut. James shone the phone light where the door handle should have been, but all he saw was a simple brass loop.

"There's no door handle!" he cried.

"I know," one of the two men said. James recognized him in spite of his blood-streaked face. It was the resort owner. Just a few hours ago James had been demanding a refund from that man, and now here they were, bracing a door together to keep alien monsters out of the lobby.

"There's got to be some way to lock it," James insisted.

"They seem to have lost interest," the second man bracing the door said. This one had a thick blond beard and was wearing a blue Chicago Cubs cap.

"They might be going around," the resort owner replied, easing his shoulder away from the door to plant his back against it instead.

"Could be," Blond Beard replied. "They're a lot smarter than they look; they were knocking on doors to get people to open up."

James stepped back from the door and cast about the shadowy lobby with his stolen phone. He saw Kayla and the kids standing at the bottom of the stairs with Eric and the teenage girl who'd been screaming a moment ago.

"What are we going to do?" Kayla asked.

He shook his head. "We have to get out to our cars. Get out of here before they come back," he said.

"I agree," Blond Beard said.

James swept his stolen phone around the lobby. Shadows flowed out of couches and chairs, flashing off the picture windows and sliding glass doors.

"Where's Toby?" the teenage girl asked suddenly. "Dad? Where—"

"You didn't see him?" the resort owner asked. "He went back to our room. He said he was going to hide with you."

"What? No," she replied, shaking her head. "He never came back."

The resort owner let out a noisy breath but said nothing.

"The aliens must have gotten him," James said, to which the girl let out a strangled sob. He swept the phone light back to the resort manager and the Cubs fan with the shaggy blond beard. This time he noticed the semi-automatic pistol in Blond Beard's hand—the source of the gunshots they'd heard on the third floor. James frowned, wondering where the other man had gotten the gun and wishing he had one of his own. "I have a minivan parked outside," James said. "But it's not big enough for all of us. I can fit three besides my family."

"I have a two-seater pick-up," Blond Beard added. "Could fit three in a pinch, with more in the back."

"I'm not getting in the back," Eric put in.

"No one's getting in the back," the resort owner added. "There's only eight of us, and I have a car, too." He pulled a jangling set of keys from his pocket with an electronic key fob attached.

"Then let's get out of here!" James replied.

The owner hesitated. "I have more guests trapped in their rooms."

"And you think you can save them?" Blond Beard asked, holding up his gun and shaking it for emphasis. "If we hadn't come to the rescue when we did, you'd be dead right now."

"Then help me. You have a gun!"

"Negative," Blond Beard said, shaking his head. "We need to get some *real* help. Besides, I've already pumped those things full of six rounds. If that didn't kill them, the other nine aren't going to either."

"We're wasting time," James said, glancing around anxiously.

"Please," the owner pleaded.

"Sorry. It's my gun, and I'm leaving. You gotta choose if you want to stay and be a dead idiot, or leave and come back as a live hero."

The owner's eyes tightened, and he wiped his bloody face on his sleeve. "Fine. Let's go." He gestured to the front entrance. "We'll need to pry the doors open and watch our backs—I left another set open on the other side of the lobby. Those things could sneak in behind us at any minute—if they haven't already."

"Shit," James said, and swung his light back around, but the phone's flash wasn't strong enough to reach anywhere close to the other end of the lobby. A real flashlight joined his, penetrating a dozen feet deeper, but James couldn't see anything besides the island tours ticket counter, the lobby bar, and more empty furniture. The far end with the restaurant was cloaked in shadows.

"I don't see anything. Let's move out," Blond Beard said.

CHAPTER 16

Bill grabbed one of the sliding doors, and the guy with the baseball cap grabbed the other.

"On three," the Cubs fan whispered.

Bill nodded.

"One, two... *three.*"

They hauled the doors open and warm fragrant air spilled in. The Cubs fan swept his gun and flashlight around the parking lot, holding them together like a wannabe police detective.

Shadows pooled between the cars, but no sign of aliens concealed within them.

"Seems clear, but it's impossible to say. We'll have to make a run for it. Each to their own vehicles."

"Split up?" Beth asked in a trembling voice.

Bill was also wondering at the wisdom of trying to reach his car alone with Beth. Neither of them had any kind of weapons. "We're going with you," Bill said, making a snap decision.

"Better keep up," the man replied. "Let's go."

With that, he ran out the open doors, leading the way with his gun and flashlight. Bill grabbed Beth's hand and tore after him, not waiting to see where Eric or James and his family went.

Bill flew across the parking lot, faster than he'd have thought possible, but Beth struggled to keep up, forcing him to drag her. She was only five two, and her legs weren't nearly long enough to keep up with two six-foot men running at top speed.

"Faster!" Bill whispered.

"I'm trying!" Beth replied between gasps. Her phone pumped up and down with her free arm, periodically flashing over the Cubs fan's blue hat and gray Hawaiian shirt. He was angling to the far right of the lot, heading for a white Chevrolet pick-up. Beth's light flashed off his shirt, then pooled on the asphalt, then back to his shirt. The man had reached his truck. Now he was fumbling with keys to open the door. Bill poured on an extra burst of speed to catch up, breathing hard.

Beth's light illuminated the vehicle again as she ran. The driver's door was open now, but the Cubs fan was gone.

Bill dug in his heels, skidding to a stop just behind the truck, his heart jackhammering in his chest. "Where is he?"

Beth's phone came up again, and Bill saw a shadow poking out just above the top of a headrest. Something was sitting behind the wheel of the truck.

"He's right there," Beth said, pointing at the pick-up.

The driver's side door swung shut with a noisy *bang,* and Bill snapped out of it. His fears were getting the best of him. He hoped his momentary hesitation hadn't been enough to get them killed. "Go!" he pushed Beth ahead of him between the truck and an adjacent car.

She yanked the door open, and he waited through agonizing seconds as she climbed in. Hairs rose on the back of his neck, imaginary hands raking fire through him. Casting a quick look over his shoulder, Bill stared hard into the darkness behind him, but saw nothing. Then something touched him, and he jumped and spun around.

Beth waved urgently and said, "Get in!"

Bill squeezed into the cab of the truck, all but crushing his daughter in the process. She slid over and Bill slammed the door shut behind them. Glancing at the Cubs fan, Bill frowned at him in the gloomy interior of the car.

"Don!" Beth's phone light flicked up to his face, making him wince from the glare. "Sorry," she added and quickly angled it down.

They both saw the slack-jawed horror lurking under Don's beard.

"What's wrong?" Bill asked.

Keys jangled in the ignition, but nothing happened. Don grimaced and shook his head. "We're fucked, that's what's wrong! My truck won't start."

"You've got to be kidding me," Bill muttered, suddenly wishing he'd gone for his Cadillac after all. "All right. It's okay. We'll head for my car. It's just around the corner." Bill's fingers grazed the door handle, but a firm hand seized his other arm and stopped him before he could open his door.

"Hang on," Don whispered. "I replaced the battery three months ago, and the alternator's brand-new."

"So? Maybe your plugs are dirty."

"The engine doesn't even turn over," Don replied. "If spark plugs were the issue, you'd still hear something when I turn the key. This is something else."

"Like what?" Bill demanded.

"The whole damn island is dark. Something took out the power everywhere, all at once. An EMP strike would do it. Look—" Don pointed out the darkened side windows of the truck, and then twisted around to look out the back window.

"Look at what?" Bill asked.

"That tourist hasn't been able to start his vehicle yet either. If he had, we'd be able to see the lights."

"Maybe he's parked out of sight," Bill said.

"Bull. You can make a run for your car if you want, but it's not gonna start either."

"So how are cell phones working?" Bill asked.

"Better insulated. The theory goes that they might survive an EMP if they're under a concrete or metal roof and not connected to the grid via a charger. These cars were outside when it hit, so they're fried."

"Then what are we going to do?" Bill demanded.

"Head back inside," Don replied.

"Hang on—" Bill said.

But Don was already pushing his door open. "Longer we wait, worse our chances get," he whispered.

And as if to punctuate that concern, a medley of terrified screams and raised voices came drifting in with the fragrant Hawaiian air.

CHAPTER 17

"You two get back to the lobby!" Don yelled as he jumped out of the truck.

"The lobby?" Beth asked, her heart spiking sharply with that suggestion. One of those aliens was out there!

"Wait! Where are you going?" Beth's dad called after him.

"To help!"

He left the truck door open. Beth watched him recede into the shadowy parking lot, the beam of her phone's flashlight shaking with her hand.

"We'd better get out," her dad said.

"Maybe we should stay..." Beth replied.

Her dad glanced at her and shook his head. "They're distracted right now. This might be the only chance we have. Ready?"

Beth breathed a shaky sigh. "Ready."

Her dad yanked their door open and jumped out. Beth was right behind him.

Raised, screaming voices drew their attention

for precious seconds. They saw a flashlight bobbing, then heard a loud voice—Don's. "Let him go!" Followed by gunshots.

"Run!" Beth's dad whispered sharply in her ear. She lurched into motion, sprinting across the parking lot to the front entrance of the resort.

* * *

"Let him go!" Don aimed with both hands, using the back of the hand holding the flashlight to steady his gun. He pulled the trigger twice in quick succession. The bullets hit with meaty *thwups,* and one of the two translucent nine-foot-tall monsters squealed and turned its head. Jagged, glass-like teeth yawned open in a jack-o-lantern grin, and a roar split the air. Both aliens stood on their hind legs, holding James aloft between them, while the big man with his tree-trunk arms and hammer fists struggled and kicked, screaming himself hoarse. His wife and children looked on from the minivan, their faces plastered to the windows, screaming their lungs out, too, while Eric lay on the asphalt with his guts coiled around him like snakes.

Don grimaced and shivered as a cold sweat prickled his skin. His head swam, and his hands began to shake. *No. Not now.*

His mind did a sharp one-eighty, veering off into the past. Blackened bodies hung out of a barbecued Humvee. The staring, empty black eyes of his buddies. Bullets crunched into the gravel around Don, zipping through the air with whistling sounds. The corporal screamed at him for help, but there was nothing Don could do; he was pinned down.

"Hang on, Peter!" Don screamed, and came back to the present with the sound of his own voice. He was back, lying flat on the asphalt, gasping for air and staring up at a starless black sky. His hands scrabbled around for his gun and flashlight. He found the light, but not the gun. Swinging the beam up, a translucent creature with jagged glass teeth appeared standing over him.

"Shit!" Don screamed. "Fuck off!" He struggled to get up, but dexterous limbs folded swiftly out and pinned him down. Sharp claws poked through his skin as if it were paper. White-hot pain coursed through him in four different places. He struggled to keep his grip on the flashlight, twisting his wrist to keep the alien in sight. He was determined to see his fate coming.

A hoof-like foot came at his face. The ringed, spongy white pad at the end opened wide, revealing a ribbed throat.

Don struggled, and claws dug deeper into his thighs and biceps. His whole body shook with adrenaline. After surviving two tours in the hellhole that was Afghanistan, this couldn't be how he died.

CHAPTER 18

Just as Bill reached the open doors of the lobby with his daughter, Don's screaming yanked his head around. The flashlight Don had been holding was lying on the asphalt in a shallow cone of light.

"Damn it," he muttered. "I have to go help them."

"You can't!" Beth whispered sharply.

"He saved my life. I have to try. Here—" He handed her his keys. "—go to the storeroom and lock yourself in."

"But what if one of those things finds me?"

"Go!"

Not waiting for a reply, Bill took off at a run. Sprinting in utter darkness, he stumbled through a planter box and nearly tripped. Sharp leaves scraped his legs.

"Hey!" Bill called out as he saw Don's flashlight flick up and cast the alien standing over him in a harsh, glaring light. One of the creature's hoof-mouths moved toward Don's face, just like it had done with him. Bill didn't hear or see Don's gun, which probably meant he'd lost it when that creature knocked him over. Bill cursed under his breath as he realized that he didn't have a flashlight to look for the weapon.

Running straight up to the alien, he kicked it in its gaping hoof-mouth. It squealed and withdrew sharply, rearing back. Don screamed as the alien's claws bit deeper into his flesh. His flashlight wavered, and a gleaming black object appeared, just to his right.

Bill dived for it, narrowly missing a swipe from one of the alien's arms. He landed hard, knocking the wind out of himself and bruising his elbows. But his hands grazed Don's gun. He seized it and rolled over just in time to see four alien arms reaching for him. Don's light illuminated the monster's jagged-toothed head and squinting black eyes. Bill fired directly between its teeth, blowing one of them out with a spray of foul-smelling splinters. The beast screeched deafeningly and thrashed, narrowly missing Bill's head with one of its forelegs. Bill pulled the trigger again, and this time the bullet hit an eye. The alien abruptly stopped screeching and fell on top of Don with a *thud.* At that, the second alien whirled around. Bill couldn't see it, but a loud, stuttering roar bellowed out of its mouth, giving Bill some idea about its location. The sound made Bill's teeth ache, and his eardrums pound painfully. He had to resist the urge to clap his hands over his ears. Instead, he took aim.

"Wait!" Don said.

Too late. Bill pulled the trigger twice in the direction of the roaring—Bang! Bang! The alien squealed, and then a human screamed.

"Fuck!" James said. "You fucking shot me!"

Bill went cold. His hands grew numb, and he almost dropped the gun. Galloping feet and skittering claws retreated, and the alien's screams faded swiftly into the distance.

"Help me get it off!" Don grunted.

Bill dropped to his haunches, set down the gun, and planted both his hands on the slick, slippery skin of the alien he'd killed. The sensation and smell were revolting. Bill heaved, and using his legs and back for extra leverage, rolled the creature away. Small as it was when crouching on all fours, it must have weighed at least three hundred pounds.

As the sound of galloping feet faded, the minivan door slid open and a pair of sobbing children spilled out. Don's flashlight made them squint and revealed their mother climbing out behind them.

James got up, clutching a bloody bicep. At least

the bullet hadn't hit somewhere more critical.

"Thanks for the save," Don said and squeezed Bill's injured shoulder painfully hard. "You can give me the gun now."

Bill bit his tongue against the pain and gave up the weapon without complaint.

"Where's your daughter?"

"I sent her to the storeroom and told her to lock herself in." A stab of dread dragged his head around to the gaping front entrance of his resort, but he couldn't see anything through the shadows.

"Big enough for all of us?" Don asked.

"No." Bill shook his head. "Two at most."

"Then we'll have to barricade ourselves in somewhere else," Don said.

Turning back the other way, Bill saw James was locked in the middle of a group hug. Don's flashlight revealed four bleeding welts on his face.

"We're too exposed out here," Don said. "Better move out before that thing crawls inside to wait for us."

Bill nodded quickly. "Lead the way."

CHAPTER 19

"That's it, all the doors are sealed," Bill said as he finished sliding a broken table leg through the silver handles on the swinging doors to the restaurant. They'd forced the sliding glass doors at the front entrance shut as soon as they got in, followed by the ones leading out to the pool. Hopefully the aliens weren't smart enough to pry the doors open again.

"Are you sure?" Don asked.

He began nodding, even as he ran mentally through his resort to double-check.

"What about a back door?"

"There's only one. In the kitchen."

"And?" Don asked, sweeping his flashlight in that direction to reveal James' waxy, blood-smeared face. He sat with his back to the wall beside the kitchen door. He had one of his kids under each arm while his wife stood beside them, her eyes wide and darting. The bullet-wound in James' arm had been bandaged with Don's bloody gray shirt, leaving the old veteran shirtless and showing off a carpet of blond hair on his chest and belly that matched his beard.

Bill shook his head. "We can't lock the back door without the keys. Same as the sliding doors."

"So where are the keys?" Don asked.

"I gave them to Beth, but Eric had a spare set."

Don's flashlight swept back around, blinding Bill with its glare. "You might have mentioned that while we were out there with him."

"We were in a hurry. It didn't occur to me."

Don let out a noisy sigh. "Well, shit. Who wants to go out and get them?"

"I can't," James said weakly.

"N-not me," his wife, Kayla added.

"Guess it's down to us, then, Billy-bob," Don said. "Should we draw straws or just measure our dicks?"

Bill scowled at the other man's sarcasm. Don's gratitude for saving his life had obviously run dry already. But they were one for one, so that was probably fair. "It's my fault; I'll do it," Bill said. "Besides, Beth should be with us." Bill made a gimme gesture. "I'm going to need your gun and flashlight."

Don chuckled darkly. "And leave me defenseless? I don't think so, Billy-bob."

"I can't go out there empty-handed!" Bill

replied, exasperated by the man's sudden attitude. "And if I don't go and get those keys, none of you will be safe in here."

"He makes a good point," James whispered.

"Looks like we're going out together, then," Don said.

"Wait, that's not what I—"

"Doesn't matter what you meant," Don replied. "The choice is between going out with a gun and a flashlight or sitting in here, defenseless in the dark. It doesn't take a genius to figure which is better. Let's go, Billy."

"It's Bill."

A firm hand landed on his shoulder, making him wince. Don turned him toward the doors they'd just finished blocking with a table leg and said, "Sure thing, Bob."

CHAPTER 20

"Wait," Don said before Bill could pull out the table leg blocking the doors. He ejected his magazine and checked the back. There was a golden bullet at the top, but the three holes in the back of the magazine were black and empty.

"How many bullets?" Bill asked.

"Less than five." Don slid the magazine back in with a click. "Three rounds left if my count is right. I personally put at least three bullets in each of them but it seems like you've got to hit them in the eyes to make it a kill shot. You got damn lucky with that."

"Yeah," Bill agreed.

"Which way to the storage room?" Don asked.

"To the right and continue straight until you reach the end of the lanai. There's an unmarked brown metal door."

"Sounds simple enough." Don nodded, and Bill pulled the table leg out, passing it to James' shell-shocked wife.

"Stay close," Don said as he pushed one of the doors open.

Bill followed him out. He heard the wooden table leg *thunking* against the doors as Kayla barred them again.

Don took long strides, weaving between overturned chairs and tables in the restaurant's outdoor dining area. Bill kept pace with him, unable to see anything beyond the narrow, sweeping cone of light that Don held in his hand. A metal railing ran around the lanai, with a gap leading to paved walkway under the eaves of the main building. At the end of that walkway lay the matte brown door of the storage room.

"Almost there," Bill whispered.

Galloping feet sounded from the direction of the pool, approaching fast.

"Damn it," Don muttered. "Pick up the pace!" They reached the door, and Bill thumped on it with both fists. "Beth! It's us! Let us in!"

"Dad?"

The galloping sound stopped, and a thunderous roar stuttered out.

"Too late!" Don cried.

Bill whirled around to see a familiar alien rearing up on hind legs just behind them. Its arms folded out, reaching for Don. He aimed and fired.

Bang!

The first shot hit a shoulder. The alien cried out and wrapped two arms around Don, lifting him into the air.

Bang!

The second shot blasted foul-smelling splinters out of its teeth.

Bang!

The third missed.

"I'm out!" Don screamed and dropped his gun with a metallic clatter.

Bill watched helplessly as Don was hoisted high into the air.

"Run, damn it!" Don said as one of those hoof-mouths dilated open and angled toward his face.

The alien let out another stuttering roar. It was almost enough to drown out the steady, galloping thunder of heavy boots thumping on grass.

The creature's head turned toward the sound, and it trilled querulously. Bill's eyes widened, and he backed away, into the corner formed between the main building and the storeroom. Dark shapes flickered in the moonlight, streaking between shadowy clumps of vegetation. They ran past the pool, approaching fast.

Terrified and defenseless, all Bill could do was watch.

Then the footsteps stopped, and a human voice sounded out.

"Weapons free!"

Boop! Boop! The hollow sounds of grenade launchers firing filled the air, and then electric blue fire crackled and sparked, coursing over both the alien and Don. The alien squealed and dropped Don. He cried out and lay twitching on the pavement.

Shotguns boomed, and more electricity flared, tracing the monstrous outline of the alien. It collapsed, shrieking and screaming, limbs thrashing spasmodically.

Footsteps thundered, and lights snapped on, blinding Bill. A pair of dark, human shapes stood over the translucent monster, studying it. "Holy shit," one of them said. "Net it!" the other replied. Two more Ms appeared, one of them holding a massive weapon. He fired, and a black net flared out over the fallen creature, pinning it in place. The alien responded by struggling to rise, but that only tangled it further. It thrashed, squealing and screaming against the net and the lingering blue crackles of whatever stun weapons the soldiers had shot it with.

Don groaned, and one of the soldiers went over to help him up. The other two kept aim on the alien, while the fourth raced up to Bill's side. "We have to go now, sir."

"My daughter—"

The metal door groaned open beside him, and Beth stumbled out, blinking wide, terrified eyes. "Is it over?" she asked.

"No, ma'am. It's not dead, just immobilized. We have a boat waiting to take you three back to the *Royal*."

"We can't," Bill said. "There are more people inside."

"We'll take care of it," one of the other soldiers said. "How many more of these things are there?"

"Just that one," Don said, limping over to them and pointing to Bill. "He killed the other."

"You killed it?" the soldier in front of them asked, sounding worried. "With what?"

"My nine mil," Don replied. "Billy-Bob pegged a lucky shot in one of its eyeballs."

"I see... well, you can tell the captain all about it back at the *Royal*."

"There's four more survivors just through those doors," Don said, pointing. "One is injured."

"Show me," the Marine said.

"This way," Don replied.

CHAPTER 21

Standing on the beach with two of the four Marines, Bill stared at their boat, a black tubular thing with an outboard motor attached.

"I've only got room for four passengers because of the gear we're packing, and one of them's gotta be me to man the tiller," the ranking soldier said. "Wounded take priority. Who are the other two gonna be?"

"I can stay here, soldier," Bill said.

The man hesitated before inclining his head in a nod. "Good—anyone else?"

Don elbowed Bill sharply in the ribs. "He's a Marine, not a soldier."

"What's the difference?" Beth asked.

Don snorted. "You mean besides the sticks up their arses?" He shrugged. "Better gear." Don looked to the corporal with a small smile and nodded. "I'll also stay. Just give me a weapon."

"Negative. Arming civvies is against protocol."

"I'm not a civvie, Corporal. I did two tours in

Afghanistan."

"Army or Marines?"

"Army."

"Well, no one's perfect. Protocol stands, however. This is strictly a recon and rescue op. We're not authorized to use lethal force."

"I'll stay, too," Bill said.

Beth balked at that. "Dad!"

Growing impatient, the Marine nodded and said, "We'll take the wounded man and his kids. Rest of you will have to wait here for the next boat."

"That's fine," Bill replied.

"Dekker, keep watch."

"Copy, boss," the other Marine replied without turning. He was already watching their backs through the night vision scope on his helmet, his shotgun at the ready.

Beth sidled up to Bill and wrapped her arms around his chest. He draped an arm over her shoulders, wincing at the sharp stabs that movement provoked from his muscles. The puncture wounds left by the alien claws hurt worse than a jellyfish sting.

Bill turned to look up the beach at his resort, but he couldn't see anything through the artificial night. His imagination filled the blanks with corpses lying in sticky puddles of entrails and blood. The Koa Kai had been a money pit from the start, but now that aliens had turned it into a human slaughterhouse, it was over. No one would want to stay in a room where the previous guests had all died horribly.

Of course, he was probably getting ahead of himself. Bill glanced up at the perfect darkness. A massive spaceship was still hovering overhead, blocking out the sun and most of the sky, and no one had any idea why they'd come or what they wanted. For all anyone knew, this was the aliens' recon mission, too, and the real invasion was yet to come.

One thing stuck out as particularly strange in Bill's brain, however: why send down unarmed, unarmored soldiers? If they could even be called soldiers. They seemed intelligent, but so far they'd only hunted and terrorized tourists. Bill wondered if that might be the point. Maybe this was some kind of recreational hunting party and humans were the stags. But that seemed like a strange goal with the vast distances between stars and the sheer amount of energy and time it must have taken to cross them. Surely recreational interests would be confined to less expensive trips.

Or perhaps these aliens were just so advanced that flying between stars was no big deal to them. They might have something like a warp drive from

Star Trek.

Bill heard splashing and muted voices behind him as Kayla said goodbye to James and her children; then more splashing as the Marine guarding the beach helped push the zodiac into the water. Moments later the outboard motor started up with a roar.

Bill glanced over his shoulder to see the boat jetting out over the gleaming silver tips of gentle swells. The crescent moon had vanished, having risen above the spaceship, but there was just enough starlight shining in from the band of clear sky below the alien craft to give them light to see by. The Marines had ordered them not to use their flashlights or phone lights, in case that proved to be a beacon drawing more aliens to them. Bill absently wondered what they thought the noise of that outboard motor would do.

He hoped they'd send more boats and more Marines when they came back. As far as Bill was concerned, *recon* was the wrong type of mission. This should have been a doomsday-style operation with the whole damn cavalry coming to shore.

And when it came right down to it, what really bothered Bill about all of this was that it wasn't an invasion or a war. It was something else. And he had no damn clue what it could be.

A terrible suspicion slithered through his

veins. He tried not to pay attention to it, but he couldn't deny what had happened to him. Whatever the aliens were doing here, chances were good that it had something to do with what they'd done to him.

His skin crawled with the memory. One of the creatures had placed a foul-smelling hoof-mouth over his, pricking his cheeks and jaw, and forcing his mouth open with a French kiss from hell; then something cold and wet had entered his mouth. It had tasted like plant nectar, sweet and surprisingly pleasant despite the revolting source.

One thing was for sure, as soon as he got to that Navy cruiser, he would have the ship's doctor check him out and make sure he hadn't been infected with any parasites or other microbes.

Visions of the movie *Alien* flashed through his mind, and he imagined a hideous creature gestating in his stomach only to tear him open on its way out.

Bill trembled.

"Are you okay?" Beth asked quietly.

He swallowed his rising bile and nodded. "Yeah, I'm fine."

Feeling watched, Bill turned and found Don staring at him—his eyes pinched into slits and gleaming with pinpricks of light. Bill wondered if Don was thinking about the same thing.

Feeling suddenly naked, Bill looked away. What would happen to him when the doctors found out what the aliens had done? Would he be studied like a lab rat until they learned *why*? What if they never let him go?

Those creatures had given the same treatment to James, and who knew how many others, but what was different about them that had caused the aliens to spare them?

Long minutes passed in darkness. At some point the Marine guarding the shore answered his radio, conversing briefly with other members of his team. Bill guessed he was talking with the two who'd stayed up at the resort to look for more survivors.

"Copy that. The beach is secure. No sign of the enemy."

"Did anyone else survive?" Bill asked the Marine when he finished speaking.

"Six more," the Marine replied.

Bill blinked in shock. He'd had over a hundred guests. To have just six survivors plus the seven that made it to the beach—thirteen in all—meant that almost everyone had been killed. "What about the rest of the island?"

"No way to know, sir. The *Royal* is sending reinforcements. Team Two is at the resort next door. They only suffered one casualty."

"Great," Bill muttered. The Marriott had escaped with a clean slate while his resort was turned into a mausoleum. *At least there'll be fewer people to write bad reviews.* Bill's conscience recoiled with that thought, and he chided himself.

"Six others made it," Beth said slowly. "Maybe Toby is one them?"

"Yeah, maybe," Bill replied.

It wasn't more than a few minutes before the survivors came tromping down the beach with a Marine escort. Flashlights bobbed beneath the Marines' shotgun barrels. Apparently they could break their own rules. Bill guessed that those people couldn't see well enough to keep up a steady pace without those flashlights. As they drew near, Beth broke the rules, too, flicking on her phone light to scan the survivors' faces—

Bloody faces with four welts each, just like Bill's and James'. Bill vaguely recognized a few of them. The bossy matriarch was there, but no sign of her family. Her eyes were glassy and vacant. Melanie was also there, with the same four welts on her face. She averted her gaze when she saw Bill. Perhaps she felt ashamed for running and hiding in her room. She'd done that twice—once abandoning Bill in the process, and the second time squandering her chance to escape.

"Where's Toby?" Beth burst into tears and

stormed up to the nearest of the two escorting Marines. "Where is he?"

"He who, ma'am?"

"A young man, tall and skinny, with long blond hair and blue eyes."

"I'm sorry, but these are the only survivors we found."

"Did you see him?"

"Can't say. Some of the bodies won't be easy to ID. Try to remain calm, ma'am. There's a chance he escaped."

The Marine brushed by her, walking down until he reached the water's edge. "Dekker, keep eyes on them until evac gets here. We need to get back to the package."

"Copy that. Is it secure?"

"Tranqued and tied up, but no way to know how long that will last."

"It's alone?"

"Negative, Team Two is standing guard."

A distant roar interrupted their conversation, echoing out from multiple sources. Bill turned to look but saw only the faintest gleam of the approaching zodiacs. By his count, there were at least five coming to shore. The Marines left, running back up the beach.

A minute later the boats rode up on shore, and five more teams of Marines jumped out. Bill and the other survivors were ushered into three of the zodiacs. They got their feet wet, but Bill was still barefoot, so he didn't mind.

In a matter of seconds, they were jetting out over gleaming black water toward a jagged silhouette on the horizon. The *Port Royal*. Bill and Beth rode with Don. Bill noticed that Don's eyes never left him. Growing fed up, he rounded on the other man, and shouted to be heard over the droning sound of the motor: "What's your problem?"

"No problem," Don shouted back. "Just curious: why did they let you live?"

"Not just me," Bill replied.

"Exactly. You all have the same welts on your faces. What did they do to you?

"Nothing," Bill replied. "You saved me before they could rip my guts out."

"I'm not so sure you needed saving," Don replied.

The Marine steering the boat watched them with dark, darting eyes, and Bill realized he was in trouble. Visions of endless interrogations, medical exams, and tests swam through his head.

PART 2 - CONTAINMENT

CHAPTER 22

"Commander Wilde has cleared the survivors for debriefing," Morris said as he entered the bridge.

Captain Reed glanced at his second-in-command. "No sign of infectious agents?"

"Not so far, sir."

Reed sighed. "Good. Unfortunately, that's not going to lift the CDC's quarantine order."

"No, sir, but it should help put your mind at ease. Would you like to debrief the survivors or should I?"

"We'll do it together. Lieutenant Peterson, how do you stand?"

"I stand ready to relieve you, sir."

"Then I stand relieved. Attention on deck, Lieutenant Peterson has the bridge."

Peterson stood at attention and saluted. The

captain returned the salute and then turned and started for the exit. "Commander Morris, walk with me," he said.

"Yes, sir."

The captain opened the door and ducked through the entrance of the bridge, heading for the stairwell. Their boots rang on the metal deck and then on the stairs as they headed down.

The survivors were all still isolated in sick bay, with Commander Wilde, the ship's surgeon, and his head corpsman, Chief Petty Officer Miller, but those security measures were woefully inadequate as far as Reed was concerned. The *Port Royal* wasn't equipped to contain a possible contagion, much less an alien one, or for that matter the actual alien they had locked in the *Port Royal's* brig. The best they could do was make sure that no one left the ship now that it was compromised. None of the other ships that had subsequently arrived from Pearl Harbor had taken on survivors or allowed their Marines to return after going ashore. Those teams were occupied securing critical areas of the island and gathering up the survivors while avoiding enemy contact as much as possible. CDC specialists from the mainland were en route to conduct more thorough testing, but it would be a while before they arrived.

Meanwhile, everyone was just thanking their

gods that the aliens had decided to land on an island. But Reed wasn't reassured by that. Just because they'd chosen to land on an island didn't mean they wouldn't change their minds and decide to land somewhere else, too. And if they were dealing with some kind of pathogen, the CDC needed to get ahead of it and develop countermeasures while they still had the chance.

Before the captain and Commander Morris arrived at sick bay, they reached a sealed bulkhead flanked by a pair of Marine privates.

The Marines saluted. Reed returned the salute but hesitated before ordering them to open the door. This entire section had been sealed off for quarantine. Were five days enough to determine that they weren't dealing with an infectious agent? And if not, would such a pathetic quarantine even matter? They didn't have Hazmat suits on board, and this door had to be opened periodically to provide rations to the people inside the containment area.

"Open it up, Private."

"Aye, sir." The door swung wide with a metallic groan, and Reed walked through. The hall was lined with bunk rooms, currently assigned to civilian survivors and the Marines from the recon teams. The captain resisted the urge to hold his breath as he strolled down the corridor with his

XO. When they reached the door to sick bay, he knocked smartly and announced himself: "Captain Reed."

The locking mechanism clunked as someone opened the door from the other side. A metallic groan issued from the hinges and Commander Wilde appeared, looking tired and miserable. "Captain," he said, saluting.

Reed saluted back. "Carry on. You don't look well, Commander. Is there something I should be aware of?"

"No, sir, just a lack of sleep. Chief Miller and I have been working around the clock running tests."

Reed stepped inside with his XO. "And?"

"Nothing, sir. No immune response. We found no foreign bodies or cells in the cultures or stains."

The captain frowned. "That doesn't jibe well with what the civilians reported when they came aboard. They all indicated that there was a direct transfer of saliva or other fluids from the invaders."

"Yes, well, be that as it may, whatever they ingested was either excreted soon afterward, or else it looks exactly like a known cell type, but that's highly unlikely. Extraterrestrials would have taken a different evolutionary path, so they wont't have recognizable cell structures."

"And what if the foreign cells are hiding in a specific place?" Commander Morris asked.

Doctor Wilde's crinkled face grew even more lined as he appeared to consider that. He shook his head. "We sampled blood, saliva, feces, and urine. We also performed ultrasounds and biopsies. If the invading cells are hiding, they'd have to be hiding somewhere that's hard to get to—in the bone marrow or the brain, for example. But even if that were the case, none of the survivors have shown any symptoms or immune response. Whatever they were exposed to, it appears that it was benign, but only time will confirm that."

"How much time?" Reed asked.

"With viruses on Earth, incubation and testing window periods can range anywhere from days to years."

"*Years?*" Reed echoed.

"Yes, sir."

"How..." Reed trailed off, his mouth feeling suddenly dry as he imagined being isolated aboard the *Port Royal* for years without shore leave. Assuming aliens didn't land en masse before then and make all their quarantine protocols moot. Working some moisture into his mouth, he asked, "Testing windows period—what does that mean?"

"It's the amount of time after initial contact with a pathogen that it takes to be able to detect it with a test."

"If viruses on Earth have testing windows anywhere from a few days to a few *years,* then you really can't say with any degree of confidence that no one on this ship is infected."

"That's correct, sir."

"Then there's no way to know for sure when it might be safe to lift the quarantine."

Wilde frowned, his pale blue eyes collapsing into anxious slits. "We've done everything we can for now. I've cleared the subjects for casual contact, but that doesn't mean we should lift any of our protocols. While we can't contain an airborne pathogen, we *can* contain just about every other type by carefully limiting contact. Many pathogens on Earth are exchanged through bodily fluids. If we are dealing with an infectious agent, then that's probably the type we're up against—based on the aliens' method of delivery."

"Yes... but why infect us in the first place? And why only some of us?" Reed asked.

"That's impossible to say without knowing more about the symptoms and side effects of infection, sir. Assuming there even is an infection to speak of."

"I want to speak with the survivors."

"Of course. Who would you like to speak with?" Commander Wilde asked.

"Which of them made first contact?"

"The owner of the resort."

Captain Reed nodded. "Then we'll start with him."

CHAPTER 23

Five days cooped up in a windowless metal box! Beth slowly shook her head. She was lying on the top bunk, facing the door. Her dad was sitting below her on the floor in front of his bed, the lowermost of the three bunks on their wall, while Don and Melanie had each taken the bottom bunks on the left and right walls respectively.

With nine beds per each of the three enlisted bunk rooms in the quarantine section, there were several empty bunks in each room, but that did nothing to alleviate Beth's claustrophobia. Doctor Wilde called the bunk rooms *coffin lockers,* and he wasn't far off. That's exactly what they looked like. Beth couldn't imagine nine people crammed into one of these rooms night after night on long deployments. Although sailors probably got to spend most of their time doing stuff in other parts of the ship, not just cooped up in their rooms.

A knock sounded on the door, interrupting Beth's pity party. The door opened, and two men in Marine uniforms walked in. Both of them had guns holstered at their hips, their hands resting lightly on the butts of those weapons as they stepped into the bunk room. Bill noticed that they wore surgical masks and blue nitrile gloves. Both of them hesitated in the open doorway.

Don climbed out of his bunk and asked, "What's going on, Private?"

"Please step back, sir," one of them said; then he glanced down at Melanie who was still lying in her bunk. "You, too, ma'am."

Melanie climbed out, but neither she nor Don made any move to back up. "Is everything okay?" Melanie asked.

"Just fine, ma'am, but for security reasons, I need you both to step back."

"Security..." Melanie trailed off.

"Now, please."

Beth's brow furrowed. Now they were being treated like criminals. Maybe they really were prisoners.

Don took three steps and nearly stood on Bill's toes. Melanie reluctantly followed.

Beth's dad rose to his feet just as she was climbing down from her bunk.

"What's with the guns?" she asked.

"Just a precaution, ma'am."

"The room is secure!" the second Marine called

out in a loud voice.

And a moment later, two decorated Navy officers walked in, also wearing masks and blue nitrile gloves.

"A captain... and a commander," Don said slowly.

"Captain Reed," the taller of the two said. "And this is my XO, Commander Morris."

"Are we being released?" Don asked.

"Not yet," the captain replied. He had dark brown eyes and a deep voice. "We have some questions we'd like to ask."

Beth glimpsed her dad shaking his head. "We've already told Doctor Wilde everything...." he trailed off.

"Humor me," Captain Reed said. "Who's the owner of the Koa Kai resort?"

Beth's dad stepped forward, brushing past Don and Melanie. "I am."

"Very well. Could you please recount for me what happened when you made first contact with the aliens?"

Beth listened as her dad recounted the experience of being pinned in place by one of the aliens and then subjected to mouth-to-mouth with one of its feet. He described the sensation of something cold, wet, and sweet entering his mouth.

"Interesting," the captain replied in a flat tone that betrayed neither the surprise nor the disgust that Beth expected. "Has anyone else here had the same experience?"

Melanie stuck up her hand. "I did."

"I see, and would you say that your experience matched what Mr. Steele described?"

"Yes," Melanie replied in a tight voice. Her nose wrinkled and her upper lip curled. She looked like she was about to be sick.

"Any symptoms since then?" the captain asked, his eyes darting between them.

"Just one," Beth's dad replied.

The captain cocked his head curiously, waiting for him to go on.

"Sleepwalking," he explained.

"Sleepwalking?" the captain asked. His gaze flicked to Melanie. "Is this something you've experienced as well?"

She shook her head. "I just have nightmares."

Don spoke up, "He's up and walking around three times a night, bumping into things and muttering to himself."

"What does Commander Wilde have to say about that?"

Don's lips curved dryly. "PTSD."

The captain stood silent for a long moment. Before he could say anything else, a loud bell sounded repeatedly from overhead speakers, followed by a voice: "This is not a drill, this is not a drill, general quarters, general quarters, all hands to action stations!"

Captain Reed and his XO looked like they'd just been struck by lightning. They hurried from the room, vanishing in an instant. The two Marines were slower to exit, keeping eyes on Bill and the others as they backed out and shut the door with a metallic *clunk*.

"What's happening?" Beth asked in the ringing silence that followed.

"The ship's getting ready for battle," Don replied.

* * *

"Captain on deck!"

"At ease. Report," Reed said as he entered the CIC.

"The spacecraft is moving away from the island, sir," an officer reported. Reed recognized him as the officer in charge of detecting and tracking air contacts, although technically this was a *space* contact. "Admiral Harris has ordered the fleet to spread out and prepare to engage."

Reed traded glances with his XO.

"Why move away now?" Commander Morris asked quietly.

"Maybe they've accomplished whatever they

came here to do," Reed replied. To the rest of the crew, he said, "Carry on. If anyone needs me, I'll be on the bridge."

"Aye, Captain."

Reed and his XO took the stairs two at a time on their way up to the bridge. As soon as Reed opened the door, he saw what was happening in the sky. The sun came creeping out from behind a sheer black spacecraft, casting a brilliant swath of light across the island. Sunlight raced across the water to greet them, and soon everyone on the bridge was squinting against the glare of broad daylight.

Reed hurried to the forward viewports and peered into the sky. Fluffy white clouds obscured some of the details, but in the gaps he could see a smooth dark surface scrolling across the sky. He hoped that meant there weren't any alien guns aiming down on them, but that was probably asking too much.

"Where are they headed?"

"Due south, sir," the OOD, Lieutenant Peterson, reported.

"There's nothing out there but open ocean," Reed replied, staring warily at the trailing edge of the massive ship as it slid across the sky. "Where the hell are they going?"

CHAPTER 24

—48 Hours Later—

"They left their people behind to die," Captain Reed said, slowly shaking his head. "And then they vanished into thin air somewhere over the Pacific. None of this makes any sense, Mike."

Commander Michael Morris frowned at him across the small table in Reed's quarters. "It's a mystery, that's for sure, sir."

Reed took a sip from a steaming mug of black coffee and winced as it burned his tongue.

Nearly the entire fleet had moved on without them to chase the alien ship across the ocean, only to watch a day later as satellites showed it vanishing into thin air. The *Port Royal* had been left behind to supervise ground operations on Kauai. So far thirty-two landing capsules had been found, and twenty-nine alien bodies recovered—all of them dead and being dissected by military and civilian doctors in a quest for answers. UV radiation exposure was their current best guess for the cause of death—meaning that they'd somehow all died of a severe sunburn. Theorists speculated that was why they'd eclipsed the island to begin with, and why they hadn't landed over the mainland or some other continent. They'd been trying to protect their people on the ground from the sun. But if that was the case, why the hell didn't they just wear spacesuits, and furthermore, why not wait to recover their people before moving off?

Reed's own conclusions were troubling at best. "The ones who came down were obviously disposable," he said, peering over the rim of his coffee mug at his second in command.

"I agree," Commander Morris replied.

"And the fact that they left the island suggests that they already accomplished their mission— whatever the hell *that* was. What's the current count for survivors of direct encounters? Two, three hundred?"

"Last I heard it was up to three-forty something."

"Okay, so they come here, traveling who knows how many miles; they block out the sun, land operatives, and target select individuals to contaminate with an unknown pathogen."

"One that's asymptomatic," Morris added.

"So far," Reed replied, before taking another sip of his coffee. "I don't like it. I want them off my ship. The CDC is better equipped to test them, and the whole island is under quarantine anyway."

"So are we," Morris said. "As far as anyone is concerned, we're equally compromised. We sent recon teams and one of them has been bunking with those civilians for the past week."

"We've taken precautions," Reed replied. "There's a good chance none of us is infected outside the quarantined section."

"What about the surviving *Crawler* in the brig?"

Crawler was the media's nickname for the aliens. "The Admiral wants us to hold onto it," Reed replied. "But the civilians can leave."

"And our people in the quarantine section?"

"They've all been exposed, so they'll have to go, too."

Morris looked uncertain.

"Something on your mind, Mike?" Reed asked.

"We might need Commander Wilde and Chief Miller on board if we have been compromised. Besides Corpsmen Reese and Diaz, they're the only medical staff we have."

"We'll make do. Right now Wilde and Miller are a bigger risk to us than I care to take. Give the order. I want them all off my ship before the next watch."

"Yes, sir."

* * *

Fresh, warm air whipped past the boat as it skipped over the water toward a familiar beach. Apprehension swirled in Beth's gut. The prospect of returning to her dad's resort, the scene of a massacre, seemed far less terrifying in broad daylight, but she still shuddered to think about what awaited them there. Who was going to clean up and remove the bodies?

No one spoke as they came ashore—much less the surly Marine at the back of the zodiac. He clearly didn't like being exiled to shore along with them.

Within minutes, the beach scraped the keel tube of the boat, and they piled out over the bow. Beth's sandals slapped wet sand as she jumped out. Another four boats roared up to either side of them, and more people clambered out. Like Beth, most of them wore borrowed blue and gray, camo-patterned Navy uniforms. She spied the familiar faces of James and his family, then Melanie, followed by the other widow, Avery Walsh, a tall woman with designer sunglasses. Beth looked away, shielding her eyes from the sun as she peered up at the Koa Kai.

Marines streaked by, dragging their boats far

up the beach, followed by Doctor Wilde with his gray crewcut and ambling gait. When he reached the tail end of the nearest boat, he turned to address them. He wore a troubled frown on his wrinkled face. His younger assistant, Chief Miller, came to stand beside him, and the four Marines who'd rescued Bill and the others took up flanking positions. They held their rifles at the ready, eyes scanning the shrubbery that hedged the beach, and the grassy palm-lined path leading up to the Koa Kai.

"All right, listen up," Commander Wilde said. "We're all stuck here for the time being, but Mr. Steele has graciously offered to provide free lodging for all of us at his resort."

"What about food!" one of the survivors asked.

Beth glanced at him. She recognized Allen immediately. He was a short, balding man with dark hair and a smooth, baby face that made him look younger than his forty-two years of age. Allen was an accountant from Jamestown, Virginia, on vacation by himself to clear his head after a messy divorce.

"The government will provide rations to the island for as long as the quarantine lasts," Commander Wilde replied.

"I have two kids waiting for me back in Virginia," Allen added.

"And they'll still be waiting for you when the quarantine is lifted, but right now, they'll be much better off with you and everyone else on this island safely isolated."

Loud grumbling issued from the group. "When will the quarantine be lifted?" James demanded.

"When the CDC decides it's safe," Wilde replied.

Silence rang like a bell as everyone absorbed the implications of an indefinite stay on Kauai.

"I don't want to go back there," a small, broken voice said. It was Avery.

"No one wants to go back," James added.

"It's not the same!" she screamed. "You didn't lose your whole family. I did!"

The group broke into a loud argument as people shared fractured accounts of their own experiences. Commander Wilde just stared at them with a deepening frown, waiting for the chaos to subside.

Beth's dad stuck his thumb and index finger in his mouth and whistled sharply for attention. The arguments stopped, and he raised his voice: "You're all free to look for alternate accommodations! But for those who can't afford it, or who would rather not suffer the expense, my offer stands."

"Thank you, Mr. Steele," Wilde added. "I'm sure everyone appreciates your generosity."

"What about the bodies? Who's going to remove them and clean up the blood?" another survivor, the resort's chef, Jenna Jones, asked. She was a tall blonde woman with green eyes and a golden tan. Her gaze flicked to the other two survivors, both local islanders who'd been working as housekeepers at the resort. Beth recognized them as Hanna Kahele and Akela Smith. The tourists began staring expectantly at them as well.

Akela shook her head. "We not goin' ta clean dat shit!"

"Then who is? Us?" James demanded.

The group burst into loud arguing once more, and Commander Wilde raised his voice. "Settle down! The CDC will handle clean-up if they haven't already. Now, please wait here while we clear the area." Turning aside to one of the flanking sets of Marines, the commander nodded and said, "Corporal Gibson, would you please scout ahead and report back?"

"Happy to, sir," Gibson said. He made a hand gesture to the Marine standing beside him and raised his rifle to his shoulder, heading for the palm-lined pathway. Both men strode up the path, quickly disappearing over the top of the stairs that led from the surf and snorkel hut to the pool area.

Beth wondered if Melanie's husband was still floating in the pool, and with that thought she remembered who else was missing—her boyfriend, Toby. During her stay on the Port Royal it had been easy to imagine that he'd run away to safety somewhere in town—to his house, maybe—but now doubt wormed through her thoughts, whispering darker possibilities. She nudged her dad in the ribs. "What about Toby?"

He turned to her with a furrowed brow. "What about him?"

"Who do I ask about him? If someone cleaned up already, how do I know if he's..." she swallowed. "How do I know if he was one of the ones who died?"

Bill sucked in a breath and blew it out slowly. He wrapped an arm around her shoulders and squinted up at his resort. "We'll ask around, but for now let's assume he escaped."

"Okay." Beth nodded agreeably, trying to do just that.

CHAPTER 25

Beth spent the next half an hour sweating through her baggy uniform under the umbrellas between the loungers at the top of the beach. Doctor Wilde and Chief Miller passed out bottles of water while the other two Marines kept watch. Beth emptied her water in minutes and promptly wished she hadn't—she needed to pee, and the only bathroom anywhere nearby with running water was the ocean. Beth stared over the sun-spackled tips of gentle swells, wishing she could be out there on her surfboard.

By the time the Marines came tromping back down the beach, Beth's bladder was bursting.

"How'd it go?" Commander Wilde asked.

"All clear, sir. No contact," Corporal Gibson replied.

"Bodies?"

"None. Blood's everywhere, though. Easy enough to clean off tiles, but the carpets are done."

"What about the pool?" Bill asked.

The corporal's gaze darted to them. "It'll have to be drained and scrubbed."

Wilde nodded to the group. "All right, let's move out and get settled. Mr. Steele will be in charge of room assignments, so if you have any concerns about that, you can talk to him."

"What about the plumbing?" Beth asked, squirming from a sharp stab of pain in her lower abdomen.

The commander's grizzled eyebrows formed a peak in the center. "What about it?"

Bill explained, "Our main water line burst before all of this began. The plumbers went out to get supplies and never came back."

"I see," Commander Wilde replied. "Don't worry, we'll get it done. What was your vacancy at the time of the incident, Mr. Steele?"

"Twenty-five percent."

"And how many rooms at the Koa Kai?"

"One hundred and twenty."

"Good. Then we should have more than enough fresh bathrooms and clean carpets to go around. Everyone, follow me."

* * *

The tiles and textured concrete around the pool were a gruesome mess. Compelled by morbid curiosity, Beth glanced into the pool as they walked by. Bits of gore floated in pink water.

Melanie cried out as she noticed that, and her sobs followed them up to the lobby. The lobby was clean, brightly lit, and refreshingly cold. The air conditioners must have come on some time ago. Besides a few bloody hand prints on the doors and walls, there were no signs of the carnage from a week ago.

Turning in a quick circle, Beth found her dad behind the reception desk while the survivors mobbed him.

A hand landed on Beth's shoulder. She jumped and spun around to see Don standing there.

She flashed a scowl at him. "Don't *do* that!"

"Sorry," he said, then jerked his chin at the reception area. "You think I can get another key card for my room? I lost mine."

Beth frowned and nodded. "We'll ask my dad. Come on." Speaking of lost key cards, she'd left hers in the suite. Had she shut the door behind her? She couldn't remember. Maybe her dad still had his.

Reaching the reception desk, she waved to catch her dad's eye. He glanced up from the computer.

"Don needs another room key."

"Room 321," Don added.

Bill looked up and shook his head. "The computer system is dead. I can't program any new room keys."

"So what's the plan?" Don asked.

"No plan needed," Corporal Gibson interrupted, walking over to the reception desk. "The doors were all open when we cleared the place. That EMP must have triggered some kind of failsafe."

"What happens when we open and shut the doors?" Allen asked. Beth glanced at the short, balding accountant. "Won't that trigger the locks again?"

"Yes," Bill replied. "Don't shut your doors unless you're inside. If you leave your room and you don't have a working key, you'd better wedge the doors open with something."

The crowd started grumbling about monsters creeping in while they were away from their rooms.

"Corporal Gibson and his men will guard the stairs and elevators at all times," Commander Wilde said, nodding to the stairwell. "Security won't be a problem."

"There's only six of you," James objected. "There are three separate buildings, each with their own elevators and stairs.

"I can help keep watch," Don put in.

"Everyone is going to stay here in the main building," Corporal Gibson put in. "In fact, I want everyone on the same floor. Level three."

"What about our belongings?" Allen asked. "I'm down in building C, second floor."

"Get your things and relocate," Gibson said.

"Alone?" Allen asked, glancing over his shoulder with wide brown eyes.

The corporal sighed. "Private Dekker!"

"Corporal?" the other Marine in the lobby asked.

"Escort the guests to their rooms. I'll watch the entrances while Clarke and Kelly bring in the supplies." Even as Gibson said that, the sliding doors on the pool-facing side of the lobby swished open and Clarke and Kelly came in carrying a heavy crate between them.

"Copy," Dekker replied. Scanning the group, he asked, "Who's on the first floor?"

"Me," Melanie croaked and stuck up her hand.

"Where to?"

She pointed to the blood-smeared door beside the stairwell. "All right, follow me," Dekker replied, shifting his shotgun to a two-handed grip, but keeping the barrel aimed at the floor. "The rest of you wait here until I come back." Grumbles and murmurs of acknowledgment answered as he and Melanie left.

Beth watched them go with a frown, then turned back to her dad. "Can I go?"

Bill glanced at the corporal. "Mind if I show my daughter to our room? We're up on the third floor, anyway, so I can help everyone get settled up there."

"Not scared of the bogeyman?" Gibson asked.

Bill hesitated. "You guys already cleared the place, right?"

The Marine shrugged and nodded.

"Then I'm not going to worry about it."

"Fair enough. I'll meet you up there once we're all set up down here."

Bill smiled tightly and turned to Hanna and Akela, the surviving housekeepers. "Would you please join us on the third floor?"

"What for, Mr. Steele?" Akela replied.

"Someone's got to mop up the blood," Don replied.

"I redy tell ya, we no gonna clean up dat shit."

"Where do you live?" Bill asked.

"Koloa," Akela replied.

"And yet you're getting to stay here for free. We could just as easily send you home."

"Not free if we gotta clean wittout pay."

Hanna nodded her agreement with that sentiment.

Bill growled. "Fine. I'll help. Get a bucket and a mop please."

"How we gonna clean wittout water?"

"She's got a point," Don replied.

"We'll use sea water for now. Mind lending a hand?"

Don shrugged. "What else have I got to do?"

"Let's go. Beth, stay here and wait until we're done, okay?"

"Okay," Beth said. She watched as her dad and Don left with the two housekeepers, all of them heading for the nearest supply closet. Dragging her eyes away, she looked to Commander Wilde and stared at him, her eyes blinking in a daze.

"Something on your mind, ma'am?"

She was trying to figure out what she should do next. She desperately wanted to know if Toby was okay, but who could she ask about that? She'd need to talk to whoever had cleared the bodies from the resort. Failing that, she could walk over to his house, but that might not be safe right now. They said all the aliens were dead, but who really knew for sure? Maybe she could find some way to call him. Beth reached into her pocket for the only personal belonging she'd taken to and from the *Port Royal*—her cell phone. The battery was long dead, but she held it up for the commander to see.

"Do you think the cell network is back online?"

"No clue, ma'am. You'll have to power your phone on and see for yourself. "My guess is that the EMP will have fried the cell transmitters just like it fried everything else."

"So how is the power back?"

"The grid probably has more redundancy built in, or at least plenty of replacement parts on hand. Everything else is going to take more time to get up and running again."

"Great." Beth's chest filled with bitter air, and she went to sit on one of the empty couches in the lobby.

While she was over there, she heard the familiar rumble of a car's engine slicing through the steady tromping of Marines' boots. Beth turned toward the sound and saw a rusty white van pull up outside the front doors of the resort. The Marines all stopped what they were doing and turned to look. Van doors slid open, and a pair of people in bulky canary-yellow suits climbed out.

"The CDC is here!" Commander Wilde announced. "Everyone get ready to provide samples."

CHAPTER 26

"How have you been feeling?" the CDC worker asked as she took a sample of Beth's blood.

"Fine."

"No symptoms?"

Beth shook her head.

"Not even psychological effects from the trauma? Have you been sleeping well?"

"Well, until today I've been sleeping in a cramped bunk room on a ship. Not very comfortable."

"Have you had any nightmares or panic attacks?"

"What's a panic attack?" Beth asked.

"Racing heart, feeling dizzy, can't breathe, sweaty hands, unreasoning fear..."

"No, but you might want to talk to Melanie. That sounds like her."

"I'll be sure to do that," the CDC worker said. "Open wide."

The woman in the canary-yellow suit came at

her with an extra-long cotton bud and swabbed her tongue with it. Beth watched as the woman slipped it into a clear plastic tube and snapped on a blue lid.

"What's your name?" the woman asked.

"What's yours?" Beth countered.

"Ashley."

"Beth."

"Beth...?"

"Steele."

Ashley nodded and used a black sharpie to scribble on both the tube with the cotton swab and the vial of blood she'd sucked from Beth's arm. "Thank you, Beth."

Ashley began turning away, but Beth stopped her. "Wait."

The other woman's eyebrows fluttered behind her mask. "Something wrong?"

"The Marines said you guys cleaned up in here."

The woman cringed. "I didn't, thank God, but some others from my team were assigned to clean-up around the landing sites."

"Landing sites?" Beth asked.

"Areas where the landers came down. They were the hardest hit. The aliens didn't wander very far. Good thing, too, or there'd be a lot more casualties."

Beth nodded absently. Those details weren't important to her right now. "I'm looking for someone," she said. "Is there any way I could get to see the bodies?"

"Are you sure you want to? It's pretty gruesome."

"One of the staff here was my boyfriend," Beth explained. "He's missing."

Ashley hesitated. "We have the bodies stored at the center right now. We haven't actively tried to ID them because of how few vehicles are still working on the island. The identification process will likely involve photos rather than physical visitation at this time. It's safer that way. We don't know if any of the bodies are contaminated."

"Can I get a look at the photos?"

"We're still collating all of the data."

"Please. I need to know what happened to him. What if you take me to the center to see the bodies?"

Ashley shook her head. "It's against protocol unless you're coming in for isolation or additional testing. But if you volunteered for some tests, maybe... you're one of the ones who came in direct contact with the aliens, right?"

"Yes," Beth lied. "They tried to suck my face off." The welts on her dad's and the others' faces were gone now, so the doctor wouldn't know that she was lying.

Ashley nodded. "That's great. Well, not great, but having a volunteer will help a lot. There are some samples we haven't been able to collect yet."

"Can't you just force people to give you whatever you need?"

"Not without proof of an actual pathogen. Orders are to wait and see if anyone develops symptoms before we start violating freedoms."

"You think it will come to that?" Beth asked.

"I hope not, but don't worry. In practice, most people with actual symptoms are happy to cooperate. Until then, blood and saliva are the only samples we can easily get. We have collected a few fecal and urine samples, though."

Beth's nose wrinkled. "Is that what I'm in for if I volunteer?"

Ashley shook her head inside her suit. "We could really use a CT scan and a spinal tap, but so far no one has volunteered for that."

Beth winced. "Isn't that dangerous?" Beth asked. "I mean, a *spinal* tap? That sounds bad."

"Not dangerous, no. A little bit painful, especially if you develop a post-lumbar puncture headache, but I can give you something for that. Anyway, if you scratch my back, Miss Steele, I'll scratch yours. You want a look at the morgue, and I want a look at your cells."

"So that's how it's going to be," Beth said.

"I'm afraid so. Do you have a parent or guardian who can sign their consent?"

"My dad."

"Where is he?"

"Getting water at the beach. We have a plumbing problem."

"I see. Well, we can see what he says when he comes back."

Beth shook her head. "Get me the forms, and I'll take them to him while you finish collecting samples." She'd forged her dad's signature plenty of times for school. Besides, it wasn't as though anyone here would actually know what his signature looked like.

Ashley hesitated.

"You don't have them with you," Beth guessed.

"No, we do, but I still need to talk to my supervisor."

"So get me the forms while you talk to your supervisor," Beth said.

Ashley favored her with a slight frown. "You must really love this boy. All right. I'll see what I can do. No promises, though."

Beth nodded. "Thank you."

CHAPTER 27

"You want to go where with them?" her dad asked, his dark brows drawing together as he leaned against their kitchen counter.

Beth stood just behind the door, arms crossed over her chest, impatient to get on her way. "To the quarantine center. It's in Lihue, next to the airport." She'd already forged all the necessary consent forms. "I have to see if Toby is there," Beth explained, swallowing past the sudden lump in her throat.

"By checking all the bodies in the morgue? That sounds traumatic."

Beth shrugged. "I've seen worse in movies."

"That's not the same, Beth. And what if he *is* there? What then? That image will be stuck with you forever."

Beth hesitated, trying to fight back the rising tide of darkness his comment triggered inside of her. She shivered and shook her head. "I need to know."

Her dad sighed. "I guess at least you'll have closure. How will you get back?"

"Ashley will drive me."

"Who's Ashley?"

"One of the doctors. The pretty one."

"Fine, you can go, but I want you back before dark."

"It won't take that long," Beth lied. It was already 4:00 PM, and Ashley had said it would take at least a couple of hours to do the tests. Add in travel time and time to check the morgue, and that put her at or past sunset.

"Good."

"Why?" she asked.

"Because Commander Wilde was saying there's a chance some of those Crawlers are still out there, and if they are, they'll be waiting until the sun goes down to come out."

A stab of dread shot through Beth at the possibility of running into one of the aliens again.

"Be careful," her dad added.

"I will."

* * *

The drive through Koloa was surprisingly normal other than the lack of cars on the streets. Pedestrians were out everywhere to make up for it, but there were no signs of the bloody massacre Beth had expected.

"How many people died?" Beth asked from the back of the van.

Ashley made an attempt to turn her head from where she sat in the driver's seat, but the hazmat suit restricted her movement. "A little over a thousand," she replied.

"A thousand one hundred and three," her colleague added from the front passenger's seat.

"Will I have to check them all?" Beth asked, swallowing thickly.

"No," Ashley said. "We have them organized by gender, apparent age, and the location they were found—among other criteria. Since about a tenth of the casualties occurred at the Koa Kai, those cadavers practically have a whole tent to themselves."

Beth felt sick at the thought of walking among those mutilated bodies to find Toby. Hopefully he wasn't there. Either way, she would definitely see some familiar faces—guests and staff from the hotel. "Do you mind if I open a window?" Beth asked.

"Go ahead," Ashley replied.

She slid the back window open and pressed her nose against the screen. Floral fragrances wafted in, and tall grass rustled loudly with the wind of their passage.

The ride to the CDC camp took Beth down a

familiar three-lane highway. It was the same route her bus took to and from school every day.

The CDC camp had been set up on a soccer field just outside the Lihue Airport. Beth knew it well. She'd played there with her team almost daily before getting kicked off for missing too many practices. Now big, rectangular white-canvas tents dominated the field. As they drove to a familiar gravel parking lot, Beth spotted dozens of CDC workers walking between those tents in their canary-yellow suits.

"Do you always have to wear those suits?" Beth asked Ashley as the driver parked the van.

"You mean the hazmats? We have to wear them whenever we leave the clean rooms. We wouldn't be much use if we got infected, too."

Infected with what? "What if no one is actually infected?" Beth asked.

The driver hopped out, followed by the worker in the passenger's seat.

"Then we'll be out of here soon, and the quarantine and travel ban will be lifted," Ashley replied as she pulled open the sliding door beside her and climbed out. Her partner went next, lugging a case full of samples. Ashley waved for Beth to follow.

She jumped out and followed Ashley and the other CDC workers through an open gate in the chain link fence that ran around the field. A pair of men in familiar blue camo-patterned uniforms guarded that gate. They glanced curiously at Beth as she walked by, probably wondering what she was doing wearing a Navy uniform.

"They're not wearing hazmats," Beth said.

Ashley shook her head. "No, they were sent to the island before we got here, so there's a chance they've already been exposed. We have them helping us guard the fence to make sure no one sneaks in and compromises the facility."

"And in case there are still any of those creatures out there?" Beth suggested, remembering her dad's warning.

"That too," Ashley confirmed.

They broke ranks with the other doctors as they crossed the field. Ashley headed for one tent, her colleagues for another. Beth began to feel nervous about what was coming. She hadn't even taken the time to read the forms she'd signed. What were they planning to do to her?

"Are we going to look at bodies first?" Beth asked hopefully.

"No. We're going to the clinic," Ashley said.

So much for that. "What about the other doctors?"

"They're heading to the lab to drop off the samples."

— 172 —

"Are they going to hurt? The tests?"

"You won't feel anything besides the needles for the anesthesia. Relax."

"Needles?" Beth asked. "How many are we talking about?"

"Two or three."

* * *

Beth lay staring up at the white canvas ceiling of the clinic, waiting for Ashley to return. Her back hurt where Ashley had withdrawn some of her spinal fluid, and her wrist was ever so slightly cold and numb where the IV had delivered a contrast medium into her body for the CT scan. Now she lay anxiously counting down the minutes until Ashley came back from taking those samples to the lab.

At least so far there was no sign of the headache she'd been warned about, but Ashley had said that symptoms could take a day or more to present, so she'd promised to go back to the Koa Kai tomorrow and the day after to check. That made Beth think the supposedly safe *spinal tap* procedure was riskier than she'd been led to believe. Then there was the CT scan. Beth was pretty sure that so-called *contrast medium* was radioactive. *Cancer one-Beth zero,* she thought dryly. She hoped she didn't live to regret forging those consent forms.

Glancing around the roomy tent, Beth saw metal shelves filled with boxes of supplies, a fridge full of vials, various types of scanners and life support monitors, along with half a dozen padded tables covered in plastic like the one where she lay. There was also a cordoned off area with a metal table that probably served as an operating room. At the far end, three big circular vents blasted cold air from air conditioners that Beth could hear droning loudly through the canvas. Flaps shuttered the transparent windows, keeping out the sun, while strings of bright LED lights blazed overhead.

Long minutes passed—thirty or more, if Beth had to guess—before Ashley came back through the simple tent-flap doorway. She still wore her hazmat suit.

"How are you feeling?" she asked, stopping beside Beth.

"Great," Beth said. She sat up and swung her legs over the side, stifling a wince as a sharp pain erupted from her lower back where the needle had gone in. "Can we go to the morgue now?"

Ashley nodded inside her suit. "Yes, if you're up to it."

Beth gingerly slid off the table to stand on her feet. "I am."

"Good. Come with me."

Ashley led her outside. The sun was sinking steadily closer to the horizon.

"What time is it?" Beth asked.

"Six-fifteen."

Beth's skin prickled, and she quickened her pace. It was the end of August so the sun would only set at around seven, but it would take half an hour just to get back to the resort. She was cutting things close if she planned to get back before dark.

"What if the sun sets before we're done here? Will I have to stay at the camp?"

"That won't be necessary," Ashley replied. "It's a big island, and there are only a few Crawlers unaccounted for."

Beth's lungs seized in her chest. "So it's true. They're still out there."

"Yes, but don't worry about it. We'll take a Marine escort with us."

They reached the entrance of another large tent and Ashley stopped to regard her before going in. "Are you sure you're ready for this?"

Beth nodded. "Yeah," she said, letting out a long breath.

Ashley pushed through the opening, and frigid air blasted out. Beth shivered and hugged herself as she walked in behind the doctor. Clouds of moisture billowed from her lips. Bodies were laid out abreast in long lines leading from the door, all of them zippered up inside white bags with tags on the zippers, like luggage at an airport. There had to be several hundred of them at least.

"The ones closest to the door are from the Koa Kai," Ashley said. "I need some details to go on. Age?"

"Nineteen."

"Build?"

"Tall and thin."

"Hair and eye color?"

"Blonde and blue," Beth replied.

"Okay, that's probably enough." Ashley walked down the front of the rows of bodies, heading for the far right of the tent. Cold air billowed from vents on both sides and radiated from the floor, freezing Beth's ankles.

Ashley led the way down the last row, stopping to check a few of the bodies along the way. How many tall and skinny blonde-haired nineteen-year-olds had there been at the resort? Beth wondered.

"Here. We'll take a look at this one," Ashley said. She was on her haunches beside one of the bags, fumbling with the zippers in her gloved hands. "Brace yourself."

Beth sucked in a breath as Ashley opened the bag. The smell of death wafted out. Ashley carefully peeled back only enough of the bag to expose the face. Bloodless gray skin and a pair of familiar blue eyes stared up at Beth. She clapped a hand to her mouth as tears sprang to her eyes. "No..."

"Are you sure it's him?" Ashley asked.

Beth nodded quickly and looked away, flinging tears away with shaking hands. "Get me out of here."

CHAPTER 28

Beth sat like a statue in the passenger's seat while Ashley drove the van back to the resort. Behind them sat a Marine with a rifle and what looked like half of a pair of binoculars strapped to his helmet above his right eye.

The headlights of the van barely revealed the shadowy depths of the vegetation along the dark, scenic road between Koloa and Lihue.

Beth stared out her side window, watching with dull eyes as the shadows seeped in behind the van's lights. Toby was dead, gutted by a Crawler. It didn't feel real. None of it seemed possible.

Koloa's street lights appeared as the van came around a dark corner. Something big and pale on four legs darted out in front of them, disappearing in the long grass and trees on the other side of the road. Ashley stomped on the breaks, tires squealed, and the van lurched to a stop.

"Did you see that?" Beth asked quietly. She twisted around to see the Marine's night vision gear folded out in front of his left eye. He peered out the side window of the van with his rifle raised to his shoulder.

"I saw it," Ashley said quietly. "Was that..."

"Hard to say, ma'am. Whatever it was, it's gone now. We need to keep moving."

"Aren't you going to go out and hunt it?" Beth asked.

"No, ma'am. My orders are to provide a safe escort to and from the resort. I'm not authorized to pursue or engage enemy contacts."

"Well those are dumb orders. Hunt or be hunted. What do you prefer?"

"My orders stand, ma'am."

Beth stared hard into the trees and long grass where the thing had disappeared, struggling to calm her racing heart.

"We should keep moving, Doctor Carter," the Marine said.

"Right." Ashley stomped on the gas, and the van's engine roared as it revved high.

Koloa's streetlights scrolled by Beth's window with far too many blank spaces in between them. "How many of those things are still out there?" she asked.

"We found sixty dead," Ashley answered in a shaky voice. "We counted thirty-two landers. Each of them has just enough room for two Crawlers, so that means four are missing."

"Four!" Beth echoed. "It only took two to kill everyone at the resort."

"Because they were unarmed," the Marine sitting in the back said. "Don't worry. We'll get them, ma'am. We have teams all over the island. You're safe now."

But Beth didn't feel safe.

Five minutes later they were pulling up in front of the entrance of the Koa Kai, as close as Ashley could get without driving through the plant boxes. The Marine escort pulled his sliding door open and swept his rifle around the parking lot before opening Beth's door. "All clear, ma'am," he said, nodding.

"I'll see you tomorrow," Ashley said in a muffled voice. "I'm sorry again about your boyfriend.

"Yeah," Beth said, not wasting time to say more. She jumped out beside the Marine, and he walked with her to the entrance. The doors didn't slide open automatically for them, but a Marine standing inside the entrance moved to open one of them manually as they approached.

Beth rushed inside the lobby, heading for the stairs and the refuge of her room. The Marines' hushed voices followed her from the entrance as they traded updates. Beth saw her dad pacing the gleaming, faux marble floors. He turned to look just as she reached the foot of the stairs, and she hesitated there.

"Beth! Where the hell have you been?" he asked, striding over quickly.

Beth looked longingly to the stairs and caught sight of another Marine guarding the bloody door and hallway to her right. It was boarded up now. Beth's mind flashed back to a week ago. She saw her dad bracing that door with Don and James as a Crawler tried to push its way in.

She shivered.

Her dad grabbed her by the shoulders and shook her. "You said you'd be back before dark!"

"It took longer than I thought," Beth explained.

He looked away, to the entrance where Ashley had pulled up. The van had already left. "Where are the people who brought you?" he demanded. "I want to talk to them."

"Gone." Beth slipped out of his grip, starting up the stairs.

Her dad sighed, then caught himself. "And Toby?" he asked, his tone hesitant now.

Beth shook her head. "Also gone."

CHAPTER 29

Beth woke up with her heart pounding and a scream frozen in her throat. She sat up and quickly scanned her bedroom for threats. The bedside lamp was on; no way she'd be able to sleep in the dark.

But there was nothing in her room. The closet's louvered doors might be hiding unseen horrors.

Thump.

Beth jumped, and adrenaline surged in her veins. The sound had come from her door.

"Hello? Dad?"

Silence answered, and Beth resisted the urge to scream.

Thump.

A powerful urge to *run* overcame her, but where could she go? The door was the only way in or out of her room. At least she'd locked it.

"Dad?" Beth asked again.

Thump.

Remembering how the Crawlers had gone around knocking on people's doors to get them to open up, Beth shivered and drew her knees up to her chest, her mind racing. If she screamed, her dad would come running out of his room and maybe get himself killed. But if she didn't, whatever was out there might grow tired of knocking and simply break the door down.

Beth hesitated, frozen with terror.

Thump.

Her brow furrowed and reason made a welcome entrance into her racing thoughts. That sound was too soft for a knock.

Then she remembered how her dad had spent the last week bumbling around their bunk room at night, bumping into things and waking everyone up. That had to be it. He was sleepwalking again.

Beth climbed out of bed on shaking legs and went up to the door. Placing her ear against it, she heard a muffled whispering, a muttering voice—words, faint but audible.

Thump! Beth jumped at the noise and reached tentatively for the door handle. She turned the lock with a shaking hand and cracked the door open with a noisy creak.

"Dad?"

He was standing there, swaying on his feet, rocking back and forth like a pendulum or a metronome. His eyes were open, staring. Beth took a deep breath to calm herself, remembering Don's advice from the *Port Royal* when her dad had begun sleepwalking: *'Don't wake him. Sleepwalkers freak out when you startle them.'* The only thing to do was to guide him gently back to his room, trying not to wake him.

Beth took her dad by the arm and gently turned him, walking slowly toward his room at the end of the hall.

He was muttering in his sleep, his words indistinct. Beth shuffled with him down the hall. She almost had him back to his bed when he suddenly stopped and grabbed her by the shoulders, his fingers digging into her like talons.

Beth froze, searching his wide eyes in the dark, wondering if he'd just woken up.

"Beth! Help me!" he whispered. "They won't let me go."

Beth tried to break free and back away, but he moved with her, pressing her against the wall. Her dad's expression twisted wretchedly. "I don't have long, Beth. They..."

A jolt of naked terror slammed into her, and Beth began to doubt her analysis of the situation. Could sleepwalkers recognize people in their sleep? "Dad?"

But he was gone again, his expression slack and vacant.

"Dad!"

He woke up with a start.

"Beth. Is something wrong?" he asked, sounding suddenly far too reasonable.

She darted down to the end of the hall and hit the lights. He stood blinking at her, his lips curved in a bemused smile.

"You said you needed help," she said, her chest heaving breathlessly.

"I did?" he asked. "I must have been having a nightmare."

"You *must have* been? You don't remember?"

He shook his head. "No." He glanced around. "I guess I was sleepwalking again. You should go back to bed."

Beth just gaped at her father, unable to believe how calm he looked and sounded. But annoyance quickly crowded out her confusion, and she stalked by him, heading for her room. "Lock your door next time," she said. "You woke me up."

"I'll try that," he replied.

CHAPTER 30

Captain Reed watched from a safe distance as a pair of CDC workers in hazmat suits moved the sedated alien into a holding cell in the Lihue police station. Police officers on the night patrol stood guard at the exits while Marines with automatic rifles and XREP-loaded shotguns oversaw the operation. Thankfully taser-based tech seemed to work just fine to subdue the aliens. So did the sedatives they'd injected this one with to safely move it from the *Port Royal*.

Reed's skin itched as he watched CDC workers lay the hairless monster on the stained cement floor of its cell. The police sergeant shut and locked the cell as soon as they left.

"Subject is secure, sir," Lieutenant Spooner said. Admiral Harris had ordered Spooner and all of his remaining men to go ashore and stay there to help capture the remaining Crawlers and guard the one they already had. But it wasn't really about guarding the subject against a possible rescue from its own kind—Reed suspected from the sheer lack of tech the aliens had brought, and the absence of a more organized invasion, that they were far more primitive than their massive spaceship would imply. They were obviously intelligent, so a rescue couldn't be ruled out, but as far as Reed was concerned, the most significant threat came from the local human population. Sooner or later one of the policemen at the station would tell his wife, and then she'd go blabbing the news to all of her neighbors. *And then we'll have a damned riot on our hands.* But that was Mayor Smith's problem. He had insisted they keep the police at the station.

Reed shook his head, his gaze lingering on the sleeping Crawler. Its translucent skin slowly rose and fell with its breath, shadowy organs shifting inside of it. If it were up to Reed, he'd just shoot it in the head and toss it in the ocean for the sharks. But then, he was a man of action, and few politicians were.

Lieutenant Spooner left the holding cell just as one of his subordinates strolled in with an update. "Sir, transport is waiting to take you to the nearest landing site."

"Excellent." Spooner's eyes flicked to Reed. "Are you still planning to accompany me, sir?"

Reed inclined his head to the lieutenant. "Let's go."

* * *

"That's it?" The lander looked depressingly analog. Floodlights shone down from the perimeter of the landing crater, illuminating a bare metal capsule, scorched black outside, padded white on the inside. It was barely big enough for two grown men, let alone two Crawlers. Strange, web-like restraints curtained what might have been a pair of seats at the back. Reed couldn't see any windows or visible controls of any kind. It was either a highly automated vehicle, or just as primitive as it looked. "The lunar lander had more tech than this," Reed said.

Lieutenant Spooner shook his head while naval engineers and their local civilian counterparts bustled around the shallow crater in which the egg-shaped lander sat.

Reed sighed. He'd exposed himself to the additional risk of contamination for this? "Keep me apprised of any developments, Lieutenant. It's time I headed back to the *Royal*."

"Aye, Captain."

Captain Reed parted ways with Lieutenant Spooner in the Nawiliwili Harbor's parking lot. Reed set a brisk pace as he and two ensigns walked under the bright lights of the parking lot, past the dry dock to the boat launch. Both ensigns kept wary eyes on their surroundings, hands on their sidearms, but Reed refused to give in to their fears. Yes, a few aliens were still unaccounted for, but Kauai was a big island, and for all they knew the missing ones were lying dead in a jungle somewhere.

A flicker of movement caught his eye. Four local women wearing colorful leis and form-fitting shirts ran toward them, giggling. Reed stopped and frowned at their approach. One of the ensigns began to draw his weapon, but Reed stopped him with a hand on his shoulder.

"Easy. Ladies, we are on official Navy business, and this harbor is a restricted—"

One of them collided with Reed, and he caught her awkwardly, stumbling back a step with her momentum. Her breath reeked of alcohol, eyes glazed. She couldn't have been more than twenty years old. In his periphery, Reed noticed both ensigns battling with their own drunken partners, while the fourth stood a few paces back, giggling.

The one in Reed's arms looked up at him with doe eyes and flashed a pretty smile. "*Aloha*, Captain." Wrapping her arms around his neck, she pulled his lips down to hers and slipped her tongue inside his mouth.

For a full second Reed was too shocked to react, but then he pushed her away. "Step back immediately, ma'am!"

She flashed another grin, and then about-faced and ran giggling into the night with her accomplices. Reed saw both ensigns wiping their lips. One of them gave him a rueful look. "We're definitely contaminated now, sir. We should report to the CDC."

Reed snorted. "We're under quarantine anyway. Besides, no one is showing any symptoms."

"Their behavior was weird," the second ensign said. "That could be a symptom—loss of inhibitions."

Reed considered it. "They were drunk. Kissing us was probably part of some bet—or maybe just end of the world madness rearing its head."

"She whispered aloha to me," the second ensign said. "Was she saying hello or goodbye?"

"Does it matter, Ensign? You want to call her back and ask for her number?"

"No, sir."

"Then let's get back to the *Royal*."

CHAPTER 31

Beth awoke to a loud knock on her door. She sat up in a rush, the covers falling away. A cold sweat instantly prickled her skin.

"Beth, breakfast is ready!" her dad announced, his voice muffled by the door.

Relief coursed through her at the familiar sound of his voice: it wasn't an alien, just her dad. Right on the heels of that relief came a crushing weight of grief. Toby's dead, staring blue eyes flashed through her mind, and she fought back a fresh wave of tears.

Knock, knock, knock! "Beth?"

"I'm coming," she said in a hoarse voice. Stumbling out of bed in her pajamas, she opened the door to find her dad fully dressed.

He flashed a smile. "Hey there, Bethy," he said. "Food's downstairs in the restaurant. Everyone else is already eating." With that, he spun away and strode off down the hall.

Beth watched him go with a wrinkled brow.

He passed out of sight, and a moment later she heard the front door open, then click shut. He was unusually upbeat first thing in the morning. Beth's thoughts flashed back to what her dad had said to her while sleepwalking last night—*Beth! Help me! They won't let me go*—and worry crept in at the edges of her thoughts. Maybe there was a reason he wasn't acting like himself.

Beth took a few minutes to get dressed before following him downs. She passed one of the Marines at the bottom of the stairs—Private Kelly. She recognized him by his young, freckled face and green eyes. He couldn't have been much older than Toby.

Beth winced at the comparison and pushed those thoughts from her head. The orange-gold rays of the morning sun streamed through the front doors, landing on the shiny brown tiles marbled with white veins. Her footsteps faltered, and she glanced the other way, out at the courtyard to the ocean beyond. The bloody pink water of the pool lay cloaked in shadows. Only the tops of the palm trees were illuminated and gleaming in the sun. Above that, the clouds were golden, not white. Maybe five or six in the morning, Beth guessed. Breakfast wasn't usually served until eight.

Crossing the lobby, she entered the restaurant

and stopped. Almost everyone was already there. Commander Wilde and Chief Miller were there, along with Corporal Gibson, though it wasn't surprising that sailors and Marines would be up this early. As for the tourists... Beth stood in the entrance, taking a silent roll call of the early risers. James, the linebacker-sized lawyer, sat with his family; Allen, the balding accountant, sat alone; The two widows, Melanie and Avery, sat together. Chef Jones sat by herself; the two housekeepers, Hanna and Akela, occupied another table with one of the Marines... Decker. Private Dekker, Beth recalled. And then there was Don, sitting alone in the farthest possible corner of the restaurant, his eyes scanning the room over a mug of coffee.

The kitchen door burst open, and her dad came out carrying a full tray of food.

Beth strode over to him just as he was setting a plate of scrambled eggs in front of Chef Jones.

"Sleep well?" her dad asked.

"No," Beth said, watching her dad pass a glass of water to the chef. Was the plumbing working again? She shook her head and regarded her dad with a scowl. "Is this a joke?"

"What do you mean?" her dad replied. He eyed her for a second, then appeared to have an epiphany. "Oh, right. You must be starving! Hang on, I'll get you a plate."

"No," Beth replied. "That's not what I meant. What time is it?"

"Six in the morning," Chef Jones replied around a mouthful of eggs.

Beth glanced around, gesturing to the others in the restaurant. "So who made all of this?"

"We did," her dad replied.

"We..."

"Chef Jones, Hanna, Private Dekker, and me."

"Okay... but why so early?"

Don walked up to them with a plate of eggs balanced in one hand and a fork in the other. "They couldn't sleep," he explained for them.

Her dad nodded agreeably, as did Jenna, their heads bobbing in unison. "The eggs were going to go bad. So I figured, why not cook them? Waste not want not."

Beth frowned. "Just eggs? Nothing else?"

"There's bread and butter, but the toasters don't work. You want some or not?"

"I guess..." Beth said.

"Good. I'll be right back." Bill wheeled away, heading back to the kitchen with an empty tray.

Don grabbed Beth's arm and began tugging her toward his table. "Let's sit," he said.

Beth let him guide her without complaint and sat beside him at his corner table. "Notice anything strange?" he asked in a low voice.

"You mean besides the fact that everyone who should be sleeping in is down here stuffing their faces with plain scrambled eggs like they haven't seen food in weeks?"

"Besides that," Don agreed. "Look closely. Tell me what you see."

Beth did, scanning the people in the restaurant. They were all eating with more gusto than they should have been considering the time, and how bland their breakfast was. But there was something else, too. Something that niggled like a grain of sand in her eye.

As she watched, a silent rhythm emerged: forks dipped to plates, up to mouths, repeat. Coffee mugs to lips, back to table. Forks dipped to plates...

"Wait, what?" Beth blinked furiously and shook her head. Maybe it was her imagination.

But it wasn't. People were eating and drinking in perfect synchrony, as if their movements had been choreographed. Simultaneous actions were staggered between the tables, but still noticeable. James, Avery, Allen, and Melanie all raised their forks to their mouths at the same instant, popped food in their mouths, and then lowered their forks again. They raised their glasses for a drink, drank for two beats, and then lowered their glasses. They weren't the only ones, either: Hanna, Private Dekker, and Chef Jones were all in sync as well.

Just then, her dad emerged from the kitchen with another plate. Jenna's hand came up to scratch her cheek. In the same instant, so did her dad's, Hanna's, and Private Dekker's.

Beth's eyes widened. "Why four?"

"So you do see it," Don replied. "I thought I was losing my mind."

CHAPTER 32

"Here you go," Bill said, setting a plate of eggs and a glass of water in front of Beth. "It's not fancy, but it will keep you going until our rations arrive."

Beth nodded, watching him with wide eyes. He didn't seem to notice her suspicion. Turning back the way he came, he headed to the kitchen. Beth eyed her eggs warily before looking to Don. "What's going on?"

"Well, it's not everything, obviously. They're not all moving in lockstep. It's more like a tell. A trace of some kind. It's like they're... I don't know, telegraphing neural signals to each other."

"Telepathy?" Beth asked.

"Something like that, yeah."

"So are they infected with something? Are they dangerous? My dad was walking around again last night. He came knocking on my door asking for help. He said they won't let him go. Then he woke up and couldn't remember any of it."

The permanent furrows on Don's brow multiplied. "That's some creepy shit."

"You're telling me," Beth replied, whispering urgently. "Do you think maybe those aliens are controlling them somehow?"

Don placed a finger to his lips and shook his head. "Eat up. We can talk after. Somewhere less busy."

Beth got the hint. She shoveled eggs from her plate and washed them down with the glass of water. "Done," she said all of a few minutes later.

They walked outside together, following the covered eaves around the resort, taking a wide berth around the bloody pool. "So?" Beth asked. "What do you think? Alien mind control?"

Don glanced around, checking to see that no one else was around; then shook his head. "I don't see how. Even if it were that, only two Crawlers attacked us that night, and of those two, only one survived. It definitely didn't infect everyone here by itself."

"Maybe the aliens don't have to be alive for it to work," Beth said.

"Intelligent, telecommunicating alien parasites?" Don said. "The CDC would have found something like that by now."

"Maybe, maybe not. The doctor I spoke with got me to volunteer for some extra tests. She said they haven't had anyone else volunteer yet."

"What kind of tests?"

"A CT scan and a spinal tap."

Don stopped walking and turned to her. He glanced back the way they'd come, then back at her, his blue eyes sharp with sudden interest. "Really?" he scratched his chin through his shaggy blond beard.

"Yeah," Beth replied. "Why, is that important?"

"It could be. Why are they waiting for volunteers?"

Beth shrugged. "Because no one is showing any symptoms of anything yet. They're trying to preserve people's freedoms."

Don snorted. "Jeez Louise. We're at ground zero for an alien biothreat, and they're tip-toeing around? I wonder what brainless bureaucrat gave those orders?"

Beth smiled in spite of the gravity of the moment and arched an eyebrow at him. "Jeez Louise?"

"I'm tryin' to spare your ears, kid. We need to get the CDC back here ASAP. Is there any way you can contact them?"

"The cell network is down," Beth replied. "But Ashley said she'd come by to check on me today. Something about a possible headache from the spinal tap."

Don blew out a breath. "Then we lucked out. Soon as she gets here, you need tell her about this."

Beth nodded slowly. "Okay."

Don glanced behind them again. "In the meantime, keep your head down. We don't want to tip anyone off. In fact, we'd better not be seen together. They might know who is and isn't one of them."

Beth frowned, feeling suddenly silly for buying into Don's paranoia. "Maybe we're overreacting. I mean, we didn't see much. Besides, we've been spending all this time together. If they're infected with something, wouldn't we be, too?"

"Not if we're immune," Don replied. "Think about it. Why did they kill some people and choose to swap saliva with the others?"

"Uck!"

"Follow my thinking for a sec, kid. Maybe they can tell who the viable hosts are just by smelling them."

"So my dad's viable and I'm not?" Beth asked. "How's that make any sense? We're related."

"Not 100% related. And anyway who the hell knows? It's just a theory, but there must be some reason behind it. That night wasn't just a random slaughter. It was a mission, and I bet they accomplished it. Their mothership never would have left otherwise."

"What mission?"

"Maybe to colonize us," Don said.

Beth shuddered. "And then?"

"We'd better hope there is no *and then*."

CHAPTER 33

Beth sat in the lobby with her back to the windows, playing with her phone and listening to previously-downloaded music from Spotify with one half of her earbuds. That left her other ear free to listen for approaching threats. Every now and then she glanced up, checking visually, too, but so far no one had thought to bother her.

Beth's eyes dipped to her phone. It was 10:30 now. She'd watched almost everyone leave the resort, walking out the front doors, headed for parts unknown. Her dad had stayed, but only because Commander Wilde had convinced him to, saying that their rations would be arriving soon, and they needed his help to put them under lock and key in one of the resort's storage rooms.

Beth's knee bounced anxiously. She felt the beginnings of a dull headache thumping behind her eyes—or maybe that was just her racing heart. Where was Ashley? She said she was coming to check on Beth today. Hopefully the doctor arrived before the rations did and her dad took off.

Long minutes passed, and Beth's playlist started over from the beginning. She barely heard the squeal of brakes over *Thunder*, a hit song from *Imagine Dragons*. Looking up, she saw the rusty white van from the CDC parked in front of the resort. Corporal Gibson cracked the sliding doors open just as someone jumped out of the driver's seat in a hazmat suit. A black Marine who might have been the one from last night walked around the front of the van, sporting a millimeters-short crew cut rather than a helmet with night vision goggles.

Corporal Gibson spoke briefly with them at the entrance before opening the doors wider to let them in.

Beth pulled her earbud out and stood up. She heard footsteps approaching and saw her dad walking in from outside. He'd been draining the pool while Hanna and Akela mopped and scrubbed the bloody surround.

"Hello there," her dad said. "Here to take more samples?"

The CDC worker shook her head, and Beth heard Ashley's muffled voice issue from the suit. "No, I'm here to check on Beth Steele to make sure she's—

Beth ran to intercept them before Ashley could

give anything away.

"—not suffering any side effects from yesterday's lumbar puncture," Ashley finished.

Beth's dad turned to look at her just as she reached them. "Her what?" he asked. Looking back to Ashley he went on. "My daughter was subjected to additional testing? Why was she singled out?"

Ashley appeared to hesitate. "You're Mr. Steele?"

"That's right."

"You signed all the consent forms."

"What consent forms?"

"I forged them," Beth said. "Sorry, Ashley."

"You did what?" her dad thundered. "Sorry, Ashley? How about *sorry, Dad?*"

Beth felt oddly reassured by the scolding. It wasn't out of character for her dad at all, making Don's theory about alien parasites affecting people's brains seem more like the product of a paranoid mind than an actual possibility.

"I can't believe this," her dad went on, shaking his head. "You mentioned something about side effects from the tests?"

Ashley's head bobbed inside her suit. "Yes." Eyes flicking to Beth, she asked. "Have you experienced any headaches?"

Beth took a moment to check. "A little. It just started."

"How would you describe the pain? Mild, moderate, severe?"

"Mild."

"That's good. I don't think it's anything to worry about, then."

As Ashley said that, Beth's phone vibrated noisily and began chirping with updates. She pulled it out of her pocket to see a stream of social media updates and e-mails pouring into the status feed on her phone.

Most of it was unimportant, but there were a lot of missed calls, and messages from her mom.

Beth? It's Mom. I just saw what's happening on the news. Call me!

Beth? Are you there? Please ANSWER.

BETH!

And then came fifty-three missed calls spread across her mom's phone and her stepdad's.

"Looks like the cell network is back," Ashley said.

Beth nodded absently. "I have to call my mom."

"You'd better," her dad said. "She's probably going crazy right now."

"I'll leave you two to get caught up," Ashley put in, turning to leave.

"Aloha," Beth's dad replied.

Then Ashley hesitated as if a thought had just

occurred to her. "Beth, in case that headache gets worse, or one of you develops new symptoms, you should save the number for the center on your phone."

Beth nodded. "Okay."

"Eight oh eight, two four four, zero six, zero six," Ashley said.

"Got it."

"I'll write it down at the reception, too," Beth's dad added. "In case someone else needs to call."

"Good idea," Ashley replied. "I'd better get going."

"Wait—" Beth said. "—what about my test results? Am I okay?"

"You're fine. In fact, as far as we can tell, *everyone* is fine."

"That's good news," Beth's dad said. "Maybe the quarantine will be lifted soon."

"Hopefully," Ashley agreed.

A niggling suspicion returned, begging for Beth's attention. "What if some people are infected, but like, maybe just in one place."

"Like where?"

"Like the brain?"

"That's why we did the spinal tap. The blood-brain barrier isolates your blood from the fluid in your brain, and keeps pretty much everything out, but we can't assume that will be true for *alien* cells.

They could be small enough to sneak through. But so far, that looks like a non-starter. Your spinal fluid was normal, and you were one of the ones infected by the aliens." Ashley shrugged. "If we couldn't find any trace of an infection in your spinal fluid, it seems unlikely we'll find it in anyone else's."

Beth's lies came bubbling back up and burned like acid in the back of her throat. "Yeah... about that..." she said in a small voice.

Her dad's hand landed on her shoulder and squeezed—hard. "It's good to hear that there's nothing to worry about."

Beth looked up at him. "But—"

He regarded her with cold eyes. "Don't think I've forgotten about your forgery, young lady."

Alarm bells went off in Beth's head. Her dad *knew* that she hadn't been directly exposed to the Crawlers the way he had. Maybe he was infected after all. It was almost like he was covering for her to avoid giving a sample of his own spinal fluid. *Like he has something to hide.*

Beth wriggled free of her dad's grasp. Retreating to Ashley's side, she shook a finger at him. "You've been acting weird all morning!"

"Weird how?" he asked.

"You and like three others. You all scratched your cheek at the same time. And another four were eating and drinking in perfect harmony like, like... zombies or something!"

Her dad's brow furrowed. "What are you talking about, Beth?"

"You're in sync!"

A bemused smile touched his lips. "The band?"

"NO!"

"Can you explain a little more?" Ashley asked.

Beth told her about the synchronized movements at breakfast, and about her dad's sleepwalking—the episode from last night in particular.

"Is there a chance you might have imagined what you saw at breakfast?" Ashley asked. "There are coincidental patterns all around us all the time, but in your heightened state, you might be more aware of them than usual."

"Well, what about the sleepwalking then?"

"Is anyone else experiencing that?" Ashley asked.

Her dad shook his head. "No."

Beth hesitated. "How do you know?"

"Because we spent a week together on the *Port Royal*," he explained. "No one else mentioned that to Doctor Wilde."

"Well, I'm not imagining things!"

"Beth, it's highly unlikely everyone except for

you is experiencing symptoms," Ashley said. "You were all infected at the same time."

"I lied," Beth blurted.

"You what?"

"I thought you wouldn't let me see the morgue if I wasn't a good candidate for additional tests."

"So you didn't come into direct contact with them."

Beth shook her head. "No." Her eyes flicked to her dad and promptly narrowed. "But *he* did—and James, Allen, Melanie, and all of the others. Only me and Don and James' family weren't exposed."

"I see," Ashley replied. She half-turned and made a hand signal to the Marine who'd escorted her to the resort. He was standing by the entrance with Corporal Gibson. The Marine ran over.

"Ma'am?" he asked.

"Please take Mr. Steele to the van."

"You're joking," her dad replied. "You can't force me. You said it yourselves. And I won't consent."

"And that's suspicious enough by itself. If you don't go willingly, we'll just zip-tie your hands and take you in anyway."

"You're wasting your time," her dad growled through gritted teeth. His eyes flicked to Beth and narrowed to angry slits.

Beth blinked in shock, watching as the Marine

led her dad away. "I thought you weren't allowed to force people to give you samples."

"We aren't. Not without justification. But you just gave me the excuse I needed. Your dad's exhibiting unusual symptoms. Sleepwalking and other behavioral anomalies—such as supporting your lie about being exposed, possibly to avoid further testing for himself and the others who were actually exposed."

"How do you know he was supporting a lie?" Beth asked. "Maybe I lied to him, too, or he just didn't know whether I came into direct contact with a Crawler."

"Direct contact resulted in bloody welts on the victims' faces that scabbed and faded within forty-eight hours. If he didn't know you lied, then he's blind. No, he knew he was covering for you. The question is, was it out of parental concern for possible consequences, or was it because he has something to hide?"

Beth's brow furrowed as she thought about that. "Can I go to the center with you?"

"What for?" Ashley asked.

"I want to know what you find."

Ashley cocked her head to one side. "Why should I take you anywhere after you lied to me yesterday? You wasted a lot of time."

Beth winced. "I'm sorry. I had to see if Toby

was there. I'll make it up to you, I swear! You can run more tests. Or..." she trailed off. "Please. I have to know what's wrong with my dad. He's all I've got left."

"It could take a while to study your father's samples."

"I can wait."

Ashley gave in with a sigh. "All right. Let's go."

CHAPTER 34

"I'm fine, Mom. I promise," Beth said.

"We've been so worried about you! The news said there were over a thousand people killed."

Her mother broke down sobbing on the other end, and Beth winced.

"A few of them landed next to the Koa Kai, but it's over now, Mom. It's okay. They didn't get me."

"They landed next to... did you see them? Did they hurt you?"

"I saw them... no, they didn't hurt me."

"Thank God! And your father? Is he..."

"He's okay."

"But what's happening? The island is under quarantine!"

"There are doctors here doing tests," Beth explained. "Dad's getting some more now." She decided against telling her mom *why* her dad was getting tested.

"Have they found anything? Are you sick?"

"No, everyone's fine. I think they're just being

careful," Beth replied as she paced the artificial-grass-covered floors of the tent. Ashley had left her here to wait with a group of others who'd come to the center.

"But when are they going to let people leave? We can't even buy plane tickets to visit you!"

Beth smiled wanly. "I think that's basically the definition of quarantine, Mom."

The reassurances and questions went back and forth for ten more minutes before the conversation waned. Beth's mom made her promise to call back as soon as she learned the results of her dad's tests.

Beth hit the red button to hang up the phone and went to sit with the others in the waiting area. The woman next to her had to be about ninety, with wispy white hair and lizard-like skin. She sobbed quietly, her brown eyes gleaming with tears.

"I'm sorry," Beth said, even though she had no idea what the woman was sobbing about.

The woman wiped her eyes and placed a tear-moistened hand on Beth's, squeezing shakily. "Have you seen my Donald?" she asked.

"Donald?"

"I h-heard you mention the Koa Kai. He went to stay there for a few days. I told him to take a vacation. *I* told him to go. Have you seen him? Is he okay?" The woman squeezed her hand again, her brown eyes pleading.

"Donald? You mean Don?"

"Don! Yes!"

"He's fine."

"Oh my. Thank you," The woman covered her mouth with her other hand, and her eyes teared up again.

"Are you his... grandmother?"

The woman nodded. "Did he tell you about me?"

Beth smiled and shook her head. "Just a guess."

Tent flaps ruffled noisily as someone came in. "Beth?"

She turned her head to see Ashley standing in the open doorway. "Did you find anything?"

Ashley waved her over, and she extricated herself from Don's grandmother.

"Wait!" the old woman cried.

Beth tossed a glance over her shoulder. "I'll be back. Maybe you can come back to the resort with us and see him."

"Oh yes! Please."

Once Beth reached Ashley, the doctor said, "Follow me."

Beth left the waiting room with her and walked down a corridor with bouncing floor panels that sounded like an old wooden dock. She stepped through another entrance at the end, and then a second one, emerging in the clinic where she'd been tested yesterday. Her dad lay on one of the padded tables. Only one other person was in the clinic. Her dad's head turned to watch as they came in, his gaze blank, his expression slack.

Ashley led the way to his side.

"Hi, Dad," Beth said, but he just smiled wanly at her. Her brow furrowed and she turned to Ashley for an explanation. "What's wrong with him?"

"Nothing. We performed all of the same tests we did to you yesterday, and took all of the same samples—along with a few extras besides. As far as we can tell, he's clear, but..."

"But?" Beth pressed, her heart suddenly pounding. "What? What's wrong?"

"Mr. Steele?"

He just went on smiling.

"Are you feeling better?"

He nodded slowly and then his head turned away from them.

"What's wrong with him?"

Ashley turned to Beth with a frown. "He had a panic attack during the last test, when we performed a head CT scan."

"A panic attack..." Beth trailed off, trying to remember what Ashley had told her about those yesterday. She'd described it as a psychological issue caused by trauma. "Are you sure? Maybe it was a reaction to the tests?"

"The CT didn't show any anomalies, nor did any of your father's samples, but his symptoms all fit perfectly with PTSD—sleepwalking and insomnia, for example. He has post-traumatic stress, and I'll bet he's not the only one."

"That's what Commander Wilde said..." Beth replied slowly.

"Well, he's a military doctor, so he should know," Ashley replied. "Anyway, I've prescribed some sleeping pills and a pill in the morning for anxiety and depression. Other than that, there's nothing more I can do, but he really should see a therapist as soon as he can. You'll need to make sure he attends regular appointments. Maybe a support group as well."

Beth's gaze slid away to study her dad's face once more. Those blank, staring eyes scared her. It was like he was *gone.* He hadn't said a word to either of them since she'd walked in. "Can he talk?"

"He's in a state of emotional shock. The panic attack broke whatever walls he'd put up to keep it bottled in. He's suffered a nervous breakdown, and I suspect it has been coming for some time. The current crisis pushed him over the edge. Has he been under a lot of stress lately?"

"Well, I mean, the resort has been having some problems, and he keeps talking about issues with the bank."

"You mean like collection agents? Does he owe a lot of money on the resort?"

Beth shrugged, then nodded. "I think so, yeah."

"Then you have your answer. This is the culmination of that stress plus the recent trauma."

Beth looked away. "But what if it's not? What if—"

"It is. Listen, if there were something alien causing neurological side effects, one of those tests should have found it. I'm sorry that you have to deal with this. I know he's your father, and he's supposed to keep it all together—not you—but he's shattered Beth, and he's going to need your help. You're going to have to be strong for him. Can you do that?"

Beth nodded slowly. "Okay."

CHAPTER 35

That night it all came crashing down around Beth like a monster wave: Toby's death, her dad's mental breakdown, the quarantine...

Her dad had been lying in bed like a paralytic ever since they'd returned from the center in Lihue. She'd made sure to bring him rations and water, but he'd barely said a word to her. He seemed to be locked in some kind of a daze.

Beth choked back tears and bit her lip hard. The pain focused her thoughts, somehow easing the emotional burden she felt. She had no one to lean on but herself.

The tears came with hot fury. Anger traded places with sadness. Fear morphed into guilt. Why was she alive while so many others had been killed? It wasn't fair. She grabbed one of the pillows on the other side of the bed and hugged it hard. Shutting her eyes, she pretended for a moment that the pillow was Toby, and they were lying on the beach together under the sparkling night, listening to the calm, summer surf polishing the shore until the sand was smooth and clear as a mirror. She could almost smell the salty water, and feel the sand tickling between her toes.

The *crack* of a branch snapping intruded, and she sat up. A feeling of hazy numbness told her she was dreaming, but that only amplified her fears. At the top of the beach where sand gave way to dense midnight-green shadows, four pinpricks of light stared unblinkingly at her. Then she heard the shrill trilling of a call to its fellows, and more sets of eyes appeared beside the first, winking through the shrubbery. Four sets of four eyes. Four.

All four of them stepped out onto the starlit sand, their wet, translucent skin flowing over muscle like liquid silver as they approached. Arms unfolded, claws clicked and scraped together in anticipation of the kill.

Beth turned to Toby and shook him by his shoulder. "Tob! Wake up! We have to run!"

He didn't even twitch. A new fear coiled inside of her, and she turned him over—Gray skin, dead, staring blue eyes.

Beth recoiled from him and jumped to her feet, backing steadily away from the monsters advancing on her. Each footstep the monsters took sounded like a hollow knock on wood. *Knock, knock, knock...* A scream built deep inside her chest and tore from her lips—

Beth woke up, bathed in sweat. She sat up, rapidly blinking her eyes to clear them. The hollow knocking sounds continued. For a minute she thought it might be her dad sleepwalking again, knocking on her door.

She froze, her heart pounding in her chest, listening...

But the sound was more distant than that, coming from down the hall. Maybe he was knocking on his own door this time?

Frowning, Beth threw back the covers and hopped out of bed. The pulsing stream of adrenaline in her veins made each step feel lighter and easier than it should. Hand on the doorknob, she slowly turned the lock, braced herself with a deep breath, and then eased the door open.

The knocking sounds continued—*definitely coming from his room,* Beth thought. The cool tiles on her bare feet woke her up a little more, and an odd notion formed in her head just as she reached her father's door, but she dismissed it. Turning the handle, she opened his door—

"Dad?"

She caught sight of a woman's naked back arching in the moonlight pouring through the open curtains of her dad's balcony. The headboard gave a final knock against the wall, and the woman's head turned, her mouth open, lips parted in silent ecstasy.

Beth gaped at her.

It was Melanie, the grief-stricken widow.

CHAPTER 36

"Four possible contacts inside the garage," Lieutenant Spooner said.

"Four? You mean they're all here? Is that confirmed?" Corporal Gibson asked.

"No. That count comes from civilian eyewitnesses in the house across the street. We won't know for sure until we flush them out."

"What's the plan, sir?" Corporal Gibson asked, staring hard at the double garage of a million-dollar mansion in the community of Princeville. Gibson's team, Alpha team, stood with team Epsilon guarding the garage doors and broken front entrance of the mansion. They were packing XREP-loaded shotguns, tranquilizer guns, grenade launchers with 40mm HEMIs, and net guns. Between them, they had enough non-lethal force to take down a T-Rex. The problem was, they couldn't crawl into that garage safely.

Bloody streaks and ragged claw marks on the white doors marked where Crawlers had tried to break in, and a splintered hole marked where they'd got it right. A trail of blood led from the shattered front door of the mansion to the garage, suggesting that one or more of the home's residents had been dragged in there. While still among the living, those residents had blocked the side entrance of the garage with a heavy pile of furniture, but it hadn't been enough to keep the Crawlers out. Now Bravo Team was watching that door to make sure none of the aliens escaped.

"We could pop a frag in there," Private Dekker suggested. He framed an imaginary explosion with his hands. "Boom."

"Negative, Private," Lieutenant Spooner said. "We aren't authorized to use lethal force."

"Well, fuck, what are we supposed to do, ask them to come out with their hands up?" Private Dekker replied.

"Can it," Spooner said. "We're gonna smoke 'em out and shoot them as they stick their heads out." Spooner clipped a smoke grenade off his belt and approached the splintered hole in the doors. "Heads on a swivel! ENVGs down. Prepare for contact."

"Copy that," Epsilon One said, and Gibson echoed that sentiment while folding down the monocular night vision goggles strapped to his helmet. Combined with the FSW-I sights on his shotgun, the goggles showed him exactly what his weapon saw without having to physically look down the sights.

A pin clinked as Spooner pulled it out, and both of Gibson's hands tensed in readiness. He didn't bring his shotgun into line yet, because Spooner was in the way. The lieutenant rolled a smoke grenade through the hole in the garage and darted out of the way, retreating to safety behind Epsilon Team.

Gibson brought his weapon up, keeping the targeting reticle from his shotgun's sights dead center on the hole. A loud hissing sound issued from within as smoke dispersed from the grenade. Alien growls and stuttering roars followed, and then smoke began billowing out. Soon it was flooding down the driveway, shifting and expanding like a living thing. The yellow bug lights mounted on the front of the garage refracted in the smoke, turning the air a deep, sunflower yellow. The ENVGs cut through all of it to reveal a faint thermal signature emerging from the hole.

"Contact, twelve o'clock!" someone shouted.

Several shotguns boomed. The alien in the opening screamed and collapsed, blocking the hole. Electric fire raced over its body in bright arcs and its limbs scrabbled for purchase on the driveway.

"Sedate it and drag it out!" Spooner said.

Tranq darts *plipped* out, and the Crawler's struggles ceased with a phlegmy sigh.

More sounds emanated from deeper within the garage: scrabbling claws and loud thumping.

Gibson's radio crackled. "Zeta One reporting, they're trying to break through the side door. Seems to be holding."

Private Dekker chuckled. "Eat smoke!"

A pair of Marines from Epsilon grabbed the Crawler they'd sedated by its front limbs and dragged it out while Gibson's team provided cover.

The thumping stopped, and a flicker of thermal signatures appeared in the gap.

"Incoming!" Gibson said.

The two Marines from Epsilon released their captive and brought their weapons to bear just as a pair of Crawlers shot out of the hole. Shotguns exploded, and XREP rounds crackled noisily in time to alien squeals. One of Epsilon's Marines got caught thrashing alien arms. Long glassy claws slashed his flak jacket into ribbons; he screamed, then fell silent, coming down hard on the pavement.

Both Crawlers lay on the driveway with him, their limbs spasming in time to electric shocks. Gibson fired off an extra XREP cartridge, just to be sure, and then tranq darts whistled out, and the aliens ceased their frantic movements.

"Man down! Medic!" Spooner said.

"On it," one of Gibson's men said. It was Private Clarke. Gibson covered him with the others as he ran over to check on the fallen Marine from Epsilon.

"Stay sharp. Three down, one to go," Spooner said.

"Copy," Epsilon One replied.

Silence fell and the smoke from the grenade dispersed with a sudden gust of wind. There was no sign of the fourth Crawler.

"Epsilon Two, check the hole," Spooner ordered.

"Yes, sir." Epsilon Two hurried out of formation and peeked around the corner. Gibson braced himself.

"All clear!"

Gibson's aim wavered as some of the tension left his muscles.

"Double check that, private," Spooner said.

"Thermal's clear, sir, but it's a shit show. Three civilians down."

"Signs of life?"

"No, sir. Plenty of guts but no glory."

Lieutenant Spooner blew out a breath and looked to Clarke who was pressing black gloves slick with blood to the fallen Marine's chest. He walked over quickly, and Gibson joined him. The man's green eyes were open, roving from face to face, but he was spitting blood, and his chest had collapsed beneath a shivering crimson pool.

"Shit," Spooner said and dropped to his haunches beside the man. "Charlie, you're going to be okay. We're gonna get you out."

Blood bubbled from Charlie's lips, but no words came out.

Spooner grabbed Charlie's hand and held it up in a tight fist. "You're gonna be just fine. Hang in there." To Clarke and Gibson, he said, "Hoist him up!"

Gibson hesitated. He knew a lost cause when he saw it, but he did as he was ordered and took Charlie's shoulders. Clarke grabbed his legs, and they walked with him toward the trio of Humvees parked out front.

Halfway down the driveway, Charlie's eyes glassed over and ceased moving. Gibson and Clarke stopped where they were.

"He's dead, sir," Clarke said, sounding confused.

"Yes he is, private," Lieutenant Spooner replied, "but he didn't have to know that." Turning aside, he nodded to the rest of Epsilon and Alpha teams. "Net and tie those bastards, and let's pack it in!"

They carried Charlie's body to the back of one of the Humvees, mopped the blood as best they could, and then laid him in the spacious trunk beside their extra gear.

Panting from the exertion, Gibson turned to see Lieutenant Spooner leading the other men as they carried three tied and sedated Crawlers between them.

Gibson eyed the cargo area where they'd laid Charlie. At least one of the Crawlers would have to ride with him. He didn't like the idea of the Marine's killers riding alongside his body. He was just about to give Spooner an earful about it when he heard the lieutenant say, "Pop smoke!" Followed by the clink of another pin being pulled from a grenade.

Purple-colored smoke poured into the night, pooling in the streetlights. Marines set their alien burdens down. The lieutenant had signaled for air evac.

Relieved, Gibson walked over to Lieutenant Spooner to address another concern. They still had one Crawler unaccounted for. "What are your orders, sir?"

Spooner glanced at him. "We wait for these assets to be collected, then continue the hunt, Corporal."

"Oorah, sir."

"Oorah," Spooner replied, nodding.

Chopper blades sounded in the distance, growing swiftly louder and nearer. The lights from two separate helicopters came tracking across the sky from the nearby Princeville Airport.

Gibson heard an exclamation from one of his men—it sounded like Dekker—and he whirled around to see a different kind of light tracking across the sky—*vertically.* More exclamations followed, and they watched a blinding, electric-blue plume of light sail into the sky.

Gibson gaped at it, shielding his eyes from the glare as it soared ever higher. The roar of its ascent reached their ears moments later, followed by an ear-splitting *boom* as it broke the sound barrier.

"Looks like we found our missing Crawler," Spooner said.

"ET go home," Dekker added.

CHAPTER 37

Corporal Lee stood guard on the darkest side of the CDC's operations center. He watched the trees rustle with the wind, heard his fellow Marines chatting to pass the time, and wondered how many of them were also infected. There was no way to tell. The differences in their behavior were so vague that anyone could miss them. Lee knew that, because he'd been analyzing his own behavior over the past twenty-four hours, watching his every move, listening to every word that escaped his lips, and he had yet to catch himself acting out of character. Such dedicated self-analysis might have been strange, or even deranged, under any other circumstances, but he had nothing better to do.

Lee had given up screaming silently in the hopes that a whisper might escape his lips. After a whole day spent clawing the walls of his numb, nerveless prison to no effect, he'd realized that there was no escape. Somehow, something had hijacked his spinal cord. He couldn't speak; he couldn't move; he couldn't even blink; he was a spectator watching helplessly as something else did all of that for him.

Lee kept going over the past week in his head, trying to decide when the switch had occurred and what had been the catalyst. The answer seemed fairly obvious. The alien organism everyone was searching for could have taken days to incubate and reach the critical mass it needed to take over his body, but Lee didn't think so. He believed it had taken mere *hours* to do so, and it had happened right after his encounter with Lily Blossom.

She hadn't introduced herself as Lily Blossom at the time; she hadn't even given him her name. She'd just sauntered up to him at his post guarding the back exit of the Lihue PD and French-kissed him until he couldn't think straight. Then she'd whispered something filthy in his ear: "First time's free." And then she grabbed his hand to pull him away from his post. He'd resisted for a moment— duty first—but his buddy, Private Nolan, had put his mind at ease.

"Relax, that's just Lily Blossom. She's harmless. Go on, Corporal, I'll cover for you. You're in for a real treat."

So Lee had followed Lily back to her room at

the Mahalo Motel, and there she had gone on to treat him to the best night of his life. She'd even stuck around afterward—not the typical wham bam typical of most working girls. Riding high, he'd nodded off, and when he'd woken up a few hours later, Lily was gone, and his body paralyzed.

At least, he'd *thought* that he was paralyzed, but then he'd watched—*watched* himself get out of the bed, get dressed, and leave the motel room. Convinced he was dreaming, he'd tried screaming himself awake, but that hadn't worked.

And it still wasn't working—Lee heard a branch snap and saw himself turn toward the sound. A pale monster crawled out of the shadows, crouching low to the ground on four bent legs. Lee screamed his silent screams as the Crawler crept toward him.

None of the other Marines guarding this side of the CDC compound seemed to care, and yet all of them were watching the alien approach the fence. Four of them lowered their shotguns, letting them hang free from the shoulder straps in a way that no Marine ever would. That was a tell right there, but none of the nine men in Lee's squad seemed to notice. Not even Sergeant Colton. *I guess that answers how many of them are infected.* But he should have known that by now. He'd watched himself contaminate their coffee this morning.

Four skinny alien arms unfolded from the Crawler's forelegs as it reached the fence. Claws clacked and scraped against the chainlink fence, making it ring and shiver in the night. Lee's head turned, and he saw his squad mates watching approvingly as the alien climbed the fence, dropped down, and then slunk silently through the grass to the nearest white canvas tent.

The doctors and lab technicians in the compound would all be fast asleep, none the wiser that their very own Lily Blossom was headed their way. Something told Lee that their encounter wasn't going to be anywhere near as pleasant as his had been.

CHAPTER 38

"I caught them doing it," Beth said, nodding through the windows of the restaurant to where her dad and Melanie sat outside at their own table making eyes at each other over their coffee.

"Doing it?" Don's grandmother, Sarah, asked in an overly loud voice. "You mean they were having sex?"

A few people looked up.

"Shhh." Beth turned with a frown to see Don whispering in her ear.

"Oh, I didn't know I was shouting," she said.

"That's okay, Nana," Don said, patting her hand.

Sarah gave him a trembling smile and took a sip of her coffee.

"Don't you think that's strange?" Beth pressed, her eyes on Don.

He scratched his cheek through his beard. "I don't know. You tell me."

"It's definitely strange," Beth confirmed.

Chef Jones came by with a tray of plates and coffee. Each plate had a brown plastic bag on it with the letters MRE in a bold black font. Don and Sarah each took a plate, then Beth reluctantly took hers.

"Mmm-mmmm Asian beef strips," Don said. "Breakfast of champions."

"Refill?" Chef Jones asked, nodding to the coffee pot.

Beth frowned and shook her head. "I don't drink coffee, remember?"

"Of course. I was speaking more to them," Jones replied.

"I'll have some more," Don said, holding out his mug.

"I still have mine," Sarah added before taking another sip.

Jones topped up Don's mug and departed the table.

"What should we do?" Beth whispered once she was out of earshot.

Don glanced around inconspicuously, then shook his head. "Your dad tested clean. We all did. If people are acting strange, it's probably just because they're living for the moment, not worrying about the future. Surviving an alien invasion will do that."

Beth frowned. "What about the synchronized

behavior we saw yesterday? Groups of four, remember?"

"Synchronized..." Sarah trailed off. "What's she talking about, Donald?"

"Don't worry; it's not important," he replied, patting her hand.

Don favored Beth with a patient smile. "Do you see it today?" he asked.

Beth looked around, taking a moment to study people's movements carefully. "No, but..."

"Then it was just an aberration."

"Like my dad's hookup with the grieving widow of a newly-wedded couple is an aberration? I can't speak for her, but he's never been so impulsive. He's not like that."

"So what are you saying? She raped him?" Don looked like he was trying hard not to laugh.

"Well, no, but..."

"Your dad's single, Beth. Maybe she came onto him, and he thought, screw it—pun intended."

"You didn't see him. He wasn't himself yesterday. He spent the whole day in bed staring at the ceiling like a zombie. *Now* look at him!"

Beth gestured out the windows to where Melanie and her dad were holding hands and staring lovingly into each other's eyes. "They're sitting like twenty feet from the pool where her fiancé died, and she's making googly eyes at him.

They haven't even tried to apologize to me, or explain."

"Are you sure they saw you?" Don asked.

"*She* saw me for sure," Beth replied.

Don shrugged and took another sip of coffee. "Okay so that's a little strange, but we all just got up. Maybe that's what they're out there talking about? How to broach the topic with you."

"I doubt it," Beth said.

"Well, the CDC is working the case," Don said. "If something's going on besides all the normal human madness, they'll find it. Meanwhile, I'm worried about more tangible threats. Hookups and synchronized cheek scratching don't fall into that category."

"What do you mean?"

"I mean no one takes a spaceship across billions or trillions of miles of space just to land a few dozen operatives, scare the crap out of the locals, and then leave."

"So what do you think they're up to?"

"No clue, but you can bet there's a lot more of those Crawlers out there waiting in the wings."

Beth frowned. "Their spaceship left. All the news reports say there's no sign of it."

"Maybe it's just too hard to spot. They had to surprise us somehow, right? Whatever the case, we need to worry about what's going to happen when the other boot drops."

Beth shook her head. "What can we do about it?"

"Hide," Don replied. "Now that they've caught all the missing Crawlers, Nana and I are going to get out of here and head for my place in the mountains. I've got enough guns and supplies there to handle whatever comes my way. It's just a damn pity I wasn't there when all this shit hit the fan."

Beth blinked in shock. "How are you going to get there?" she asked. "Your car doesn't start."

"I fixed it yesterday while you were out. It's an old truck, not a lot of electronics. Once I bypassed the ignition, she purred to life."

A prickle of dread skipped down Beth's spine at the thought of him leaving. Don was her anchor to sanity in the middle of all this craziness, the only one who seemed to be acting normally, the only one she felt she could trust.

Unless he wasn't. Why wasn't he suspicious anymore? Maybe this was *his* way of acting strange—by dismissing her dad's odd behavior.

"Looks like your dad's come to offer the olive branch," Don said, nodding over her shoulder.

Beth turned to see him and Melanie coming inside, making a beeline for their table.

"I'll leave you guys to talk," Don said. "Time

for me to bug out."

Beth heard his chair pushing out, followed by Sarah's, and turned to see both of them standing.

"How do I find you?" Beth asked, searching Don's eyes desperately.

Don smiled sadly back. "You don't, kid. That's the point of a bug out shelter. Can't have people knowing where it is."

"But—"

"Beth?" Her dad's voice interrupted them, and she reluctantly tore her eyes away from Don and his grandmother to see her dad and Melanie standing a few paces behind her. Melanie's cheeks were flushed, and she didn't seem to know where to put her eyes. "Can we sit down?" her dad asked. His tone and expression were apologetic, hesitant. "We need to talk to you about last night."

Beth nodded but didn't say anything. Her dad and Melanie were holding hands. He pulled a chair out for her beside Beth, and then sat facing her. Beth glimpsed Don and his nana disappearing through the French-style glass doors of the restaurant, strolling off through the lobby.

"I wanted to explain what you saw last night," Bill began.

Beth snorted. "What's to explain? Seems pretty obvious. You two hooked up." She shrugged. "No biggie."

Bill's eyes flicked to Melanie, then back. "Well, it's more than that, Beth. And it wasn't as sudden as it looked. Mellie and I—"

"Mellie?" Beth echoed.

"Melanie and I," Bill amended. "We spent several hours together yesterday while you were out. We got to talking, and it turns out we have a lot in common. But besides that, I guess we were both feeling lonely and vulnerable, and—"

Beth stood up, almost knocking her chair over in the process. "What you guys do is your business," she said.

"Beth..." Bill said.

"Bill..." She replied in a sarcastic imitation of his tone. His eyes flashed, but he didn't say anything. "It's okay," Beth said, fighting back tears with a smile. Don had left her. Toby was dead, and her dad was... someone else. "You're both consenting adults, right? It's not like she forced you."

Bill nodded slowly.

"Then you didn't do anything wrong. Just good fun. But try to keep it down. The walls are thin." Beth stormed off before either of them could say anything else.

CHAPTER 39

Commander Morris stood on the bridge of the *Port Royal*, listening to Captain Reed bark orders to the crew. Admiral Harris had sent them to investigate some anomalous weather patterns at two degrees and five minutes north of the island. The air temperature there was apparently five degrees colder than everything around it and had been so for at least four days. Those readings had been recorded by weather satellites, but Harris wanted them to take supplemental ones from sea level. It seemed like a strange errand for a warship, but Kauai's harbor was on lock-down. Even the coastguard had been grounded. Only USN ships were allowed to navigate the quarantine zone, and the *Port Royal* was closest to the anomalous weather region.

"ETA?" Reed asked, glancing at Morris.

He checked his watch. "We are five minutes out from the specified coordinates, sir."

"Then we should already be able to measure

the phenomenon," Commander Morris said. "The coordinates put us one hundred miles into the low-temperature area."

"Yes," Captain Reed replied, nodding. "Let's go down to CIC and check in with Petty Officer McCown, shall we?"

"Aye, sir,"

Reed gave the conn to Lieutenant Peterson, and they left the bridge together, heading down the stairs to CIC. The CIC was dark, as usual, to help sailors see the information on their screens. Reed walked straight over to McCown's station. "Petty Officer," he said. "What are conditions like out there?"

"Temperature and pressure readings are within the normal range, sir," McCown reported.

"Interesting," Reed replied while stroking his chin.

Commander Morris noticed McCown stroking his chin, too. He frowned at that, but quickly dismissed it as irrelevant and forced himself to focus on the task at hand. "What's the temperature?" Morris asked.

"Just three degrees colder than expected, not the five that satellite data indicated."

"That's still a difference," Morris said.

"Yes, sir, but meteorology is hardly a precise science. There could be a million reasons why this area of the ocean is colder."

Morris nodded. "Including an alien spaceship hovering overhead and blocking out three to five degrees worth of sunlight."

One of Reed's eyebrows arched up as he turned to regard Morris. "It's three degrees, Commander. Not ten or twenty."

"The difference could grow more pronounced as we sail deeper into the area. We need to report this to Admiral Harris."

"And we will," Captain Reed replied. "But it could be caused by ocean currents or cloud cover, or a thousand other things. We shouldn't feed into mass hysteria by suggesting darker possibilities. Next minute the Admiral will be ordering us to launch missiles into thin air to sound out your invisible spaceship. And even if you're right, all that would do is start an interstellar war. No, I'm not going to jump at shadows, Commander, nor should you." He scratched his cheek. McCown scratched his.

Morris frowned. "Are you being insubordinate, Petty Officer?"

"Sir?" McCown asked.

"You keep copying the captain behind his back!"

"I do?"

Captain Reed turned to regard McCown.

"Doing what?"

"Just now. You scratched your cheek, and so did he. And before stroking his chin."

Captain Reed frowned, and then flashed an apologetic look at McCown. "Carry on, Petty Officer."

"Aye, sir."

Reed led Morris away with an arm around his shoulders. "This is what I'm talking about," he began in a soothing tone. "We're all on edge, Morris, and being under an indefinite quarantine doesn't help, but we need to be careful that we don't allow it to affect our judgment. Bad judgment leads to bad choices, Commander."

"Aye, sir," Morris replied, nodding. "And if the temperature readings do line up? What then?"

"Whatever the readings are, I will report them to the admiral, but I'm certain that even in the heart of the anomalous region we'll find temperatures are already on their way back up. It's just a passing weather phenomenon. Not a cloaked spaceship." Outside the CIC Captain Reed shut the door and turned to face Morris. "The reality is, they're gone, Commander. They probably didn't like what they found down here." A smile curved his lips. "Maybe we didn't taste as good as they thought we would."

Commander Morris grimaced. "I hope you're

right, sir."

"I am. You'll see. A few weeks or months from now the quarantine will be lifted, and everything will go back to normal."

"But what if the CDC finds something?" Morris asked.

Captain Reed snorted. "They won't."

"How can you be so sure?"

"Logic, Morris. If they planned to infect us with something, why the hell would they make a small, underpopulated island their target? They'd start with a big city like New York, someplace where an infection couldn't possibly be contained."

"Unless they're not that smart; they could be just as bestial as they seem," Morris replied.

"Have you ever seen a lion build a spaceship, Morris?"

"No, sir."

Captain Reed nodded and reached out to clasp one of Morris's shoulders. "Exactly."

Some of the tension in Morris's chest eased, and he blew out a breath.

A small smile appeared on the captain's lips. "You look relieved, Morris."

"I am, sir. All this time, I've been secretly preparing myself for the worst. It's good to know there are other possibilities."

"Indeed there are, XO. Come." The captain

released his shoulder. "We'd better get back up to the bridge."

CHAPTER 40

Corporal Gibson peered into the egg-shaped alien capsule, watching as engineers in yellow hazmat suits bumbled around inside. Ever since that final Crawler had somehow blasted off in a pod last night, efforts to study and guard the alien landing craft had kicked into high gear. Gibson didn't have a high enough rank to know why, but he could guess. If the capsules could be used to return to the alien ship, then they could be used to locate it and maybe even to destroy it.

But Gibson wasn't optimistic about their chances of figuring it out. He'd seen more knobs and dials on an old analog radio than there were on those pods.

A thundercloud rumbled overhead, drawing Gibson's gaze away. "Looks like rain," he said. As if summoned by his words, fat droplets came splatting down to the muddy crater where he stood with his team.

Private Dekker threw his head back and spread

his arms to the sky as if waiting for aliens to beam him up.

"Hands on your weapon, Deks," Gibson said.

"Sure thing, Corporal."

Gibson turned back to the pod just in time to see a crooked flash of lightning crack open the sky right in front of him, dazzling his eyes. A split second later, a titanic peal of thunder shook the ground.

"Shit! Any closer and I'd have to paint on my eyebrows!" Dekker said.

Gibson frowned. Blinking spots from his eyes, he stared at the metal pod in the crater. Sitting at about 15 feet tall, and having blasted out all the trees in the immediate vicinity, that pod was a lightning rod. Feeling the hairs on the back of his neck prickle, Gibson started forward.

"Hey!" he said, calling out to the engineers poking around inside. One of them looked up and cupped a hand to their ear. "We need to clear the area until the storm passes! That pod is probably conductive!"

The man in the hazmat suit shook his head as if he couldn't hear—or maybe in disagreement. They probably thought their suits would protect them if lightning struck. Gibson cast about, searching for Sergeant Rathers. He was in charge of security for the site, so it was his call. Gibson spied him standing on the rim of the crater, watching a nearby road with binoculars. A white pickup truck was rumbling along it.

Gibson jogged up the side of the crater to reach him. "Sergeant," he said. "I think we need to clear the site."

Rathers lowered his binoculars. "And why do you think that, Corporal?"

Gibson explained his reasoning. "If lightning strikes that pod, it could ignite whatever fuel it has left."

"Does it look big enough to use chemical rockets, Gibson? If the engineers aren't worried, then I don't think we should be either. Orders are to work around the clock on this. That means rain or shine."

"Copy." Gibson sighed. He was about to head back down to join the rest of his team when he noticed that they were standing at the top of the crater, too—just over the rim and down the other side, actually. They were keeping their distance after that lightning strike. *Smart,* Gibson thought.

Another flash of light dazzled his eyes, and this time he heard a deafening roar through the thunder. A plume of bright blue fire leapt a hundred feet into the air. The shockwave hit a split second later; a blinding wave of superheated air picked Gibson up and tossed him down the hill.

He rolled to the bottom, fetching up against a tree. Bits of debris and clods of dirt rained down, hammering the grass flat.

Sergeant Rathers lay face down some five feet away with a branch as thick as Gibson's arm sticking out of his back.

"Sergeant!" Gibson called, his own voice sounding distant to his ringing ears. Rathers didn't even twitch. As his hearing cleared, Gibson heard that roaring sound from before, followed by a loud *boom*. He twisted toward the sound to see the egg-shaped lander trailing a dazzling blue engine glow and streaking across the sky at a sixty-degree angle, heading due North.

A large black bird pin-wheeled away from it, expanding as it swooped toward the ground. But it wasn't a bird. It had arms and legs. Gibson shivered. It was one of the engineers who'd been inside the pod, his mustard-yellow hazmat suit charred black.

Gibson pushed off the ground with one arm to see Dekker, Clarke, and Kelly cutting a path through the long grass to reach him.

"Clarke!" Gibson roared. "The sergeant's down!"

The three of them picked up the pace.

Dekker grabbed Gibson's hand and pulled him to his feet, while Clarke and Kelly ran on to the sergeant's side.

"He's dead, Corporal," Clarke announced.

"Shit," Gibson muttered. "On me. We need to check the area for survivors." He led the way up to the rim of the crater to find the ground steaming and blasted smooth. There was no sign of the engineers except for one smoking boot.

"No one lived through that," Clarke said.

"Spooner is going to lose his shit," Dekker said.

Gibson looked back up to the sky, squinting and holding up a hand to shield his eyes against the glare of the landing pod's thrusters. "They didn't die for nothing," he said. "Now we know how they work."

"With lightning?" Kelly asked.

"Not exactly," Gibson said. "Lightning hit the pod, and the electrical surge must have triggered the thrusters."

"Like jump-starting a car," Dekker put in.

"Yeah." Gibson frowned. He doubted it was that simple, but the engineers studying the other pods could probably do something with that info.

"Where do you think it's headed?" Dekker asked.

"Back to their ship, where else?" Gibson replied. "Some kind of autopilot."

"I thought their ship was gone," Kelly put in.

The pod zipped behind a cloud and disappeared. Gibson waited long seconds for it to return, listening to raindrops hissing on the super-heated ground like water in a frying pan, but the dazzling blue plume of the pod's thrusters never reappeared.

"Must have run out of fuel," Dekker mused.

"That, or it disappeared inside their carrier," Gibson replied, bringing his gaze back down to regard the others with a grave expression. "We'd better get back to base and report. With any luck, someone had eyes on that pod and command already knows where that carrier ship is hiding."

"What makes you so sure they're hiding?" Dekker asked. "Maybe they jumped to the next star system, and the pods are set to follow. That would explain why they haven't tried to land more of them."

"For all our sakes, I hope you're right, Deks," Gibson replied.

PART 3 - HAVOC

CHAPTER 41

—Three Months Later—

Ashley Carter sat at a long table, created by pushing four smaller ones together in the CDC center's mess hall. Seated with her were seven other senior physicians, and the director, Dr. Dean Coben. They'd all gathered here at the director's request to discuss the elephant in the room—or in the tent, in this case.

More than thirteen weeks had passed since the Crawlers had arrived, and almost as much time since the CDC had begun looking for signs of infectious agents, and so far, no one had come up with anything. All of the so-called *infected* remained asymptomatic, and the aliens themselves were long gone. Apart from the sixty dead ones and the four live ones at the missile testing facility at Barking Sands on the west side of the island, there was no sign of the Crawlers anywhere, and no one had any clue about why they'd come.

Efforts to study the Crawlers were being conducted by an agency that Ashley had never even heard of—the AATIP, which stood for the Advanced Aerospace Threat Identification Program. They were also the ones who'd handled recovery and relocation of the thirty remaining landing pods to the same facility at Barking Sands. All of it was being kept out of the public eye, much to the outrage of the public and the media. The alien assets on the island were the reason for the mountain of political pressure now sitting on Director Coben's shoulders. A week ago Washington had given him an ultimatum: find evidence of an infectious agent, or lift the quarantine.

Anyone with half a brain could figure out why: they were anxious to get the alien tech to a more secure facility before some other country came along and tried to steal it out from under their noses. Worries of a second Pearl Harbor-style sneak attack played on an endless loop across every news channel, but this time everyone expected the attack to come from China, since they were the ones with a fleet massing to challenge the US Navy in the Pacific.

"Can anyone here give me a reason to maintain the quarantine?" Director Coben asked.

None of the other doctors spoke, so Ashley

filled the silence. "Just because people are asymptomatic, doesn't mean we should let down our guard. There are plenty of viruses on Earth that have longer incubation periods than three months."

"Granted," Director Coben replied, nodding. "But by now we should have found some sign of alien cells. We've tested everything we can think of, and still come up empty-handed." Coben began shaking his head, and Ashley saw several other doctors doing the same. "It's time to admit we're jumping at shadows," he added.

Ashley frowned, her eyes scanning the others around the table, feeling unnerved, but unable to put her finger on the reason.

"We need more time. One more week."

"We were given one more week a week ago," the director replied. He steepled his hands on the table and leaned toward her, his brown eyes hard, crow's feet pinching together. "It's time to call it. Let's take the vote."

Three other doctors steepled their hands on the table, and Ashley frowned, a distant memory trickling to the fore. She recalled the girl from the resort telling her about synchronized behavior. At the time Ashley had dismissed it, but now...

"By a show of hands, how many believe we should lift the quarantine?"

The director raised his hand at the same time as the other three who'd been steepling their hands and shaking their heads with him. The other three appeared to hesitate, then two of them raised their hands. Ashley kept both of hers in her lap, watching the director and his three copy-cats with narrowed eyes.

Coben lowered his hand, and the other three did, too. "Let the record show seven out of nine in favor of ending the quarantine."

Ashley couldn't believe what she was seeing. This went beyond ordinary coincidence or unconscious mimicry. But even if it was a symptom, how was it possible? The center was isolated, and all of them were trained to take strict precautions. They'd observed every protocol. Could it be that the center had been compromised without them knowing it? And if so, by what? All the test samples had been clean.

"It's settled then," Director Coben said, shuffling the test result papers in front of him to slip them back into a blue folder.

"Wait," Ashley said.

All eyes turned to her.

"I just thought of something else we could try."

"And that is?" Director Coben asked.

Ashley hesitated, scrambling to think of

something. She hadn't actually thought of anything, but she had to buy time somehow. "It's a long shot, but maybe if we take new samples from the contaminated individuals and test them again, we might find something."

Director Coben scowled. Ashley's eyes skipped around the table. More than just the three copy-cats were scowling with him. "What do you think you'll find this time?"

"Some of our samples are more than ninety days old," Ashley said. "Alien cells might take longer to divide than human ones. Maybe we were looking too soon."

"We have more recent ones, too," Director Coben pointed out. "As I recall we gathered fresh samples from a subset of the contact group just a week ago for that exact reason."

"True, but as you say, it was only a subset."

"We selected the subjects at random, Carter, and there isn't enough time left to re-test the whole group."

"Not the whole group," Ashley insisted. "Just a few outliers."

"You have someone in mind?" the director asked.

Thinking back to Beth Steele's account of synchronized behavior at the Koa Kai, Ashley nodded. "I do."

"Then get it done. You have until midday tomorrow. If you still haven't found anything by then, I'm pulling the plug."

"Yes, sir," Ashley said, nodding quickly. "I'll work around the clock if I need to."

"That's your prerogative, Doctor." The director's gaze roved around the table. "Meanwhile, I want everyone else to start packing. If Doctor Carter doesn't find anything, we're all going to be on the first flight out of here. Meeting adjourned."

Heads bobbed, and Ashley's colleagues traded eager smiles as they pushed out their chairs and stood up from the table. As far as any of them were concerned, the job was done, and the outcome was as good as it could be.

Ashley studied them all carefully, especially the director and his three mimics, but they all stood up at separate times, their behavior once again appropriately staggered. She frowned and massaged her temples to knead away an encroaching headache. Maybe she was just imagining things.

As she stood up and pushed out her chair, Ashley heard the director's radio chirp, followed by, *"Director, this is Corporal Lee, I have a Mr. Donald Hale here at the fence asking to speak with Doctor Carter. Over."*

Director Coben grabbed the radio and said, "Coben here. Turn him away. This is a restricted area."

"Hold on, Director," Ashley said. "I know him."

Coben's brow furrowed curiously. "You asked him to come?"

"No, sir, but while he's here, he can save me some time by giving samples."

"Very well." Into the radio, Coben said, "Escort him to the clinic, but make sure he doesn't enter it until Doctor Carter joins you."

"Yes, sir. Over."

CHAPTER 42

Beth sat in Math class, pretending to listen as Professor Abbot taught them how to solve polynomials. She had bigger problems than learning algebra—like being forced to share a six-hundred-square-foot hotel suite with her dad and his fiancé, Melanie. It was driving her crazy, and thanks to the quarantine she couldn't run away to live with her mom in LA. Christmas break was coming up—the perfect excuse to leave—but it was impossible to even buy a plane ticket.

The alien invasion was a distant memory; she was one of the lucky ones who'd been able to get over it without lingering effects from the trauma, but she'd been left with a different kind of trauma. Ever since that horrifying night when she'd walked in on her dad and Melanie—no, not her dad, *Bill*; he was Bill to her now—she'd had to watch the two of them walking around on a cloud and making everyone feel uncomfortable with their public displays of affection. The last straw had come with her dad throwing a big party at the resort, inviting strangers off the street to enjoy snacks and an open bar to celebrate their engagement. He'd gone through all of the Koa Kai's canned goods and their remaining supply of liquor in a matter of hours. There must have been a thousand people at the resort that night, and they'd trashed the place.

It was all Melanie's fault. She was only twenty-one, so of course she'd thought it would be cool to throw a kegger at her dad's place to celebrate the engagement. It was like her dad had lost his mind. He was acting like a teenager, leaving Beth to be the adult.

And somehow, neither of them had even given a second thought to Melanie's dead husband. As far as Beth was concerned, that was all the characterization she needed: twenty-one-year-old widower hooks up with divorced forty-three-year-old resort owner one week after her husband died. It was a pathetic joke, and Beth felt like she was the only one who wasn't laughing.

"Beth *Steele!*"

She blinked the glaze from her eyes to see that Mr. Abbot was staring at her. "Yes?"

"Your uncle is waiting for you in the Main Office."

"My Uncle?" Beth asked. That was impossible.

Her uncles were all living in LA and on the east coast. Had the quarantine been lifted and she'd somehow missed hearing about it?

"Yes, a Don Steele, I believe. He needs to speak with you. He said it's urgent."

Don. Beth jumped to her feet, sweeping her notebook and math textbook off her desk in one smooth motion.

The teacher watched with a disapproving glare. "I hope you'll be back, Miss Steele. You can't afford to miss any more of this class."

"Yes, Mr. Abbot." Beth burst out of class and hurried down the hall. She had to force herself not to run. The last time she'd seen Don, he'd been on his way with his grandmother to his *bug out shelter* in the mountains. She couldn't begin to imagine why he had come to see her at school in the middle of the day. The only thing she could think of was that it had something to do with their mutual suspicions of her dad and the others at the Koa Kai. That gave her hope. Maybe her dad's crazy behavior really was a result of some alien infection messing with his head, and if so, maybe there was some way she could get him back.

* * *

"Is there somewhere private we can talk?" Don asked Mrs. Newman, the office clerk. Beth was bouncing on her feet with the burning need to know why he was here, but so far Don had refused to say anything.

"Well..." Mrs. Newman glanced around. "I suppose you could use Vice Principal Morgan's office. He's out at the moment." She pointed to the darkened door.

"Thank you," Don replied, and practically dragged Beth over there.

Once they were inside with the door shut, Don stepped out of view of the door's window and ushered Beth into the corner of the room. She backed into a filing cabinet with a noisy thump.

"What's going on?" she asked.

"Keep it down and listen up, kid. You need to get out of here. Now. Is there some way you can cut class and meet me in the parking lot?"

"What? Why?"

"I can't explain here. Yes or no, Beth?"

"I can, but—"

"Good. I'm driving the same old white Chevy. You remember it? You'll find me parked out front in the far corner of the lot, northwest of the main entrance. The engine will be running.

Beth nodded absently, then shook her head. "Hang on. I'm not going anywhere until you tell me something."

Don glanced around, checking the ceiling, and Beth realized he was looking for cameras.

"Relax. No one's listening," Beth said.

But Don shook his head. "We can't be too careful." He glanced behind him to the door, as if worried someone might have their ear pressed to the other side. "Are you going to meet me or not?"

His mysterious behavior left her no choice. "Give me five minutes."

Don nodded. "Good call."

As they emerged from the vice principal's office, Don pasted a sunny smile on his face. Beth's heart pounded in her chest, and she was afraid some of that tension had bled through to her features.

"Everything all right, Mr. Steele?" Mrs. Newman asked.

"Just peachy, thank you."

"Glad to hear it..." She replied with a bemused expression. "Beth you'd better get back to class."

She nodded quickly and hurried out after Don. He headed straight for the main entrance, while Beth arced right to the girls' bathroom. The window in there was small and hard to reach. It was locked from the outside, but the lock was old and easy to jiggle loose. It was also one of the few places in the school with no security cameras, making it the perfect place to sneak out.

CHAPTER 43

Beth jumped down from the jimmied window and raced around the side of the school, staying clear of windows and darting between trees. With the wind in her hair, she felt like she'd broken out of jail. It reminded her of when she and Toby used to sneak out together—before he'd dropped out and found a job at her dad's resort.

Beth's throat tightened at the memory, and shook her head to clear it. She ran down the side of the gymnasium to reach the parking lot. There, shadowed by an umbrella-shaped tree and the soaring window-less edifice of the gym, Beth scanned the northwest end of the parking lot.

She found the glowing red tail lights of Don's truck peeking out behind a green minivan at the furthest extent of the parking lot. Glancing around to make sure no one was watching, Beth darted out of cover to reach the cars. She crouched low to hide behind the vehicles and not be seen through their windows. At the end of the parking lot, she sneaked between Don's truck and the minivan.

"That was ten minutes, not five." Don regarded her with a look of strained patience. He had his windows rolled down, and to Beth's surprise someone in a familiar canary-yellow suit sat beside him.

"Ashley?"

"Hi, Beth," the doctor replied.

"Get in," Don added, waving her around to the passenger's side.

Beth pulled open the door, and the doctor shuffled over to sit in the middle of the bench seat.

"Thanks," Beth said, then climbed in and shut the door. "So, now can you explain what's going on?" Beth asked. She tried to lean around Ashley to catch Don's eye as he began reversing out of the parking space.

"I'll let Ash tell it," Don said. "Ash?"

"It's Ashley," she replied. Turning to Beth, she said, "He's been working with chickens."

"Chickens?" Beth asked.

Don hit the accelerator, and the Silverado's engine roared as he left the parking lot and joined the street.

"He infected a group of chickens by mixing blood from someone he believes to be infected into their food."

"Not someone I *believe* to be infected. She *is*

infected. That woman is not my grandmother."

"Sarah?" Beth asked. "What's wrong with her?"

"She's off," Don said. "Everything she says and does is just a little *off* like she's trying too hard to be herself and put me at ease."

"How did you get her blood?"

"Slipped a sedative into her tea and then I took it."

Ashley went on, "Anyway, he infected the chickens and then studied their behavior over the past nine weeks, all the while comparing them to a control group of uninfected animals."

Beth shook her head. "And?"

Don chose that moment to interject: "And, I discovered the same synchronized behavior we saw at the resort. It wasn't a coincidence, Beth. The difference is, the chickens can't help themselves. Maybe their brains are too tiny; I don't know, but I've got a whole coop full of them playing follow the leader in groups of four—well, except for the immunes, Donnie and Bethy."

"You named your chickens after us?" Beth asked. She was beginning to wonder if maybe Don had lost his mind.

"You're missing the point," Don sighed. "This is important, Beth."

"Do you have any proof?" she asked, her eyes

flicking between him and Ashley.

"He showed me videos," Ashley said. "He came to the CDC to turn over his notes, the recordings, and all of the samples from his work, but Director Coben brushed us off. He's going to lift the quarantine tomorrow if we can't find proof of a dangerous pathogen in *humans.*"

"Isn't lifting the quarantine a good thing?" Beth asked.

"It would be if there were no reason for alarm," Don replied.

Beth watched as Don drove them past a suburban development in Lihue. She recognized where they were; he was heading for the airport, or rather, for the CDC complex in the soccer field next to the airport.

"He thinks the Crawlers have secretly taken over the minds of almost everyone on the island," Ashley explained. "He thinks they're all doppelgängers."

"That's crazy..." Beth said, but her voice sounded unsure even to her own ears. Maybe that explained her dad's and Melanie's madness. "By taken over, you mean... what exactly?"

"I think they're pretending to be the people they were while consciously pursuing the Crawlers' agenda."

"What agenda?"

"Infect as many people as possible as a prelude to a real invasion. Then when they come, instead of going to war with them, the infected people will all be bending over backward to give them whatever they want like good little slaves."

"But..." Beth shook her head. That explanation didn't make sense to her. She looked at Ashley and asked Don, "How do you know *she's* immune? Or me?"

"Because both of you described your suspicions to me before I had to say anything. You, Beth, at breakfast that day, and Ashley now when I went to see her at the CDC. If either of you were infected, you wouldn't be trying to draw attention to the Crawlers' business."

Beth's eyes flicked to Ashley. "Does this make any sense to you?"

"I might not be immune," Ashley said. "I've been observing all the protocols. It's possible I just haven't been exposed yet. And he's just guessing about this being a prelude to a bigger invasion. But I do think that *something* is going on."

"It's a damn good guess," Don said. "And it fits with everything else that the Crawlers have done."

"Not everything," Ashley replied. "If this is phase one and it's designed to spread a pathogen to as many people as possible, then the Crawlers should have invaded the mainland—not an island in the middle of the Pacific. If you're right, then it's almost as though they wanted the spread to be contained, and that doesn't make any sense when you plug it into your theory of an alien bioweapon."

"Maybe it's a weapon *test,* to see if they can get away with it, or to lull us into a false sense of security while we knock ourselves out trying to find their invisible weapon. Hell, if they made their whole damn spaceship invisible, they can probably do it on a microscopic level, too."

"Not necessarily," Ashley replied.

"Well, maybe you missed something. Besides, you said yourself that the quarantine center might have been compromised, which means you could have people on the inside actively working to hide evidence."

"The center was compromised?" Beth asked. "How do you know?"

"I saw the same thing this morning," Ashley explained. "The director and three other doctors were all syncing up, just like Don found with his chickens—and like you saw with your dad."

Unease crawled through Beth's gut, making her feel queasy. She could see the white canvas tents of the CDC complex growing larger in the distance. "If the center is compromised, then *why* are we going there?"

"Because I need to run more tests, and because Don found a cure, and we need to see if it works."

"You found a *cure?*" Beth asked. She stared at Don with wide eyes.

"Damn right." He nodded absently as if it were no big deal.

Hope exploded inside of Beth like fireworks. "What is it?"

CHAPTER 44

"What's the cure?" Beth asked again just as Don parked in the lot outside the center. A pair of Marines immediately peeled off the fence to intercept them.

"Radiation," Don said.

"What kind of—"

"Not now, Beth," Ashley said, cutting her off.

"Does the director know?" Beth whispered.

"No. I told Ash to be careful, just in case. Seems I was right."

One of the Marines came up to Don's open window.

"Is there a problem, Corporal?" he asked.

"This is a restricted area," the Marine replied.

"It's okay, Lee," Ashley said. "They're with me. I'm taking them to the clinic for testing."

Beth saw the man frown, but then he nodded and stepped back. "Yes, ma'am."

Don shut off the engine, and they climbed out of the truck. Corporal Lee escorted them all the way to the entrance of the clinic tent.

"You can leave us now, Corporal," Ashley said when it looked like he wanted to enter the clinic with them.

"My orders are to keep eyes on any civilians you bring to the center."

"Since when?" Ashley asked. "Whose orders?"

"The director's. Since this morning, ma'am. I'll be sure to stay out of your way."

Ashley looked like she wanted to argue further, but she gave in with a nod. "Very well, you can help with the testing."

"Help, ma'am?"

"I could use another test subject."

"My orders are—"

"You're not hiding something are you, corporal?" Ashley asked.

Beth felt her whole body go cold, and Don appeared to tense up, but then the Marine shook his head. "No, ma'am."

"Good. Then let's get started."

Don caught Beth's eye and gave his head a slight shake. They followed Ashley and the Marine inside the tent and each hopped up on one of the examination tables while Ashley dug around in a box on one of the metal shelving units.

"You first," Ashley said, nodding to the Marine. She had a needle and a stretchy blue tourniquet in her hand. He frowned, but shifted his shotgun to a one-handed grip and allowed her to roll up one of his sleeves. Beth watched his blood pour into the vial at the end of the needle.

"Thank you," Ashley said, marking the vial and placing it in a clear plastic stand.

It was Beth's turn next. She winced as the needle went in. Don didn't even blink as Ashley took his blood.

"Now what?" the Marine asked.

"Now, we get a look at your blood counts to see if there's any sign of an infection."

"Right." He nodded slowly, and his gaze strayed to Beth and Don.

They spent a long time waiting while Ashley studied slides of their blood under a microscope and made notes on a pad. Then she placed the slides on a padded table under a machine that Beth vaguely recognized as an x-ray machine. *Radiation. That's the cure.*

"What's that for?" the Marine asked.

"Just a routine diagnostic test," Ashley said, but Beth could tell she was trying too hard to be nonchalant.

Ashley stepped away and ducked behind a screen. The machine buzzed once, twice... three times before Ashley stepped back into view to retrieve the samples. She returned to her microscope to study the samples. Don got up from the table and stretched his back and legs while they waited. Beth noticed that he was getting closer to the Marine in the process.

At some point, Ashley grew very still.

"Is everything okay, Doctor?" Corporal Lee asked.

But she didn't reply.

"Doctor?" The corporal shifted his grip on his shotgun.

Don inched a step closer to him, and Beth held her breath. The tension in the room was stretched to the limit, just about to snap. The Marine was definitely acting suspicious.

"Everything is fine," Ashley said, retreating from the microscope and turning to them with a frown. "You're all clean, but I still have a lot of tests to do. It could be a while. Corporal Lee, would you please escort these two to the waiting area? I may need them for more tests later."

Lee nodded slowly. "Of course."

Beth frowned, wondering if Ashley was telling the truth or hiding something because of the Marine. "How long do you think you'll need?" she asked. By now the school would have discovered her absence and reported it to her dad.

"A few hours," Ashley said.

"A few hours!" Beth echoed.

"I'm sorry. I'll try to be as quick as possible."

"This way," Corporal Lee said, gesturing to a tent-flap door opposite the one that led outside.

Beth and Don followed him through and down the hall to the waiting room where Beth had met Don's grandmother for the first time. But unlike it had been back then, the room was empty now.

Corporal Lee stayed with them, standing guard by the door to the clinic. His presence made a candid discussion impossible. If that Marine was infected and Don was right, then talking openly in front of him would be a very bad idea.

Unable to talk about what was really on her mind, Beth passed the time in silence, alone with her thoughts. Those thoughts ran in anxious circles, wondering about the so-called infection they were investigating, and who they could actually trust.

The time passed with agonizing slowness. Beth's stomach growled, and her mouth felt dry. That gave her an idea. "Hey, can I get something to drink?" she asked.

Corporal Lee glanced at the door he was guarding, then back to her.

"What do you think we're going to do if you leave us alone?" Don asked in an amused tone.

"You could compromise the integrity of the center," Lee replied.

"Relax, Corporal," Don said. "I did two tours myself. The last thing I want to do is get you into trouble. I get that you have a job to do."

Lee sucked in a breath and let it out slowly. "All right. Don't go anywhere." With that, he turned and pushed out through the waiting room doors. The flaps sealed themselves behind him along a magnetic seam.

"Come on," Don said, pulling Beth to her feet and heading for the door to the clinic. "This is taking too long."

"But he just said—"

"He's infected, kid. The director sent him to keep an eye on Ashley and us."

They swept into the clinic to find Ashley still peering into the microscope, scribbling notes furiously on a pad of paper. She was so absorbed in her work that she didn't notice their approach.

"Ash," Don said.

She jumped at the sound of his voice and whirled around. "Don't *do* that!" she whispered. "Where's the corporal?"

"Out to get us water, but he'll be back soon. What's the verdict?"

"You were right. The samples were all normal until I irradiated them with the CT scanner. Yours were all fine, but it was like the Corporal's blood short-circuited. The radiation killed one in ten of his cells, and they started changing as they died."

"Changing how?" Beth asked.

Ashley shook her head and shrugged. "Becoming alien." She gestured to the microscope. "Take a look for yourself."

"We don't have time for this," Don said.

Beth hurried to peer into the lens. She saw light pink circles and larger purplish ones. In between, were amorphous blue structures, smaller than the other cells, with delicate, web-like structures inside of them.

"See the blue ones?" Ashley asked.

Beth nodded. "They just appeared out of nowhere. Gradually changing from red and white cells into *that*. I call them chameleon cells."

"Enough with the biology lesson," Don said. Lowering his voice to a whisper, he said, "What have you been doing all this time? We should be getting the hell out of here before we get caught. We need to get this information out before it's too late and they lift the quarantine."

Ashley nodded quickly. "I've been checking old samples." She pointed to the microscope beside Beth. "That one is your dad's. He's definitely infected, and so is almost everyone else from the resort. I only found two other immunes—Corporal Gibson and Commander Wilde."

Beth felt hope stirring inside of her again. "But

we can cure them, right?"

Ashley shook her head. "I don't know. I hope so."

Don let out an impatient sigh and glanced around quickly. "Let's cut the chatter," he said. "We need to bug out, *now,* while we still can."

At that moment the tent flap doors leading from the waiting room flew open, and Corporal Lee stormed in with two bottles of water dangling from one hand, his other holding his shotgun at a threatening angle.

"I told you not to move," Lee said.

"Sorry," Ashley replied in a bright voice. "My fault. I called them in for more tests."

"I see... find anything interesting?" he asked, his eyes flicking between them.

Ashley shook her head. "Same as ever. Empty-handed. It looks like I'm going to have to go back out into the field to gather more samples."

Ashley removed the slide from the microscope and tossed it into a tray with the others for cleaning.

"Where are you going?" Corporal Lee asked.

"Not sure yet," Ashley replied. She walked over to a big rectangular black bag and started packing it with medical supplies.

"You should have an escort," Lee said.

"That won't be necessary, Corporal. You've

done enough."

He walked over to them, and Beth watched his approach with wide eyes and a pounding heart.

"Your water," he said, handing each of them a bottle.

"Thanks," Don replied. "We should get going, too."

"Yes, we should," Beth agreed.

Ashley finished packing her bag and zipped it up. "I'll walk you out," she said.

The Marine Corporal shadowed them across the trampled, overgrown grass to the fence. He was about to follow them to the parking lot, too, when Ashley turned to him and nodded. "Thank you, Corporal. You can return to your post now."

He nodded back hesitantly, and the three of them walked the rest of the way alone.

"I'll follow you in one of the center's vans," Ashley said in a low voice.

"Follow us where?" Don asked as they reached the side of his truck. "If you're looking for suggestions, I have a boat in the harbor with our name on it."

"No." Ashley shook her head. "The harbor is under heavy guard, and the whole island is still under quarantine. We won't even reach it before we get arrested."

"Then what are you planning?" Don asked.

"We go to the Koa Kai and speak to Commander Wilde and Corporal Gibson. They're also uninfected, and they might be able to help us get off the island."

"I guess we could use some reinforcements," Don replied. "But how are you going to convince them?"

Ashley patted her case of supplies. "Wilde is a doctor. I'm going to show him." Ashley glanced back to the fence, probably checking to make sure none of the Marines had followed them to the gravel parking lot. "On the way there I'm going to call HQ in Atlanta to see if I can stop them from lifting the quarantine."

"Good idea," Don said. "Let's go."

CHAPTER 45

"This is what Doctor Carter was doing?" Director Coben asked, picking through the bin of slides next to the microscope.

Corporal Lee nodded. "Yes, sir. She claimed that she didn't find anything, but she seemed to be acting suspiciously."

The director wore a hazmat suit, but they both knew that was just to keep up appearances.

"Let's take a look, shall we?" Coben said, fishing one of the slides out of the bin at random. He checked the label. "Private Nolan Dekker. Blood sample." He placed the slide under the microscope and peered through the lens. "You were right to be suspicious." Coben withdrew from the microscope. "She knows."

"What are we going to do?"

The director appeared to think about it. "We need to proceed carefully. Who was with her?"

"Two civilians. Immune like her."

"Then it's safe to say they're working

together," Coben said.

Lee struggled to recall more details. "Beth and Don, I believe, were their names."

"Beth Steele and Donald Hale," Coben clarified.

Lee cocked his head. "You know them?"

"Only by name. They're both from the Koa Kai group. Beth is the owner's daughter. Did Doctor Carter have contact with anyone else at the facility while she was here?"

"No, sir. She was in here by herself the entire time."

"Good. She probably doesn't know who to trust. That will make this easier. Did they say where they were going?"

"Negative," Lee replied.

"Hmmm." The director pawed through the bin of slides once more, checking labels. "These samples are all from the Koa Kai group. Check there first. Take a team. Our kind only."

"Yes, sir," Lee replied. "What do we do when we make contact?"

"Wait for them to make the first move. We don't want to look like the bad guys. If you can, bring them back here. Tell them I want to follow up on their test results."

"Copy that. What if they have a chance to tell someone what they know before we catch up with them? This could spread beyond our ability to contain. Especially if one of them makes a call to someone on the mainland."

"I'll take care of the phones, but you're right about the potential for this to spread. We can't have any loose ends, and we also can't be seen tying them off."

The director drummed his fingers on the table, and Corporal Lee fought the urge to do the same.

"What about the Seeders?" Lee asked. "There's still one of them out there. If it were to somehow free the others, they could hunt down the immunes and take care of the problem for us. That would give us an excuse to explain any casualties."

"Yes," Coben replied. "Unfortunately we can't release them until nightfall, and we have no contact with the missing Seeder, but it's still a good idea. I'll have Sergeant Colton take another team to Barking Sands. They'll release the Seeders once the sun goes down. In the meantime, you'd better hurry out, Corporal. We don't want to lose track of Doctor Carter. Be discreet, but do what you must. We can always have the Seeders cover it up afterward."

"Understood."

* * *

Ashley drove like a maniac down Route 50. Her helmet lay on the passenger seat beside her.

Hopefully, she was immune and not just one of the lucky ones who'd somehow escaped contamination. Her right hand held the wheel as she followed the winding road behind Don's truck. She used her other hand to clumsily search through the contacts on her phone. She needed to reach someone from the CDC headquarters in Atlanta, someone senior enough to override Director Coben's authority. She glossed over the number for the Director of the CDC; he was impossible to reach directly. But Principal Deputy Director Schuman was more promising. They'd met on several occasions, and Ashley actually had her cell number.

Ashley stabbed Dr. Schuman's name with her left thumb and placed the phone to her ear. The phone rang and rang, and...

"Hello?"

"Dr. Schuman!" Ashley said.

"Yes? Who is this?"

"It's Doctor Ashley Carter from the CDC. You might remember me from the 2017 STD Prevention Conference in Washington. We went out to dinner together to discuss my research."

"Ah, *that* Ashley. Yes, I remember you. What can I do for you, doctor?"

"I'm currently assigned to the quarantine zone on Kauai," Ashley explained.

"Oh, that must be fascinating work—unprecedented, I would say. It's just a pity you haven't found anything. Did you have a chance to study any of the... extraterrestrials?"

"No, not directly—"

"That's a shame. I imagine there's a lot we could learn about infectious disease from alien biology. For instance, how do their systems react to our viruses and bacteria?"

"I'm sure that would be interesting, Madam Director, but I'm actually calling about a much more urgent concern..." Ashley trailed off as a familiar beep sounded in her ear. "Hello?"

No reply.

Ashley removed the phone from her ear to check it. The call had dropped, and now she had no signal. Seeing the dense foliage and lack of civilization on both sides of the road, Ashley could guess why. Blowing out a shaky breath, she tossed her phone onto the passenger's seat. The island's spotty cell coverage might have just cost the human race their survival. *Calm down, Ashley. There's still time. The quarantine doesn't end until tomorrow.* She'd call again once she reached the town of Koloa.

CHAPTER 46

Beth listened to long grass rustling as they drove by. Don focused on the task of driving while Beth thought about everything she'd just learned. If radiation was the cure, how would that even work for her dad? Would they have to give him a lethal dose, or would it just be like getting an x-ray to look for cavities? She thought back to the CT scan they'd performed on him and remembered how he'd been afterward—a zombie with dull, staring eyes—until later that night when Melanie had revived him through carnal means. The pieces snapped into place, and Beth's eyes widened. "It wasn't a panic attack..."

"What?" Don asked, glancing at her.

She explained about the CT scan and her dad's reaction to it. "That was his reaction to the die-off of alien cells, not a delayed reaction to trauma."

"Makes sense," Don replied. "But what's your point?"

"We just have to get him to a CT scanner, or

something like it, and we can probably cure him. That's why he and Melanie hooked up. I think she was trying to re-infect him. And now they're engaged, so it obviously worked."

"They're engaged?" Don asked.

"Yeah. We have to find some way to get him away from her."

"One thing at a time, kid. First we have to make sure we live through this."

Beth blinked. "Live through this?"

"If Ashley stops the CDC from lifting the quarantine, we become enemy number one to the infected who would rather spread their alien spores far and wide, and we're *inside* that quarantine zone, so we'll be stuck on an island full of hostiles. Not to mention, once the Crawlers realize that the jig is up, they might just skip ahead to the real invasion. We need to play this carefully, or we're dead."

Beth took a minute to process the implications of that. "But... what are we supposed to do?"

"I'm not sure yet. My place in the mountains is an option if we can get there before they realize we're onto them."

Beth nodded slowly, silently and stared out the window at a blurry wall of grass and trees.

"Maybe we don't need the CT scanner. How did you irradiate those chickens? You have something that emits radiation? Would it work on my dad?"

"I didn't irradiate them. Not exactly. I got to thinking about what killed the Crawlers. Why did they all die when their ship moved away from the sun? Radiation was the answer."

"But the sun isn't radioactive."

"UV radiation, kid. It's milder stuff, sure, but the Crawlers obviously don't get a lot of sunlight where they came from, so they don't have any defenses. I took blood samples from the infected chickens and laid them out in the sun; then I examined them under a microscope, and bingo, I found the alien cells, just like Ash."

"So you're saying all we have to do to cure the infected people is get them to lie out in the sun?"

Don snorted. "I doubt it. Blood doesn't have protection from UV, but our skin does, and we can't exactly turn people inside out to cure them."

Beth's heart sank. "Then it won't work."

"Sorry to burst your bubble, kid."

Beth studied Don curiously.

He noticed her scrutiny and asked, "What? Do I have a monkey on my face or something?"

"It's just that you don't seem like the type to own a microscope."

Don smiled at that. "What's the type?"

"I don't know... academic? You were a

soldier."

"A helicopter pilot, to be specific, and more recently an EMT—until the PTSD got me fired."

"I'm sorry."

"Don't worry about it. I was planning to retire anyway."

The highway curved away and down, and the town of Koloa appeared in the valley below.

"Almost there," Don said. "Remember, play it cool. The minute they figure out we're onto them, they'll kill us to shut us up. Best let me and Ash do the talking."

Beth nodded agreeably. "Sure." But she had a feeling that rescuing her dad wasn't their priority, and she had no intention of leaving him behind.

CHAPTER 47

Don parked in front of the Koa Kai and then reached over Beth's lap to the glove compartment.

"What are you doing?" she asked.

"Getting my insurance policy."

"You..." Beth trailed off as he withdrew a gleaming silver pistol with a brown grip. "What's that for?"

Don leaned forward and tucked the weapon into the waistband of his jeans. "I told you. Insurance." He opened his door and hopped out, making sure to cover the pistol with his loose-fitting Hawaiian shirt.

Don slammed the door. *Bang.* Beth jumped with the noise, then opened her door and jumped out, taking a moment to close it more gently than Don had. Beth went to stand by the tailgate with Don while they waited for Ashley to park her van beside them. Staring up at the entrance of the Koa Kai, everything looked so normal. The brown roof gleamed in the sun; palm trees waved in the breeze with the muted clattering of their fronds; plenty of cars were parked out front—well, there was one thing that broke the illusion of normalcy: a green Humvee with a machine gun mounted on the roof.

"Looks like Gibson's team is here," Don said, nodding to the Humvee as Ashley came to join them.

"Remember, we need to speak with him alone," she said, her voice muffled by her hazmat suit's helmet. "The other three are infected."

"Yeah... or maybe we should just go," Don said. "Would be nice to have extra guns and boots, but the risk might outweigh the reward."

Ashley wasn't listening. She was busy fiddling with her phone, frowning deeply at it behind the glass faceplate of her helmet.

"What is it?" Beth asked.

"Do you have a signal?" Ashley asked, looking up from the phone.

"I don't know," Beth replied. "Phones aren't allowed at school, so mine's up in my room."

"Hmmm," Ashley replied, and her gaze roved on to Don.

He held up his hands. "Don't look at me. Cell phones can be tracked. I don't own one."

"Great," Ashley replied. "Well, let's go."

Beth led the way to the entrance of the resort—

And almost walked straight through the

automatic doors. They didn't open for her as she'd expected.

"Power's out," Don said. He turned to Ashley. "You said the cell network is down?"

"Yes, why?"

"Then it's not just the Koa."

"Another EMP?" Ashley asked, her gaze snapping up to the sky.

"No. If it were an EMP, your van would have crapped out before we got here, and your phone is powered on and exposed, so it would have, too. Even the amplifier in your suit that you're using to talk to us would be offline. This is just a garden variety blackout. Unless..."

Beth's brow furrowed. "Unless what?"

"Unless they're on to us already."

"Shit," Ashley muttered.

"That's it," Don said. "We need to get out of here."

Just then the doors slid partway open, and Beth's dad peeked out. "Beth! Where have you been?" He came out and fixed her with a dark look. "The school called to say you took off."

"Your phones work?" Don asked.

Bill shot him a frown. "Until recently. What's going on? You know what happened to the power?"

Don shook his head. "No clue. Sorry."

"What are you doing here?" Bill's eyes flicked to Ashley, then back to Beth. Her chest grew tight, suddenly realizing that they had no good reason for the three of them to be together.

"It's my fault," Ashley said. "I called them in for additional tests at the center."

"Oh?" Bill asked. "Why them?"

Ashley shook her head. "They were selected at random."

"I see. And what are you doing back here?"

"I gave Beth a ride from the center," Don explained. "I hope that's okay."

"It's fine," Bill replied.

"And I'm here to take more samples," Ashley added. "Is Corporal Gibson's team here?"

Bill stared silently at her for several seconds before offering a reply. "No. They're at Barking Sands."

"Oh, I see..." Ashley trailed off. "What about Commander Wilde?"

"Yes, he's here. Why?"

Ashley patted her black case of supplies. "I need to take samples."

"The commander was also selected?" Bill asked.

"Yes," Ashley replied, but Beth could hear the strain in her voice.

"He's upstairs," Bill said. "Room three oh six."

"Thank you," Ashley replied.

Bill's gaze found Beth, and she flinched at the intensity of his stare. "You should go upstairs too. You're grounded."

"But Ashley needed me to—"

"I don't care. You could have gone after school instead of sneaking out."

"Fine," Beth replied, pretending annoyance as she pushed by her dad in the entrance. Ashley followed, but Don hesitated. He was just Beth's ride. He didn't have a reason to be there.

"How's the old gang?" Beth heard him ask. "Everyone still mooching off your generosity?"

"Everyone's fine," Bill replied.

"Mind if I come in? There's something I wanted to ask Wilde about."

Beth stopped just inside the entrance to listen to their conversation.

"The commander?" Bill asked.

"Yeah, he and I go way back. We served in Afghanistan together."

"You did?"

"You didn't know?" Don countered.

"No, I didn't."

"Well, I guess you and I didn't spend a whole lot of time chatting. So, may I?"

"Go ahead," Bill said.

Beth darted out of sight and up the stairs

beside the elevators before he could catch her standing there. She caught up to Ashley on the second floor.

"Where's Don?" Ashley whispered.

"Right here."

Beth jumped at the sound of his voice and glared at him.

"What?" he asked.

She looked away with a frown, and they climbed the rest of the way to the third floor. "I have to go to my room," Beth said, pointing to the end of the hall. "Come get me when you're done?"

Don shook his head. "We need to stick together so we can make a quick exit."

"And make them suspicious?" Ashley asked. "Not worth it. We'll get you afterward."

"On what pretense?" Don asked.

"I'll think of something," Ashley said. "Go to your room, Beth. We'll see you there soon."

"Okay," Beth replied, nodding hesitantly before hurrying down the hall. When she arrived at the door, she ran her keycard through the battery-operated scanner and opened the door to find Melanie sitting on the couch, watching her as she came in.

"Beth! Where have you been? Your father and I have been worried sick!"

"That's none of your business," Beth replied,

smiling thinly at her as she walked around the dining table, heading straight for the hallway to the bedrooms.

"Whether you like it or not, I'm going to be your stepmother!"

We'll see. Beth shut and locked the door to her room behind her, feeling suddenly trapped. What if Ashley and Don couldn't come up with an excuse to get her out? She'd be stuck here, surrounded by infected human impostors. Don's warning came to mind: *the minute they figure out we're onto them, they'll kill us to shut us up.* Beth shuddered. She could imagine that Melanie might try to gut her with a knife, but surely her dad wouldn't try to kill her, too.

She hoped Ashley would be able to convince Commander Wilde to help them. He probably had a gun with him, and Gibson's team was out, so they'd be the only ones armed with actual weapons. With luck, that would be enough to give them a chance if it came to a fight.

CHAPTER 48

"Some people just came here from the CDC. Where are they?" Corporal Lee asked as he and his team strode into the lobby.

The owner of the resort pointed to the ceiling. "Upstairs. Room three oh six. They're with Commander Wilde. Is something wrong?"

Lee glanced about, then nodded. "They know."

"What do they know?"

"Everything," Lee replied.

"What are you planning to do about it?"

"We're going to take them back to the center, and then let the Seeders take care of them for us."

"Good," the owner replied, nodding.

"Where's room three oh six?" Lee asked.

"This way. I'll take you."

Lee motioned to his team, and they followed the man to a nearby stairwell, then up those stairs to the third floor. Room 306 was just a few doors down from the top of the stairs. The owner led them there, then turned to them and said, "My daughter was with them. Do you need her as well?"

"Beth Steele?" Lee asked. "Yes, we need her."

"She's in our room. What do I tell her?"

"Orders are to be discreet. Tell her she's infected with something and has to return to the center for analysis. No need to go into details."

"All right. I'll go get her."

Lee nodded, then turned and rapped loudly on the door. "Doctor Carter? It's Corporal Lee from the center. I need to speak with you urgently."

* * *

Ashley froze at the sound of the corporal's voice.

"Shit," Don said.

"I can tell them to leave," Wilde said.

"Something tells me that's not gonna work," Don replied. He drew a silver pistol from the waistband of his jeans.

Ashley's eyes widened. "You brought a gun?" she whispered.

"That shouldn't even be a question," Don said.

"Hang on," Wilde said, shaking his head. "Let's all just calm down."

Bang, bang, bang! The door thundered with someone's fist. "You've got three seconds to open this door," Corporal Lee announced.

"Guess I'm not the only one losing their head,"

Don said.

"I'll take care of it," Wilde insisted. "Give me a second."

Don caught Ashley's eye and shook his head. "Pack your stuff. If they see that microscope, they'll know you weren't just here to collect samples."

The door clicked open, and Ashley heard the chain rattle as it snapped taut. "What's the meaning of this, Corporal?"

"Sir, we need to take you all to the quarantine center immediately. Doctor Carter is infected with a dangerous pathogen of alien origin. You and anyone else she has been in contact with may have also been exposed."

"Fascinating. That's what Doctor Carter said about you and everyone else."

Ashley grimaced at that. She'd barely had the time to finish explaining and demonstrating everything to Wilde before the corporal had shown up. She wondered who he would believe: this Marine, or her.

"Isn't that exactly what an alien collaborator *would* say, sir?"

"Collaborator?" the commander echoed. "I thought we were talking about infections, not allegiances."

Ashley was halfway through packing her bag

when Don stopped her. "Jig's up," he whispered. "Doesn't matter what they see now."

She finished packing anyway.

"Open the door, sir. We need to escort you all to the center immediately."

"Stand down, Corporal. I'll escort them to the center. Leave it to me."

"Negative, sir. They're dangerous. You need backup."

Ashley saw Commander Wilde's hand stray to his sidearm. She held her breath and glanced around quickly, looking for a safe place to hide if the bullets started flying.

Don raised his voice, "If we're infected with something, we should do as the corporal says."

Commander Wilde glanced back at them with a frown, and Ashley noticed Don tucking his gun behind his back once more. They traded silent glances beyond the corporal's line of sight.

The commander sighed theatrically. "One minute, Corporal." He shut the door, but hesitated before opening it. His eyes were fixed on Don. "What are you planning?"

Don whispered, "You can still take us in your vehicle. Make sure that you do."

"Open the door!" Corporal Lee demanded, pounding on it with his fist again.

Commander Wilde slid the chain off and

opened up to find Lee pointing a rifle in his face.

"Get that weapon out of my face, Corporal!" The commander's face flushed bright red.

But the corporal made no move to obey the order.

"Did you hear me?" Wilde asked darkly.

"Yes, sir, but I can't do that, sir."

Ashley saw three additional Marines standing behind the corporal, all of them aiming their rifles, too.

The corporal's gaze found Ashley, and his eyes narrowed, but his aim never wavered from Commander Wilde. Ashley wondered if that was because the doctor wore a sidearm.

"Everyone out," the corporal said.

Before Ashley could reply, she heard Beth's voice, "Let me go!" Followed by her father's—

"You're needed at the center, Beth. They think you could be infected with something dangerous!"

Both Beth and her father stepped into view beside the Marines. Her dad had her trapped in a white-knuckled grip, and he seemed oblivious to the deadly confrontation with the Marines.

"Step outside, sir," Lee said.

Commander Wilde looked like he was about to argue more—or burst a blood vessel—but then his cheeks returned to their normal color, and he nodded. "Very well."

The Marines backed up, and Wilde stepped out. Don went next, followed by Ashley. She caught Beth's eye as she stepped into the hallway. "Beth, it's okay," she said. "They just want to run a few follow-up tests on us."

"Are you fucking *kidding* me?" Beth demanded. She kicked her dad in the shins. He winced but didn't let her go.

"Trust me," Ashley replied. She hoped Don's plan was a good one. Her gaze skipped to the insubordinate corporal. "This is just a precaution, right? They don't think we're contagious. Otherwise, the CDC would be here—right, Corporal?"

His aim didn't waver, but he blinked and nodded. "That's right, ma'am."

"Fine," Beth harrumphed and jerked her arms free of her father. She turned to him with a scowl. "But you have to come too."

"They don't need me," Bill said.

"They do," she insisted. "I'm a minor, remember? They might need you to sign consent forms. Unless you just want me to forge your signature again..."

Bill frowned, and Ashley's pulse sped up. She knew what Beth was doing—trying to sidle her father off in the hopes that they could cure him—but right now they had more pressing problems, like finding a way to escape from Corporal Lee before they wound up at the bottom of the harbor with bullet holes in their heads.

"Fine," Bill said with a tight smile. "I'll go."

"Negative," Corporal Lee said. "We don't have room for five."

"You won't need it," Wilde said breezily. "I'll take them in my vehicle. You're just the escort, remember?"

Corporal Lee looked uncertain. "Our orders are—"

"To take them back to the center," the commander interrupted. "And I'm going to help you. Move out, Corporal."

Lee hesitated before giving in with a nod. "After you, sir."

CHAPTER 49

"We can take two in each of our vehicles, sir," Corporal Lee said once they were all out in the parking lot.

Beth resisted the urge to turn and run while she still could.

"Negative, Corporal. They all ride with me," Commander Wilde replied.

"Sir, with all due respect you don't even have seatbelts for—"

The commander cut him off with a wave of his hand. "I've been tolerant of your insubordinate demands this far, but I won't take another. The civilians ride with me. There's no sense exposing yourselves to whatever they've been infected with any more than you have to."

Corporal Lee had the look of a man who'd boxed himself into a corner. Beth resisted the urge to smile smugly at him. Staying together sounded a lot safer than riding with those impostors—even if it did nothing to change their destination. Beth hoped the others had some kind of plan.

"Very well, sir," Corporal Lee said. "We'll take point and rear."

"Of course," Commander Wilde replied.

"Move out!" the corporal said.

"Oorah!" his men replied in unison, and the four of them marched off in synchrony, their feet pounding the asphalt at exactly the same time.

Don looked like he wanted to say something about that, but then he glanced back at Beth's dad and clamped his mouth shut.

"Let's go," Commander Wilde said, pointing to his Humvee. It was the one they'd seen when they arrived.

The five of them piled in. Ashley took the front seat to make room for her bulky suit, while Beth and Don each sat by the back doors, leaving her dad to perch on the flat-topped storage compartment running between their seats.

Don looked to be sweating through his shirt. His eyes were wide and darting. He laid his head back and gasped, squeezing them shut. "Fuck, not now..." he muttered.

"Are you okay?" Beth asked.

He shook his head quickly, his skin pale and waxy.

"What's wrong with him?" Beth asked, her eyes flicking to Ashley.

The doctor twisted around as best she could. "Don?" she asked. "Don! Look at me. What's going on?"

"I can't..."

"Just breathe, okay? Deep, slow breaths."

"What's wrong with him?" Beth asked.

"He's having a panic attack," Commander Wilde said, and Ashley nodded inside her suit.

"Great timing," Beth said.

"He can't help it," Ashley replied.

"Harden up, son!" Commander Wilde said.

"Yes... sir," Don replied through clenched teeth. The glazed look in his eyes passed, and some of the color returned to his cheeks.

"Rolling out," Commander Wilde said as he started the engine. Beth heard another Humvee rumbling along behind them and saw a third one flash its lights at them through Don's window—the vehicle didn't have a rear window. Beth noticed the third Humvee hanging back, giving them space. Commander Wilde reversed out and then accelerated after the lead vehicle.

Minutes later, they were rolling down the streets of Koloa at forty miles per hour, pinned front and back between their escort.

Apprehension constricted Beth's throat. How were they going to get out of this? "Guys..." she began but trailed off when she saw her dad staring curiously at her.

"Yes, Bethy?" he prompted.

"Let's not distract the driver with conversation right now," Don interrupted. "Wait until we're out on the highway."

"Okay," Beth replied in a small voice.

They passed the next ten minutes in silence. The town of Koloa fell away, replaced by the dense foliage of the three-lane highway between Koloa and Lihue.

Don stretched his arms...

And grabbed her dad in a choke hold. Bill's feet began kicking and strangled noises spluttered from his lips as his face turned red.

"You're killing him!" Beth cried.

Don shook his head. "He's fine."

"Let him go!" she screamed.

Bill struggled to pry Don's arm away. When that failed he swiped blindly at Don's face. Beth grabbed Don's arm, trying to help Bill break free.

"Stop it!" Don said.

"Beth, he's trying to knock your dad out," Wilde added.

Beth withdrew, biting her lip, and watched miserably as her dad's struggles became progressively weaker and more desperate. Ashley watched them with wide eyes.

"Ash, tell me you packed some kind of

sedative in that bag of tricks!" Don said.

"Give me a minute..."

Wilde's eyes flicked up periodically to watch them in the rear-view mirror, but he said nothing else. Bill's eyes rolled up in his head, and he batted lazily at Don's arm one last time before going limp.

Horror stabbed through Beth once more as she watched Don check her dad's pulse with two fingers on his neck.

After a few seconds, he nodded. "He's good, but he could wake up any second."

"Here!" Ashley passed a needle to him loaded with clear fluid and capped with a blue lid.

Don pulled the lid off with his teeth and stuck the needle into her dad's thigh, depressing the plunger with his thumb.

"How long will this give us?" Don asked.

"Four to six hours," Ashley said.

"Good enough."

"For what?" Commander Wilde asked. "I'm assuming you have a plan."

Beth looked from the commander to Don. Apparently she wasn't the only one in the dark.

"The same plan you had when you insisted we all ride together," Don replied. He pointed up to a circular hatch in the ceiling. "That's a Ma Deuce you have on the roof. And neither of the corporal's vehicles have one."

"If we open fire on our own men, they'll have all the right and reason to hunt us down, dead or alive."

"And if we don't, we're dead anyway. In case you haven't noticed, we're being led off to the slaughter."

"Maybe not," Wilde said. "Maybe they really do just want to run some tests on us."

Don glared at the back of Wilde's head. "You don't really believe that. You saw the blood samples. They're the ones infected—not us. And even if it were us, the CDC would have been knocking on your door—not an insubordinate, trigger-happy corporal who thinks he can give orders to a superior officer. You and I both know what that smells like, and we need to ditch them before we're up to our necks in it."

"You have a secure location we can head for?" Commander Wilde asked.

"Yes, sir," Don replied.

Wilde let out a shaky breath. "All right, soldier. Light 'em up."

CHAPTER 50

Don opened the hatch, jumped up, and swiveled the gun around to face the back. Metallic thunder chugged out from the weapon, and sparks kicked off the hood of the Humvee as Don riddled it with holes. The driver immediately began to swerve out of the way, and Don's aim drifted down to the front tires. One of them exploded, and shreds of rubber flew out. Sparks leapt from the naked rim as it kissed the road, and then the Humvee swerved off into the long grass on the side of the road.

"One down!" Don yelled as he ratcheted the turret back around. His ears were ringing.

"Heads down!" Wilde called out from below.

Don caught sunlight winking off the scope of a rifle as it popped out the passenger's side window of the lead vehicle. The Humvee was armored from the back, so the only sure way to stop it was to aim for the rear wheels, and even those were going to be hard to hit.

Don pressed down on the butterfly-switch trigger with both thumbs just as the rifle aiming at him began rattling out rounds—but it wasn't aimed at him. Screams sounded from below, and Don thought he heard glass shattering. Then he scored a lucky hit on a tire. It exploded with a *bang*, and the remaining tires squealed as the driver swerved, trying to correct. That gave him a momentary view of the other rear wheel, and he blew it out with another *bang.* The Humvee came up fast, losing speed, and Wilde swerved around it. Don gave them a passing volley through their windows and saw blood splatter the inside of the vehicle. *Jackpot.*

He fell back into his seat just as the commander accelerated to put distance between them.

"Clear," Don said. "What's our status?"

The roar of weapons fire still echoed in his ears.

"Doctor Carter's hit!" Commander Wilde said.

"Shit. Ash, can you hear me?"

"I... I can't breathe."

Don leaned over Bill to peek around the front seat. Ashley's suit was slick with blood and covered in shattered glass. Wind gusted in through the broken windshield, making it hard to see without blinking constantly. "Where are you hit?" he asked.

"Between the ribs... upper right side," Ashley said between gasps.

"We have to get your suit off," Don said. "How do we... shit," he cast about for something he could use. Unable to find anything he settled for pressing his hands against the bubbling wound in Ashley's side. With her suit in the way, that did nothing to staunch the flow of blood. "She's going to bleed out. We have to pull over somewhere."

"If I pull over, we're dead," Wilde replied. He passed a bayonet to Don. "Cut the suit off."

Don grabbed the knife in a bloody hand and folded out the first blade he could find. He made short work of the rubbery material, as well as Ashley's clothes underneath. A grisly hole appeared just below her right breast.

"I need bandages, gauze, something!" Don said.

"In the bag," Ashley said, gasping as she pointed to the black case at her feet. Don's eyes flicked up to Beth, who was peering around the other side of the front seat. "Can you reach the wound?"

"I-I think so," she replied.

"Good. Put pressure on it."

Beth reached out tentatively.

He grabbed her hand with one of his. "Here, where my hands are. Hard as you can." Once her hands had taken over for his, Don strained to reach Ashley's bag, yanked it up, and dropped it on her lap. He zipped it open and began pulling out bandages and gauze.

"I need directions, Don," Wilde interrupted.

Don looked up briefly. "Stay straight until you see a dirt road appear on your left."

"Got it."

To Beth, Don said, "Lean her forward. I need to check for an exit wound."

Beth pushed Ashley forward until her forehead was bouncing on the dash, and Don cut more of her suit away at the back, revealing a huge, golf-ball-sized hole. "Clean shot. That's good," he said. "Just missed your spine, though." He began wadding up gauze and wrapping it with compression bandages around Ashley's chest to cover the exit wound.

"She's losing too much blood!" Beth said. She struggled to keep her hands on the entry wound.

"Just hang on a second," Don replied.

"Dirt road up ahead," Wilde interrupted. "That it?"

Don muttered a curse as he glanced up. "Yes! Take it!"

Wilde hit the brakes, and both Don and Beth lurched forward. Don had to hook his legs to avoid flying out the broken windshield. Then came the turn and both of them were thrown to the side. Beth knocked her head on the window, and Ashley flopped around like a rag doll. Adding injury, a huge bump knocked their heads into the ceiling as they joined the dirt road.

"Make her sit up straight!" Don said.

Beth pulled back on Ashley's shoulders. Her head lolled inside the suit.

"Shit. She's lost consciousness," Don said. "Probably a sucking chest wound."

"A what?" Beth asked.

"It means her lung collapsed! Just keep pressure on the wound!"

Don cut a square of material from Ashley's suit, then brushed Beth's hands away and began taping it over the entry wound. He saw the plastic sucking into the hole, then pushing back out with a river of blood as Ashley exhaled.

"Shit. This isn't going to work."

"Do the best you can," Wilde said. "I've got a fork in the road. Which way?"

Don looked up. "Right! Go right!" He pawed through Ashley's bag again. "Damn it! Tell me you packed one, Ash..."

"One what?" Beth asked.

"Found it." Don withdrew the glinting tip of a large bore needle with a green plastic fitting on the back. He turned and stabbed the needle between

Ashley's ribs. Air whistled out. "Good." He let out a breath. "You can do it, Ash," he said in a shaky voice as he wrapped a compression bandage around one hand. Ripping off the taped square of plastic he'd placed over the entry wound with his other hand, he replaced it with a thick layer of gauze. "Hold it there," he told Beth. She placed a shaking hand over it. "Apply pressure, damn it!"

Beth did, and the gauze turned red.

"Good. Now, push her forward."

As she did so, Don began wrapping the compression bandage around Ashley's chest, the same as he'd done with the exit wound. By the time he finished, two lines of bandages crisscrossed Ashley's chest.

Don withdrew and wiped the sweat from his brow. "That's all I can do for now. The rest is up to her."

Don sat back down with his head pounding in time to his pulse.

"Where are we going?" Wilde asked.

"My place. It's off the grid, about ten miles from here. In the mountains."

Commander Wilde shook his head. "At this speed that'll take us at least twenty minutes." He glanced at Ashley but said nothing. They both knew she was going to need a miracle to survive this.

The Humvee skipped through a pothole, and Don knocked his head against the roof. He winced and hauled his seatbelt out to prevent an encore.

"They're going to send choppers as soon as they realize what happened," the commander said.

"Let's hope the blackout took out their comms."

"Wouldn't bet on it. They'll have radios in their vehicles," Wilde said, "and the receiving stations at the CDC and Barking Sands have backup generators."

"Yeah..." Don replied, peering up through the open hatch as they skipped through another pothole. He was half surprised not to see a helicopter already hovering over them.

CHAPTER 51

When his cabin came peeking through the trees, Don could hardly believe it. There was no sign of pursuit. By some miracle, they'd made it. Had he killed all four Marines? If so, that might explain it.

Commander Wilde pulled to a stop in front of the cabin and Don said, "This is it. Everybody out." He opened his door and jumped down. Commander Wilde was close behind him. "I'm going to need your help with Ashley," Don said.

"Count on it," Wilde replied.

They ran to the passenger's side and hauled Ashley out together. She stirred and groaned as they did so. A good sign. It meant she was still alive and at least semi-conscious. "Let's get her inside," Don said.

Wilde nodded.

"What about Bill?" Beth asked as she jumped out.

Don glanced at her. "We'll deal with him in a

minute."

They pushed through the front entrance of the cabin into a messy living area. "Beth! Clear the table!" Don said as they approached an old wooden dining table. She did as asked, picking dirty plates and half-empty glasses off. Don spared an arm to help and swept the remaining items off onto the floor with a crash and clatter. The table was barely big enough for Ashley, but it would have to do for now. Don stared at her, blinking sweat and breathing hard.

"I need equipment," Wilde said. "I don't suppose you have a bag of saline?"

He nodded. "I do."

"Get it!"

Don nodded and took off at a run, heading for one of the storage rooms at the back.

As he went, he heard banging on the hatch to the basement. *I guess someone's awake.*

"What's that?" Beth asked, running into the storage room behind him.

Grabbing an IV bag full of saline, Don glanced at her and shook his head. "That's Nana."

* * *

"You have your grandmother locked in the basement?" Beth asked as she chased him back to the dining room.

Don hurriedly passed items to the commander.

"I wasn't going to let her run around free once I realized what she was."

Commander Wilde hung the IV bag from a nearby curtain rod while Don fitted the catheter to Ashley's wrist.

"Get her helmet off," the commander said.

Don hurried to do so.

Beth waited in silence, watching as they worked. Realizing now wasn't the time for questions, she bit her tongue and spent the time checking her surroundings. Don's place was a simple wooden cabin, dark and dirty inside, surrounded by trees. It wasn't even on the road. They'd left the dirt road and driven down what looked like a trail for horses for another five minutes just to get here. Wondering if Don had power, Beth flicked a nearby light switch. Nothing happened. She frowned, and her thoughts went back out the open door to her dad, lying in the back of the Humvee, unconscious and abandoned.

Beth went to check on him. Dead leaves crunched underfoot. Birds chirped and sang from the trees. Bugs hummed and buzzed. Chickens clucked.

Bill lay half on, half off the storage compartment between the back seats. His legs dangled off the edge and his arms were folded up at an awkward angle. Just then he gave a big sigh in his sleep. At least he was alive. She thought about Don's grandmother, locked in the basement like an animal. Was that what Don had planned for her dad?

There had to be a cure. If radiation killed the alien cells, then surely it would be a simple matter to fix them. That CT scan had done *something* to him. Maybe if they could get her dad to one of those scanners...

But they were fugitives now. They'd fired on Marines and killed at least one—or Don had, anyway. But more to the point, everyone on the island was probably infected by now. There was nowhere they could go that would be safe.

Beth crawled into the back of the Humvee and laid her head on her dad's hip, waiting for Don or Commander Wilde to come out and get them.

She dozed off while waiting and dreamed she lay in bed at the Koa Kai with Toby's arm draped over her, and her dad safely distracted downstairs while he managed new arrivals. Toby smiled sleepily at her. "Hey." It was a real memory, not just a dream, but even in her sleep Beth's chest ached to remember him.

Beth awoke to the sound of thunder. She sat up and rubbed her eyes. It was dark outside, the ground scarcely lit with moonlight. How long had she slept? She twisted around to look at her dad, but he was still sedated. *It can't have been that long, then...*

More thunder sounded, booming endlessly in the distance amidst the roar of airplanes. *Airplanes?* Beth frowned. That wasn't thunder.

Don and Wilde ran out and stared up at the sky. Beth climbed out of the truck to join them in time to see a pair of jet fighters scream by at a low altitude, making the ground tremble. A second later, two missiles streaked after them, and then another fighter appeared, giving chase.

An explosion illuminated the sky and pounded Beth's eardrums, silhouetting the trees with fire. Beth cringed, holding her ears, and ducking low to the ground. "What's happening?" she asked. "Is it the Crawlers?"

Don turned to her with big black eyes and shook his head. "No, it's just us humans."

CHAPTER 52

"Let's get him inside," Don said and pointed to Bill.

Beth helped them pull him out of the truck and carry him into the cabin. She noted that lanterns hung from the ceiling, illuminating the cabin in strategic places.

"Lay him out on the sofa," Don said.

"What if he wakes up?" Beth asked as her dad stirred and hugged a couch cushion.

"You could hit him on the head with something..." Don suggested.

"Are you crazy?" Beth replied.

"There are more sedatives in Doctor Carter's bag," Don said. "Why don't you go out and get it for us?"

"It's raining hellfire out there, and you're sending her?" Commander Wilde asked.

"They're not going to waste a missile on her. Besides, you and I have more important things to do. I've got a two-way radio out back. We need to see if we can pick up something on the emergency bands."

The commander gave in with a grudging nod. "Lead the way."

Beth ran back to the Humvee and retrieved Ashley's bag. It was heavy, but she'd manage. Surfboards weren't exactly made of feathers.

Explosions still boomed distantly, accompanied by the occasional flash of light. Just as she headed inside, a trio of missiles arced above the tree line. One of them exploded in mid-air, blooming like fireworks.

Beth hurried back inside the cabin. She made sure to shut and lock the door behind her—not that it would offer much protection. Hearing muffled curses from the others, Beth set Ashley's bag down by the door and ran toward the sound of the voices. She emerged in a stuffy room with a desk and stacks of equipment. Loud static crackled from speakers somewhere in the room.

"They're jamming all the bands," Don said while turning a dial.

"Who is?" Beth asked from the doorway. "You have power?"

Commander Wilde and Don both turned to her with grim looks in the silvery glow of an LED lamp.

"Battery-backup," Don explained. "Won't last

long with the generator off, though. And as to *who*, that's anyone's guess, but I'd say the Chinese."

"A good guess," Wilde added. "They've been posturing and making threats for months."

"They have?" Beth had made a point to avoid watching the news or talking about any of it. Sticking her head in the sand might not have been the smartest move, but it had kept her sane.

"They're going to break the quarantine for us if they make landfall," Commander Wilde said.

"And play right into the Crawlers hands—or claws," Don added. "At least it's going to take the heat off us, and I've got enough supplies to last a few months."

Beth cast about. "Where?" The cabin didn't seem big enough to store three months' worth of anything.

"In the basement," Don explained.

"With your infected grandmother?" Commander Wilde asked with arching eyebrows.

"There's an outdoor entrance, and the supplies are locked up out of her reach."

"You have an armory?" Beth asked.

Wilde let out a breath and ran a hand back through his crew cut gray hair. "At least there's that. What have you got?"

"Everything you could need and more," Don replied.

"Show me," Wilde replied.

Don switched off his equipment, then grabbed the lantern off the desk and stood up. He and Wilde brushed by Beth in the doorway. She followed them to a rickety wooden door at the back of the cabin.

"Not exactly a defensible position," the commander remarked, and Beth had to agree. That door wouldn't stop a determined squirrel.

"It's meant to be safe because it's hidden," Don replied. He walked around the side of the cabin to a particular spot, then bent down and cleared away a mess of dried leaves. A rusty metal hatch appeared with a loop of steel for a handle. He hauled up, and the hatch opened with a screech of rusty hinges.

"It's not even locked," Wilde said.

"It locks from the inside," Don replied. "The storage area doubles as my panic room. It wouldn't be smart for me to lock myself out."

"I suppose not," Wilde replied.

Don led the way down a metal staircase, his lamp illuminating a bare, musty-smelling concrete basement. Metal shelves full of canned food, bottles of water, and various other types of supplies lined the floor.

Weaving a path through the shelving units, Don took them to a metal rack on the far wall covered with rifles and handguns. A standing metal tool case below that housed boxes of bullets.

"What do you think?" Don asked.

Commander Wilde grabbed a rifle off the rack and stared at it as if it were made of gold. "That's a full auto M16! How did you get your hands on that? Fully automatic rifles are illegal in the state of Hawaii."

Don tapped his head and winked. "Dark Net's good for something after all."

"You realize that's another crime," the commander replied.

Don grabbed a matching rifle off the rack and armed it with a smooth pull on a handle near the back. "You can arrest me for it later."

Beth snorted. A loud clanging sound made her flinch and drew her eyes to a metal door beside the gun rack.

"Donald! Let me out!"

"Is that..." Beth trailed off.

Don placed a finger to his lips and shook his head.

"I can hear you talking in there! Let me out of here, right now!"

"No can do, Nana," Donald replied.

The voice on the other side broke down sobbing, and Beth felt a sudden pang of sympathy for the old woman. "Maybe you should let her out.

How do you even know she's infected?"

"I just know, okay? I caught her trying to contaminate my coffee—among other things."

Beth frowned, and Wilde gawked at him. "Contaminate?"

"She spat in it!"

Commander Wilde smirked. "Maybe she just doesn't like you."

"That's not all. When I asked her to help me with my experiments, she refused."

"That's hardly proof," the commander replied. "What about clinical evidence? What you and Doctor Carter showed me was conclusive. You find anything like that with her?"

"Of course! I didn't just test the damn chickens. And remember, she was the one who infected them in the first place."

"Then she stays put," Wilde replied.

"But we can cure them right?" Beth asked.

Don and the commander both looked at her.

"Radiation. That's the cure. All we have to do is irradiate them, right?"

"You have an x-ray machine in your pocket that I don't know about?" Don asked.

"No, but..."

"Then it's not that simple," Don replied. "Those machines are all in medical clinics and hospitals—and the quarantine center, but that's a non-starter."

"But my dad..."

"Will have to bunk with Nana. Besides, in case you haven't noticed, there's a war going on out there. We're not going anywhere until it's over, and maybe not even then. Sorry, kid, but your dad and my Nana are not the priority right now."

Beth planted her hands on her hips. "So we're just going to sit around here while they claw their nails out on the walls of your dungeon?"

"You got it," Don said.

Commander Wilde shook his head. "We can't do that. We have to tell someone what we know."

"Who are you going to tell?" Don asked. "The radio doesn't work, power's out all across the island, and something tells me the Chinese will shoot us on sight—not to mention our own people, who will probably do the same."

"Everyone is distracted right now. We might have a chance to get away," Commander Wilde said. "If we wait until the Chinese take the island, it will be too late."

Beth slowly shook her head. "What makes you think they'll win?"

"Our fleets are spread out across two oceans, while theirs is focused on one—and they had the element of surprise because they attacked first. You can bet they made that count." Wilde shook his head. "We'll be lucky if we last the night. And when our lines fall, so does the quarantine. If the world doesn't know what's happening here before then, it will be too late to stop the spread of whatever the Crawlers infected us with. We can't just stay here and let that happen."

"What about Ashley?" Beth asked.

"Beth's right," Don said. "Ash is in no shape to leave. We should at least stay until she's stable." He grabbed a handgun off the wall. Pulling back on the slide to check the weapon, he handed it to Beth. She took it with shaking hands. "Careful, it's loaded."

"Wha-what am I supposed to do with this?" Beth asked, staring at the weapon with wide eyes.

"In case you need to defend yourself," Don explained while grabbing spare magazines from a drawer in the tool chest.

Beth was busy trying to figure out how to hold her gun when Commander Wilde reached over to help her. "Always aim it at the ground when you're not using the weapon, and keep your fingers clear of the trigger. Wrap them outside the trigger guard." He tapped the loop of metal around the trigger. "When you want to shoot—" He turned the weapon slightly to show her a little metal lever on the side of the gun. "—you have to disengage the safety first. Flick it up with your thumb." He illustrated the process for her. "Flick it down again, and it blocks the trigger. Got it?"

Beth nodded.

"Good. When you want to shoot, use both hands to steady the weapon. Hold it out directly in front of you, dead center of your target, and aim by looking down the sights to the tip of the muzzle." He tapped a little metal flange at the end of the gun.

"Got it... how do I reload?"

"You've got fifteen rounds. You can keep pulling the trigger until you've used them all. Hopefully, you won't need to reload, but..." He trailed off, hunting through the tool chest. "Here's a spare mag." The commander handed her a rectangular black container with shiny golden bullets peeking out at the top. "Put that in your pocket."

Beth did so. Looking around for Don, she found him hunting around on one of the shelves in the storage room. "Now what?"

"Now, we tie up your father and see if we can get some answers out of him," Don said, holding up a packet of zip ties and a set of jumper cables.

"What are those for...?" Beth asked in fading voice.

"You'll see," Don replied.

CHAPTER 53

—Half an Hour Ago—

Commander Morris stood beside the captain in the CIC, peering over the SONAR operator's shoulder.

"Their subs are everywhere," Morris said.

"Yes they are, Commander," Captain Reed replied. His hand twitched beside his sidearm. He'd taken to wearing one ever since the Chinese Fleet had shown up making demands to have access to the alien technology and the creatures housed at Barking Sands. Every now and then Morris was tempted to get a pistol of his own, but then he chided himself for being paranoid, and subsequently wondered about the captain's own paranoia. Captain Reed was usually a level-headed man, and like Morris he should have known that world powers like China and the US wouldn't go to war over the handling of the alien assets, especially not when those aliens were likely still in orbit somewhere. No, China would posture and threaten, and apply pressure until some kind of international sharing agreement was established. But that was the politicians' job. Old ship drivers like Morris just had to hold the line without blinking while they played their games. Wearing a sidearm to ward off the possible threat of Chinese boarders felt too much like blinking to him.

"Don't they realize the island is under quarantine?" Morris asked. "We'd have to break it to give them what they want."

"I doubt they care about that, Commander. It's been three months, and not a single case of infection has been reported by our media. And for all we know they have their own agents on the inside reporting the same. No, they've almost certainly concluded by now that the quarantine zone is an excuse to give us exclusive access to alien tech."

"An elaborate excuse, sir. They're obviously not thinking clearly."

"People in a crisis rarely do, but perhaps we should do something to help clear their heads. Lieutenant Nielson—"

Captain Reed strode through the CIC to reach Nielson's station. Commander Morris followed with a furrowed brow. Nielson was the gunnery officer in charge of the *Port Royal's* various weapon control systems.

"Sir?" Nielson asked.

"Arm a mark 46, and pick a target."

"Yes, sir," Nielson replied.

Adrenaline shot through Morris like fire, but everyone else in the CIC went on as if nothing were amiss.

"Captain!" Morris exploded. "You can't open fire on them! We haven't been authorized to—"

"I just authorized us, Commander." Captain Reed drew his sidearm and aimed it casually at Morris's chest.

Morris blinked and shook his head. "What are you doing? Have you lost your mind?!" Morris shook his head numbly. "You're going to start a war!"

"That's the idea."

A bang sounded and a bullet tore through Morris's gut like fire. Scarcely able to believe it, he clapped a hand to his stomach to check. It came away bloody. "You shot me?" This couldn't be real.

"I'm sorry, Morris. You're not one of us," Captain Reed said, and slowly shook his head.

None of the other officers even bothered to look up from their stations.

Except for Lieutenant Nielson. "Torpedo armed, sir," he said.

Captain Reed smiled, and Commander Morris

stumbled back a step, shaking his head in disbelief. Pain wracked his gut, making his legs weak.

"Fire," Reed said, and then he pulled the trigger again, and Morris's confusion ended with a singular moment of stunning clarity.

* * *

"Fuck, it's like the fourth of July out here!" Private Dekker said, yelling to be heard over the sound of the air raid sirens.

Corporal Gibson cast about the darkened complex of the Pacific Missile Range Facility. The water gleamed darkly, alternately lit by fire and the moon. Just offshore the flaming ruins of the *USS O'Kane* slowly sank. Not far from it, the *Port Royal* also burned, but it went down fighting, steadily belching missiles into the sky. Fighter jets roared as they chased each other through the night, tracer rounds stitching bright lines across the clouds.

"We need to find cover!" Private Clarke said.

Corporal Gibson glanced back at the main bunker they guarded. The Crawlers were inside, locked in makeshift cells. They'd be safer inside, but they'd been assigned to guard the entrance. They couldn't just abandon their posts....

"We hold here and wait for further orders," Gibson said.

"But—"

Jasper T. Scott

"End of discussion!" Gibson snapped.

"Well, shit," Dekker said.

A few minutes later a Humvee came roaring down the access road in front of them. Tires skidded as it slammed on the brakes.

All four doors flew open, and a team of Marines came jogging out. Gibson straightened as they approached.

"Corporal!" one of them said.

Gibson couldn't see anyone's rank, so he came to attention and said, "Sir!"

"Don't you sir me, I work for a living."

Gibson smiled crookedly as he recognized the voice. "It's good to see you, Sergeant Colton. What are our orders?"

"Stand down. We've got the bunker. Subjects are to be released."

"What? But they're—"

"I'm not asking, Corporal. We've got Chinko landers inbound, and this facility appears to be their target."

"What about the landers?"

"Let 'em have 'em! If we couldn't learn jack in three months, then they won't either. It's the Crawlers they might get something out of, and we're not going to make that easy for them, are we, Corporal?"

"No, sir?"

"Good. Then I suggest you clear out before you become the Crawlers' first meal."

"Copy..." Gibson cast about. "Where to?"

"To hell for all I care! Get a vehicle and get to the harbor. Orders are to fall back and pull up stakes."

"That can't be right. We have to fight!"

"Negative. We've lost this one, Corporal. Fight another day." Sergeant Colton patted him on the shoulder as he said it. "Now move aside!"

Gibson stepped away from the doors without further complaint and watched blankly as the sergeant and his team ran in.

"Gibs, let's move!" Dekker prompted.

A cracking-roar followed by an explosion thundered overhead, and he snapped out of it. His head jerked up to see the flaming bits of a fighter jet raining down.

"We need a ride!" Gibson said and sprinted around the side of the main building. The parking lot lay dead ahead, with half a dozen Humvees and transport trucks waiting in the moonlight. They must have closed to within thirty feet of the nearest vehicle when a familiar roar drew Gibson's gaze to the sky. Two dark, jagged shapes were swooping down on the base from above. A split second later, Gibson heard the telltale *hiss* of missiles streaking down.

"Incoming!" Gibson threw himself to the ground just before a massive explosion tore through the parking lot. Glass shattered, and heavy trucks rolled like bowling pins. An intense wave of heat washed over Gibson with violent force, sending white-hot shards of shrapnel biting into his hands and arms. The shock-wave passed, leaving Gibson's ears numb and ringing. He looked up to see the parking lot on fire. Not a single vehicle was left for them to use.

"Shit, change of plans," Gibson said, but he could barely hear his own voice. He got up and twisted around to check on his men—

Dekker stared back at him, bleeding from a cut on his cheek, but otherwise fine. Clarke and Kelly lay face down on the concrete. "Team, report status!" Gibson bellowed.

They didn't stir. Gibson jumped to his feet and ran to Clarke's side. He rolled the man over and saw dull staring eyes. "Clarke!" No response. "Dave!" Gibson tried using his first name, choking back tears. "Damn it!"

Dekker dropped down beside Kelly and checked him, but he was an easy call. A piece of glass the length of Gibson's foot stuck out from the side of Kelly's head.

"Fuck! Now what?" Dekker asked.

"Back to the main entrance!" Gibson said.

"We'll pack in with the sergeant."

They got up and ran. A sharp pain exploded in Gibson's calf, but he ignored it. Taking inventory of scrapes and bruises could wait. He'd just lost two men. Two *brothers.* The pain was good. It helped him focus.

When they came back to the entrance of the main bunker, they found the doors hanging open, and the ground slick with a trail of blood. A dark shape lay slumped just beyond that.

"What the fu..." Dekker trailed off.

Gibson tightened his grip on his rifle and yanked it up to his shoulder. "NVG down!" he said, switching to a one-handed grip to yank down the monocular night vision goggles clipped to his helmet. As soon as he did that, the shiny red thermal overlay of a four-legged monster appeared, watching them from the bushes beside the entrance.

"Contact, twelve o'clock!" Gibson said and squeezed the trigger. Just as he did so, the Crawler darted out of sight. "Dekker, on me!"

"Wait—" Gibson felt a hand haul him back. "Let it go, Corporal. We need to get out while we can."

Gibson wheeled around. "Lay hands on me again and I'll break them off, Private. You got rocks in your head? We're in combat. You follow *my* lead."

"Copy that," Dekker replied in a small voice.

Looking around for the sergeant's vehicle, Gibson couldn't find it. "Looks like they evac'ed, already."

"We could use one of the pods."

Gibson arched an eyebrow at him. "That's not going to improve our position, Deks." The engineers had figured out how to activate the landers less than a week ago, but no one knew where they were programmed to go. Best guess was back to the mothership—if it was still around. They'd been about to send up a probe up to find out when all of this shit had rained down. Shaking his head, Gibson went on, "Best case we'd be up there on their ship, surrounded by millions of Crawlers. Worst, we'd be drifting through space on autopilot."

"But what if we could sabotage their ship?" Dekker asked. "We're dead anyway. What have we got to lose? We should go out guns blazing. For Clarke and Kelly."

Gibson ground his teeth, scanning the night for any sign of more Crawlers creeping up on them— or Chinese marines, for that matter. So far he couldn't see either, but the battle still raged with distant peals of thunder. "Fuck it," he said, giving in with a nod. "I guess it's worth a shot."

"Oorah!" Dekker cheered. "Let's go!"

"Hold up. Let's hit the armory and switch up our loadouts first. We're gonna need some heavy firepower if we do make it to Grand Central Crawler."

"Right, yeah. Good point..." Dekker said slowly.

Gibson frowned at his sudden lack of enthusiasm. Dekker was usually the first one on board when it came to blowing stuff up. "On me and watch our six. We're goin' in."

"Copy," Dekker replied.

CHAPTER 54

"Wake up!" Don yelled, slapping Bill's cheek repeatedly to rouse him.

Beth watched with a wary frown. "Why don't you interrogate your grandmother?"

"Because she's too old to take much of a beating," Don replied.

"I'm not going to let you torture him," Beth said.

"It's not your dad anymore, kid. Anyway, don't worry, we won't leave any permanent damage."

Bill's eyes cracked open, and his head lolled. He sat on the living room floor leaning against one of the couches. "Where..." He glanced around and appeared to work some moisture into his mouth. "Where am I?"

"My place," Don replied. He snapped his fingers at Commander Wilde, and the commander brought over the car battery and jumper cables they'd carried up from the storage room. "Get his shirt open."

Beth's palms grew sweaty. "Did you hear me? I said I'm not going to let you torture him."

"You don't have to be around for this," Don replied. The commander set the car battery down beside him and handed him the cables.

Beth looked to Wilde, her eyes pleading. "You're a doctor. You have to take an oath, right? Do no harm or something like that. You can't be okay with this."

Commander Wilde grimaced and shook his head. "I'm also a Marine, and I'm sorry, but Don is right. We need to know what's going on. You can step outside if you can't stand to watch."

Bill's eyes were wide and darting now. "What's going on? Why would you want to torture me?" He struggled to free his hands, but they were secured behind his back with three zip ties. His ankles were similarly bound. But he could still move his legs.

Don hooked up the jumper cables and sparked the ends together. "Where should we start? Earlobes, or nipples? you pick, Bill."

"Fuck off!" Bill kicked both legs up, aiming for Don's face, but Don caught them and forced them down by sitting on his ankles.

"Get his shirt open," Don said.

Commander Wilde stepped forward and

ripped open the shirt. Bill tried to bite him, but Don touched the sparking ends of the jumper cables to either side of his face, and he screamed.

Blackened scorch marks appeared on Bill's cheeks.

"Stop it!" Beth yelled.

"That was just a taste," Don whispered darkly.

"What is *wrong* with you?" Bill asked, shaking his head. "First you strangle me, and now you're going to electrocute me?" His eyes flicked to Beth. "Bethy, it's me, Dad! Don't let them do this. *Please.*"

She bit her lip and shook her head. "There has to be another way," she said, catching Commander Wilde's eye from where he stood behind her dad.

"I don't think there is," he replied.

"You're not Bill," Don said and sparked the jumper cables together once more. "So who are you?"

"What makes you think I'm not Bill? Ask me anything!"

Don turned to Beth with eyebrows raised. "Go ahead. Something only he could know."

"Uh..." Beth cast her mind back. "What was my favorite stuffed animal as a kid?"

"Elle, the Elephant," Bill said. "But it was actually Dumbo. We got him for you at Disneyland."

"That's right!" Beth said.

"Ask me something else," Bill prompted.

"Okay, what's mom's favorite restaurant?"

"La Strega, an Italian place back in LA."

Beth frowned and slowly shook her head.

"Is that true?" Don asked.

"Yes, but... that doesn't make any sense. Maybe we made a mistake. Maybe he really isn't under the influence of anything."

Bill's lips curved into a smug smile. "I told you."

"Look at him!" Don said. "He's screwing with us." He touched both ends of the jumper cables to either side of her dad's chest. Bill screamed and all of his muscles spasmed at the same time. Tendrils of smoke curled off his skin, and sickening burnt smell reached Beth's nose.

"Stop it!" Beth said and ran over to Don. She pulled him back as hard as she could, knocking him over. The cables touched him in the process, and he yelped.

Bill laughed. "Exhilarating, isn't it?"

Don lay glaring at him. "Does he *seem* normal to you?"

"No," Beth said. "But we're not going to get anything out of him like this. And he might not even know anything."

"She might be right," the commander said.

Ashley groaned, drawing their attention to the

dining room table where they'd left her. All three of them hurried to her side. Ashley's blue eyes cracked open to sleepy slits.

"What's going on?" she asked.

"They're torturing my dad," Beth said.

Ashley's eyebrows scrunched together. "What? Why?"

"We need to figure out what the aliens are up to," Don explained.

"Torture doesn't work. Don't you idiots know anything?"

Bill laughed. "Apparently not."

"In certain cases it does," Commander Wilde said.

"No, it doesn't," Ashley insisted, rocking her head from side to side.

"We could do passive torture," Don suggested. "Don't give him any food or water until he talks."

Beth scowled. "And what if he doesn't know anything?"

"Let's forget about it for now," Commander Wilde said. "Our priority is to get the word out about what we're dealing with, and we're not going to be able to do that from here. Ashley's awake. She's stable enough that we can leave her here with Beth."

Don nodded slowly. "You're right. We'll be back with help as soon as we can."

"Sure..." Ashley said.

Commander Wilde grabbed Beth's sidearm from the kitchen counter and handed it back to her. "If your dad tries anything, don't be afraid to use it. And whatever you do, don't cut him free."

Beth swallowed thickly and nodded, feeling the cold weight of the weapon against her palm. Both men headed front door. Along the way Don grabbed the car battery and disconnected the jumper cables. He stuffed the cables in his back pocket and went to join the commander. They grabbed their rifles and a lantern from an armchair near the door and then Don opened it.

"Wait," Bill said just as Don stepped outside. "I'll talk."

Beth frowned, and Commander Wilde shot her father a skeptical look.

"He's stalling," Don said from the front step of the cabin. "He doesn't want us to go out and tell anyone about the infection."

"Maybe," Bill replied. "But you want answers, right? And what are you going to tell people, anyway? Your story would be more convincing if you had something significant to say."

"All right, I'll bite," Don said, bringing his rifle up to aim it at Bill as he stepped back inside and shut the door behind him. "But you had better make it good."

CHAPTER 55

"Everyone who is infected is part of a plan," Bill said smilingly.

Beth could hardly believe what she was hearing. "Who are you?" Holding her gun in both hands, she flicked off the safety, and pointed it at his chest. "What did you do to my dad?" she demanded.

"He is still here, but he cannot speak to you as long as I am in control."

"Then let him go!" Beth said and shook the weapon at him. "Let him go, or I'll shoot!"

Bill cocked his head. "And kill your father?"

Don walked over to her and gently pushed the weapon out of line. "Don't," he said. To Bill, he added, "You said the infected ones are part of a plan—what plan?"

"We have no weapons. This was the only way to take your planet."

"No weapons?" Don snorted. "I don't buy that for a second."

"Me neither," Beth added.

"It is true," Bill insisted. "We never needed weapons before. It is not our way. Direct conflict is too messy."

"We *who?*" Commander Wilde asked. "The Crawlers?"

"We, the ones aboard the vessel you saw in the sky," Bill said. "It is a colony ship. Your planet is the only one within many light years that is capable of supporting us. We have come a long way. We didn't expect to find your world already inhabited, much less by an intelligent species."

Don began nodding slowly. "So you found Earth from afar with some kind of telescope, and you thought, that looks nice! Let's go there! So why infect us? Why not just tell us all of this from the start? We could have made a space for you and shared the planet."

"How would we communicate? The only way I am able to speak with you now is because I am sharing the mind of the human you know as Bill Steele. That is also how I know that your people would never give up anything without a fight, and even if they did, they would only come against us later. As I said, this was the only way to take your planet."

"So that's the plan, is it," Don said, nodding slowly to himself. "Kick us out of our homes and take them for yourselves. Then what? Kill us all?"

"No. Our goal is to live in peace with you," Bill replied. "We only sent down a small number of Seeders, and we picked a relatively unpopulated island to avoid unnecessary casualties. We are not the hostile invaders you imagine."

"Bullshit," Don said. "Corporal Lee and his men were acting pretty damn hostile, and they shot Ashley."

"You fired first," Bill replied, smiling patiently at them.

Don shook his head. "He's a snake. We can't trust anything he's saying."

"Maybe not," Commander Wilde agreed. "But I think at least some of what he's saying is true. If they had weapons they would have used them to invade us by now. Instead, they chose to invade our minds."

"That's even better!" Don said. "Who needs to fight a war for Earth when you can turn the locals into mindless zombies and make them vacate their homes peacefully? After that, who knows, they'll probably make us all walk into the ocean and drown ourselves."

"Our goals are peaceful, I promise you," Bill said. "Once we are settled, and a proper government established, you'll be released and allowed to go on with your lives."

Ashley interrupted from where she lay on the kitchen table: "If the goal was to infect us with something, why start with an island that's easily contained?"

"We could not afford to be careless," Bill said. "In the past, other hosts have reacted badly to the... *infection*, as you call it. In some species, all of the hosts died. Others went insane. Mortality rates have been as high as ninety-nine percent. We have had time to perfect the symbionts since then, but we could not be sure of your reaction. That is why we had to start on an island. To make sure we didn't accidentally kill all of you."

"So nice of you to think of us," Don said.

"It would be a lonely planet without you," Bill replied.

"You need us...?" Commander Wilde asked.

"Need? No, but your species has a certain usefulness to us. No one can be king without subjects. Who would serve us if you all died?"

Don snorted incredulously. "You want us to be your slaves."

"Is that not what you have done with the inferior species on this world? You raise them for food and keep them as pets. You hunt them for sport. I assure you, we will be far kinder than you have been."

Beth shivered. "You're going to keep us as

livestock?"

Bill laughed. "No. We don't want to eat you. That would be a horrible waste. No, all of our meat is grown artificially."

Silence thickened the air as they absorbed the implications of everything the alien controlling Bill had said.

"Something just occurred to me..." Commander Wilde said. "Don, when you mentioned Ashley getting shot, he said that we fired first. But how would he know that? He was unconscious at the time. The only way he could know that is if he somehow knows what Corporal Lee and his men know. And if that's the case, then your grandmother has been sharing what she knows, too. Does she know exactly where we are?"

"Shit," Don said. He shook a finger at Bill. "You were stalling for a reason!"

Bill grinned at them. "I'm sorry. You know too much. We can't allow you to escape."

Don hoisted his rifle to his shoulder, and Beth heard the safety click off.

"Wait!" This time she was the one pushing the gun away from her father. "Don't. He's still in there."

"Assuming he was telling the truth," Don replied. "There might not be any way to bring your father back."

"Forget about him," Commander Wilde added. "We need to leave while we still can."

A *rustling* noise like dried leaves dragging sounded on the other side of the living room window. It was open. Beth recalled the commander opening it after they'd come up from the storage room.

"Did you hear that?" Don asked quietly.

Beth's heart froze in her chest.

Commander Wilde brought his rifle up to his shoulder, too. "It's too late. They're already here."

CHAPTER 56

Corporal Gibson stepped into the alien lander carrying an arsenal with him: grenades, C4, an FN SCAR rifle with a grenade launcher attached, a whole belt of spare magazines, a bandoleer of grenades for the launcher, a combat knife, and two Berettas. The collective weight of all that ordnance would stagger a SEAL.

"How do we launch the pod?" Gibson asked. He cast about quickly, looking for the launching mechanism that the engineers had ultimately found behind one of the panels inside the pods.

"Here." Dekker slid open a panel, revealing a recessed compartment with a simple lever inside.

"Hold up, Deks. We'd better secure ourselves first."

"It's on a ten-second timer."

Gibson frowned. "How do you know?"

"I overheard the engineers talking about it," Dekker said. "Ready?"

Gibson blew out a breath and dropped into

one of two seats inside the pod. He grabbed web-like straps and looped his arms through them. "What about the hatch?"

"Closes during the launch sequence," Dekker replied just before throwing the lever. The hatch slid shut, and Dekker hurried to sit in the remaining seat. Gibson regarded him with a knitted brow. "You overheard the engineers talking about that, too?" he asked, jerking his chin to the hatch just as it sealed with a loud *hiss*.

"Yeah, why?"

Gibson shook his head. "Just curious. I guess it's a good thing you're a nosy bastard."

Dekker grinned and said something else, but his words were stolen by the deafening roar that began underneath them. The lander leapt upward violently, squashing them into their seats. Vertebrae popped and ground together in Gibson's spine, and his back arched painfully. Blood rushed into his feet, and he saw stars. The sensation eased sometime later, and Gibson realized that he'd blacked out. He came to, and his vision cleared, only to see that they were soaring freely through the air. The pod had vanished, all except for the black webbing of alien restraints that he clung to.

"Fuck..." he muttered, staring down at the dwindling speck that was Kauai. Wisps of cloud concealed the water and ground like the lingering drifts of snow at the end of spring. All around them, flickering golden specks blazed against the black velvet of the ocean—*ships on fire. Our ships.*

"It's some kind of hologram or projection chamber," Dekker said, shaking his head as if to clear it.

Gibson nodded wordlessly, still staring at the ruined fleet.

"Mother of..." Dekker trailed off with a whistle. "You see what I'm seeing, Gibs?"

Gibson followed his gaze to the sky. A blue outline hung above them, shaded to reveal details—a massive spaceship hovering over the North side of the island.

"That wasn't there before we took off," Gibson said.

"It must be cloaked or something," Dekker said. "We're headed straight for it. I told you it was there!"

"Yeah." They'd all heard about the strange cooling effect over the water on the North side of the island.

As they drew near the spaceship, the blue-shading that marked its position took over the entire sky. The shivering and shaking of friction with the atmosphere gradually faded, and Gibson looked down once more. Now he could see the whole planet curving away darkly below them, the far edge limned in sunlight.

"Here we go..." Dekker said.

Gibson looked up to see what looked like a shaded blue city rushing up—or down?—to greet them. The pod stopped accelerating, and suddenly he was weightless, bobbing around in the air as if it were water. Gibson's stomach flipped threateningly. He ground his teeth and clenched his fists around the webbing until the sensation passed. Moments later they went sailing between towering structures on the underside of the spaceship. There were no glittering lights to mark the hull, but a dark, funnel-shaped portal opened up directly above them.

"Into the belly of the beast..." Dekker remarked.

"Ready up," Gibson said, grabbing his SCAR in both hands. It was blessedly light in zero-*G*.

"Oorah," Dekker whispered as the alien spaceship swallowed them and hazy, blue-shaded walls streaked by them, growing narrower and narrower with every passing second. Unseen forces gripped the pod, nudging it down the throat of a tunnel that looked no wider than the head of a needle...

And then they shot out into a vast, spherical chamber lined with thousands of pods just like theirs. A pale silvery light illuminated the interior.

Landers, packed together like eggs clung to the walls and ceiling. The spaces between them looked like the hexagonal cells of a honeycomb. "They could have landed thousands of Crawlers," Gibson said, slowly shaking his head as their pod angled for a tiny gap in the honeycomb of landers. "But they sent down less than a hundred. Why?"

"Who cares?" Dekker countered.

Their lander twisted around as it approached the empty space and retro thrusters fired, pressing them into their seats. Gibson craned his neck to keep their destination in sight. The honeycomb gaps between pods snapped into focus, and he saw them for what they were—a transparent scaffolding around the pods, a deck. Their pod slid slowly into a hexagonal berth... then snapped suddenly into place with a ringing *clunk. Magnetic docking clamps?* Gibson wondered as he peered through the transparent walls of the pod, staring hard at the see-through deck that wound between and around their landers. The inside of the hangar was dimly lit, no brighter than a full moon. Gibson caught a glimpse of shadowy beings coming around the corner of an adjacent pod, walking toward them on... *two legs? Walking?* Gibson couldn't detect any kind of gravity, and he remembered that Crawlers preferred to walk on four legs, not two, but before he could get a good look, the walls of their lander grew opaque.

"Looks like we've got incoming," Gibson said as he looked away—

Only to find himself staring straight down the barrel of Dekker's rifle.

"What the hell, Deks? Mind your sights!" He tried to bat Dekker's rifle out of line, but Dekker grabbed Gibson's hand and twisted it painfully to one side. Cold fear coursed through Gibson.

"I am sorry for the deception," Dekker said. "But we need your help."

"We? Who the fuck is we, Dekker?"

Dekker smiled. "We, your new rulers."

CHAPTER 57

Don crept to the living room window, pasted himself to the wall beside it, and then peeked around the corner with his lantern. "Clear," he said.

Beth held her pistol in shaking hands, her eyes darting and wide.

"Wait here," Don whispered to her as he walked by. He signaled to the commander, then to the front door. Wilde nodded and turned to the door with his rifle raised.

Don edged past the kitchen and down the hall to the back door. Unable to just stand there, Beth took a few steps to follow him.

Don came within a few paces of the door, then froze, his head turned, as if listening. Beth hurried up behind him. "What is it?" she whispered.

He glanced back at her—

A bang sounded, and the back door flew open in a hail of splinters. A pale monster leapt through with four bony arms reaching. Jagged glass-like teeth parted. Don opened fire. A handful of rounds rattled out before the creature knocked him over and pinned him to the ground.

Beth backed up quickly, aiming her pistol at the Crawler.

"Shoot it!" Don cried as he wrestled with the alien.

Beth pulled the trigger, the gun kicked hard against her hands, and the bullet whistled harmlessly over the alien's shoulder. She fired again and this time hit it in the shoulder with a sickening *thwup*. The alien squealed and partly collapsed as the leg below the shoulder gave way.

"Again!" Don screamed—then gasped as alien claws bit into his shoulder.

"Get out of the way!" Commander Wilde pushed her aside and brought his rifle to bear with a rattling roar. The alien shrieked, writhing and lashing the air. Failing to reach the commander, it reared up on hind legs and crouched.

Pale fluid streamed from the alien's torso in dozens of places, but it just kept going. Rear legs bent, and the monster sprang forward, knocking the commander over.

Just a few feet away, Beth brought her gun to bear once more, this time aiming for one of the four black eyes at the top of the Crawler's head. She fired twice in quick succession, and the Crawler collapsed with a shuddering sigh, pinning both Commander Wilde and Don beneath its bulk.

As the creature exhaled, it shrank dramatically until it was barely larger than her.

Commander Wilde rolled out from under it, flinging thick, colorless alien blood from his hands and wiping it from his cheeks. "Nice shooting," he said through a grimace as he struggled to rise. Beth went to lend him a hand.

"We have to get out of here now!" Don put in.

"Agreed," Commander Wilde said.

"What about my dad? And Ashley?" Beth asked. "We can't just leave them here!"

"We can put Ashley in the back of the Humvee," Don replied. "But your father will have to stay. He's a liability."

"But—"

"Kid, wake up, he almost got us all killed! You included."

Bill's laughter trickled to their ears from the hall. "You'll never escape the island!"

Don growled and hefted his rifle in a one-handed grip. "Just be glad we don't shoot him in the head before we leave," he said and shouldered roughly past Beth.

Afraid that he might change his mind, Beth followed him and the commander to Ashley's side. They removed the catheter from her wrist and helped her to a sitting position.

"Where are we going?" Ashley asked sleepily.

Don grabbed her under the arms and Commander Wilde grabbed her legs, leaving their rifles to dangle by the shoulder straps.

Beth stared uncertainly at Ashley's pale face. "She doesn't look too good. Are you sure we should move her?"

"No choice," Don replied. "And she'll look worse with her guts ripped out by a Crawler."

Don and the commander hoisted her up and carried her to the front door. Beth hurried after them.

"Door," Don grunted, nodding to Beth.

"Wait," Commander Wilde said. "We don't know if there's more of them out there. I'd better check first."

Don nodded, and the commander set Ashley's feet down, leaving Don to carry her full weight. He leaned heavily against the armchair beside the door for support.

Wilde grabbed a lantern hanging from the roof and then cracked the door open. Holding the lantern in one hand and his rifle in the other, he peered outside. "Clear so far," he whispered.

Then he stepped out the front door. Beth waited, her ears straining for the slightest noise, but all she heard was her pounding heart and ragged breathing.

The seconds dragged like hours. Finally, the door creaked, inching open—

Beth aimed her gun at the door.

The commander stepped back inside. "Seems clear," he whispered.

Beth let out a shaky breath and slowly lowered her gun. Commander Wilde passed the light to her and grabbed Ashley's legs.

"Let's go."

"Beth, you lead the way," Don said.

"Me?"

"You've got the light. And a free hand to shoot."

Beth gave in with a scowl and went outside. The thunder of war had grown sporadic and distant, leaving the crickets and bugs to fill the night with noise. Beth led the way across the dry, crunching leaves and jutting roots that passed for Don's front yard. The Humvee sat in the shadows beneath tall trees, broken wedges of glass gleaming darkly where the windshield should have been.

They reached the vehicle, and Commander Wilde set Ashley's feet down again to open the trunk. Beth watched the trees, sweeping the lantern around with her gun. Ashley groaned weakly, drawing Beth's gaze back in time to see Commander Wilde and Don laying her in the back of the truck.

"All right, let's go," Commander Wilde said, and slammed the metal hatch.

A flicker of movement caught Beth's gaze, and she saw her father hopping out onto the front step of the cabin.

"To hell with it," Don said and brought his rifle up to his shoulder.

"No!" Beth jumped in front of Don's rifle, putting herself between him and her father.

"Hello?" Bill called out to them. "Is anyone out there?"

"Get out of the way!" Don said.

"Leave him alone!" Beth replied.

"Pack it in, Don!" Commander Wilde added from the front seat of the Humvee. The engine roared to life a split second later.

"Commander Wilde?" Bill called into the darkness. "Is that you, sir?"

"Sir?" Don echoed. "He's trying to be funny again!"

"It's me! Corporal Gibson!"

"Gibson?" Commander Wilde echoed.

* * *

—Half an Hour Ago, The Mothership—

The hatch opened to reveal a pair of pale-skinned monsters standing on two legs. Corporal

Gibson gasped at the sight of them. "Those aren't Crawlers." These creatures wore shimmering suits. Only their heads were exposed, and they had four of them bobbing at the end of long, serpentine necks. They reminded Gibson of the mythical Hydra. Each head had two pale, silvery eyes, and evidently controlled its own pair of skinny, three-jointed arms which branched from the base of the necks.

Which head controls the legs? Gibson wondered. The faces were angular with slightly protruding snouts and dark slits for nostrils. Transparent needle-like teeth protruded from the upper jaw, overlapping a matching set of teeth in the lower one.

Dekker backed out of the pod to join the Hydra on the see-through deck, his aim never wavering from Gibson as he did so. A Hydra opened one of its mouths and spoke to him in a guttural voice of watery growls, clicks, and trills.

Dekker nodded along, as if he understood perfectly. "Pass the rifle out slowly," he said. "Butt first."

"You're with them?" Gibson asked as he passed his SCAR out the hatch. He was too shocked by the appearance of the *Hydras* and Dekker's mysterious allegiance to them to try anything. "How?"

"You'll see," Dekker replied, taking the rifle and slipping the strap over his shoulder. Now two barrels pointed at Gibson.

"Now the Berettas," Dekker indicated.

Once again Gibson gave up his weapons without a fight, but he still had a belt full of frag grenades and C4. All he had to do was pull a pin and it would be over.

"Now the ordnance," Dekker said.

Gibson's fingers hesitated over the silver loop of a frag grenade's pin.

"Don't even think about it!" Dekker yelled, raising both rifles threateningly.

Gibson's hand opened, and he began removing the belt instead. One grenade wasn't going to take down a ship the size of Texas. But there might be a better opportunity later. If nothing else, he wanted to know what all of this was about.

He passed the explosives through the hatch along with his combat knife and spare magazines, but he didn't volunteer the extra blade he'd tucked into his right boot. Maybe Dekker hadn't seen him hide it while they were in the missile range's armory.

"Now your turn," Dekker indicated. "Slowly."

He didn't know about the hidden knife. Gibson's heart pounded with the thrill of that small victory. He untangled himself from the web-like restraints and drifted weightlessly toward the transparent floor where Dekker and the two Hydras stood. As his hands reached through the threshold of the hatch, the three of them backed away, and Gibson passed through a disorienting transition from zero gravity inside the pod to a significant fraction of Earth gravity on the deck. He wound up having to crawl out of the lander. He struggled to stand under the sudden weight of his body and remaining gear.

Gibson looked around the alien hangar, then glowered at the Hydras. "What do you want?"

"The same thing anyone wants," Dekker replied for them. "Peace, prosperity, and a good life."

"Peace." Gibson snorted and shook his head.

"The war will be short-lived. It was a regrettable necessity. Your government was about to attack us."

"Hang on—*you* started the war with the Chinese?"

Dekker nodded. "Of course."

Gibson gaped at him, unable to believe what he'd just heard.

"But as I said, it will not last long. Once the symbionts finish spreading through your population, only the immunes will seek conflict, and they are few in number. It will not be long before your planet is united under a common purpose."

"*Our* planet?" Gibson echoed. "It's your planet, too! And united under what purpose? Fighting them?" Gibson's eyes flicked to the Hydras.

"No, serving them. Serving *us*."

Gibson felt the acid burn of bile rising in his throat. He cleared it and spat in Dekker's face.

Dekker just smiled. "It is unfortunate that some of you are immune. We had hoped to avoid pointless strife during this transition."

"Fuck you!" Gibson said. One of the Hydras trilled something and then stepped forward to grab him with eight arms. Those bony limbs with their dainty hands looked fragile—easy to snap. Gibson resisted, but the Hydra were stronger than they looked.

One of the Hydra's heads hissed in Gibson's ear, and another snapped its jaws in front of his face. That one gave him a look that made him shiver—silvery eyes wide, lips peeling back in a grin around needle-sharp teeth. The other two heads looked on, swaying hypnotically as if to unseen music. Sharp claws at the ends of spindly fingers bit through Gibson's uniform, and then he was pushed along. The Hydras wound through the labyrinthine hangar past countless landing pods. Dekker walked beside them, keeping one of the two rifles trained on Gibson at all times.

"The Crawlers aren't the real invaders," Gibson said.

"You're surprised? Did they seem capable of building something this magnificent?" Dekker gestured to the yawning hangar.

Gibson bit his tongue and walked on in silence. The Hydra holding him stank like a dead fish, but that was the least of his problems.

At last, they came to the end of the hangar and walked through a broad pair of doors into a yawning corridor no better lit than the hangar had been. The silvery glow radiated from a long strip along the ceiling that reminded Gibson of old office lights. Everything else, the walls and floor, were glossy, pale, and colorless—all silvers, whites, and grays.

Before long, the Hydras stopped and turned him toward another set of doors. One of them reached out and placed a palm against a glossy black panel beside the doors. The doors parted to reveal a glass-like capsule and rows of strange, high-backed chairs with wide headrests. Black webbing like Gibson had seen in the pods draped each chair. Ahead of the capsule, visible through the clear sides and front, lay a long tunnel with multiple forks curving away in all directions. Gibson realized that this was some kind of mass transit system. He supposed they'd have to have something like that on a ship this big.

The Hydra holding him pushed him into the capsule and forced him into the nearest seat. It barked and trilled something at him in a voice that alternated between guttural and musical, then grabbed the webbed restraints to either side of his chair in four hands for emphasis.

Dekker translated, "Strap in if you don't want to become a puddle of jelly on the windshield."

Gibson looped his arms through the restrains as he'd done in the landing pod. Dekker snorted as if that wasn't how they were supposed to be used. "Good enough," he said and took a seat behind Gibson.

The Hydras sat together in the back. Gibson twisted around to see Dekker wrapping the webbing around himself, attaching each half to metal hooks on opposite sides of the chair. Gibson did his best to copy Dekker.

"Where are you taking me?" he asked, just as the doors to the corridor and the capsule slid shut.

"To the control room," Dekker replied.

Before Gibson could inquire further, the capsule lurched into motion, accelerating so rapidly that it knocked the wind out of him. Gibson struggled to breathe. Gasping for air, he watched dark spots gathering before his eyes. Then came the first fork in the tunnel, and the capsule darted left. Moments later, it leapt up and fell in behind another capsule. They raced along, still picking up speed. Gibson was convinced they'd broken the sound barrier several times, but no sonic booms had sounded from either capsule. The tunnels had to be vacuum sealed. Why fight air resistance if you didn't have to?

Half an hour must have passed before their capsule finished twisting and turning through the ship. Gibson felt it slow, then stop, and the doors slid open. He fought to un-hook his webbed restraints and rose on shaking legs. One of the Hydras came loping up and grabbed him with eight spindly arms. Eight silver eyes stared fixedly at him, watching, and those needle-sharp teeth were a constant reminder that these aliens were not some pacifistic race of herbivores. They were born predators. Perhaps the only reason they hadn't invaded in force was that they didn't need to. Winning over the hearts and minds of humanity and making them into willing slaves would be far better than simply killing all of them.

The Hydra holding Gibson pushed him along, and Dekker kept both rifles trained on him once more. The second Hydra led the way through the open doors of the transport, and they emerged in a vast chamber with thousands of desks and chairs arrayed in long rows, with aisles running between. It was like the CIC of the *Port Royal,* but on a far larger scale. Some of those control stations were empty, while others were populated by more of the four-headed Hydras. Gibson noted that the monstrous four-legged Crawlers were nowhere to be seen. He supposed that they were also slaves of the Hydras.

As they walked down one of the aisles between control stations, Gibson got a closer look at what was happening in the room. Each of the Hydras sitting at those stations was perched in an egg-like chair with high, curving headrests for each of their four heads. They wore glossy black helmets on their heads that covered their eyes, while their arms and hands remained free to drape down their torsos like a horrid form of dreadlocks. Thick cables snaked from each of the helmets to four distinct sections of each control station, and above those connections were ghostly, holographic images of people with two legs and arms and just one head — *humans.*

Suddenly Gibson understood Dekker's inexplicable treachery, and the isolated occurrences of odd behavior he'd witnessed over the past months — people making the same motions and gestures in suspicious synchrony, as if somehow communicating signals to each other's brains. The reason was evident now. Four heads per Hydra meant they could control four different human avatars each. The people in the holograms were all being remote-controlled by the Hydras.

"So this is your big plan?" Gibson asked. "Use us like puppets and live vicariously through us?"

"No, this is only the initial phase," Dekker explained. "Once your people are pacified and disarmed, it won't be necessary to directly control all of them, and most of them will return to their senses. Only the law enforcement officers will remain under direct control, and even then, only while they are on duty."

Gibson slowly shook his head. "Why show me this? Why bring me here?"

"Because there is a group of immunes who have uncovered what we are doing and found a way to stop us. You are going to help us eliminate them."

"The fuck I will," Gibson replied.

They came alongside a control station with four familiar-looking holograms hovering above it. Gibson scanned the faces, and his eyes widened in surprise. One of them was Bill Steele, another was Private Dekker. The other two Gibson recognized as the chef and one of the housekeepers from the Koa Kai Resort.

The Hydra sitting at that station removed one

of its helmets. The free head turned to look at Gibson. It hissed and bared its teeth as it passed the device to the Hydra who wasn't already pinning Gibson's arms and shoulders in eight different places. That alien took the helmet in two hands and walked toward Gibson with it.

He struggled anew, trying to break free. He managed to elbow the Hydra in the gut, drawing a satisfying hiss from one of its heads. Alien hands flexed, and claws dug deeper into his arms and shoulders. Gibson bit back a scream. He refused to give them the satisfaction.

"Don't worry," Dekker said. "This won't hurt."

Gibson's eyes darted to the remaining three holograms hovering above the control station. "You're going to make me control one of them?"

Dekker laughed lightly. "Why would we do that? No, we just need to see inside of your head for a minute."

The Hydra holding the helmet lowered it over Gibson's ears and eyes, blocking out everything. The helmet smelled like sardines, and it was far too big. For a minute Gibson allowed himself to hope that meant it wouldn't work for whatever the Hydras had planned. But then he heard a sharp shriek of metal, like a thousand swords unsheathing all at once, and needles pricked through his scalp on all sides, pinning his head inside the helmet. A rush of thoughts, memories, and images swirled through Gibson's mind. He could have sworn he felt things crawling around inside his brain, hunting through the kaleidoscopic swirl for useful tidbits.

Dekker was right; it wasn't painful, but the sheer speed of his racing thoughts and the invasion of privacy made his skin crawl and his stomach churn, pushing him to the edge of insanity. This time Gibson didn't hold back. He screamed long and hard, until his voice failed and his eyes streamed with tears.

CHAPTER 58

"Bullshit! He's stalling!" Don said, trying to get around Beth for a clear shot. "That's not Gibson."

"I swear it's me! I can prove it. Ask me something only Gibson would know!"

"We don't have time for this!" Don roared.

"Get in the truck," Commander Wilde added. "Let's go."

"Wait," Beth replied. "Maybe he's telling the truth, maybe..." Beth trailed off, unable to finish that thought.

"How the hell could he be telling the truth?" Don demanded.

"Dekker and I escaped the island in one of the landers!" Bill answered. "We launched ourselves, and it took us up to their ship. We were right. They never left! They're hovering over the ocean just north of the island. Dekker turned on me, but I... he's dead. I found them up here. The ones controlling us. They're all sitting in some kind of life support pods with these VR helmets on... one for each of their four fucking heads. They're like fucking Hydras. And there are holograms of us hovering above each of their control stations. Four of us for each of them. They're controlling us somehow! I killed one of them and tried on one of the helmets to see what would happen... and now I'm here, but I can't get the fucking thing off! I can't wake up!"

Beth listened to her father's rambling explanation with growing disbelief.

"You believe any of this, Commander?" Don asked.

"No, but if by some miracle it *is* true, he might have valuable intel. Let's sedate him and load him up." Commander Wilde jumped out of the truck, and both he and Don advanced on her father with their rifles raised. Beth followed them on shaking legs.

"It's me, I swear to God, Commander. Ask me anything!" Bill said again. "Something only I would know."

"Fine. You asked for it," Wilde said. "What's your sexual orientation?"

"I don't have one! I'm asexual!"

Don's footsteps faltered. "Is that true?"

"It is..." Commander Wilde trailed off, sounding confused.

"And no one else knows that?" Don asked.

"Does that sound like something he'd go blabbing to his buddies?" Commander Wilde shook his head.

"So how do *you* know?" Don asked.

"I'm the *Port Royal's* doctor. He asked me if I could prescribe something to fix it."

Don frowned. "I don't trust him."

"Neither do I, but somehow that's him. It has to be."

"Unless he's infected."

"Ashley said he wasn't," Beth put in. "She tested his samples, remember? He's one of the immunes, like us."

"We'll have to sedate him anyway," Commander Wilde decided. "Just in case."

"We'd better hurry," Don added. "If my Nana led a Crawler to us, there could be infected Marines right behind them. Whoever or whatever is controlling the infected people, it's clearly desperate to keep us from telling others what we know."

"Agreed," Commander Wilde said.

Beth watched them shove her father roughly back inside the cabin, knocking him over in the process. They disappeared and returned a moment later with Ashley's bag of medical supplies. Commander Wilde crouched beside her dad to inject him with a sedative, and then the two of them picked him up and carried him out to the truck. "Open the back door," Don panted as they drew near. "Bill's riding with you."

Beth nodded and put the lantern on the roof so she could pull the door open. She stepped back as they shoved her father inside, leaving him lying half on, half off the flat-topped storage compartment between the seats at the back of the Humvee.

"Get in!" Don said. Beth grabbed the lantern and jumped in next to her dad. Don slammed the door behind her and then he and the commander both climbed in the front. Commander Wilde popped his head out the window as he reversed out. The bumpy road made Beth worry about her pistol going off accidentally, so she wedged it between her seat and the compartment where her dad lay.

"Someone should man the M2," Don said. Not waiting for permission, he climbed into the back, nearly stepping on Bill's leg in the process.

"Watch it!" Beth snapped.

"Move him!" Don replied.

She wrestled her dad's legs and arms out of the way, and Don stood up to grab the machine gun on the roof.

The commander turned the truck around and

drove back up the rough track that led to Don's place. As soon as they hit the dirt road, they careened down the mountain, flying over potholes and slapping through overgrown vegetation. Ashley groaned with each bump, and Beth found herself wincing in sympathy.

"Where are we going?" she asked.

"That's a good question," Commander Wilde said, ducking as a leaning tree branch came through the broken windshield. "We need to find the Chinese, but if they see us coming in a Humvee, they'll shoot us before we can surrender. Nawiliwili Harbor is probably our best bet. If we can steal a private boat, we can head for Oahu, or a surviving ship, and if need be, use the boat's radio to announce our surrender."

"I have a boat in the harbor," Don said, "But the Chinese are jamming the radios, remember?" Don called down from the roof.

"They might not be by then!" Wilde shouted back. "What would be the point of jamming after they've already taken out all of our ships? They'd just be hindering coordination of their own assault."

"Unless it wasn't them jamming the radios," Beth said. "What if it was the aliens?"

Silence answered her question for several beats.

"She makes a good fucking point," Don said.

"We'll wave a white flag if we have to," the commander replied. Either way, it's still our best bet."

"Copy that," Don replied.

But Beth wasn't so sure. They were in the middle of a war zone, and the Chinese were the enemy. What if they blew them out of the water before they ever got a chance to explain what was really going on? And even if that didn't happen, what could they hope to do about any of it?

"What happens after we surrender?" Beth asked. "What are you hoping the Chinese will do?"

"Ideally, we convince them to fire on that spaceship with everything they've got. If they don't have weapons, and the real invasion hasn't landed yet, then this might be our only chance to stop them."

"Fire on them with *what?*" Don asked. "Cannons won't reach space, most missiles won't either."

"They'll have to use ICBMs," Commander Wilde replied.

"ICB-whats?" Beth asked.

"Nukes," the commander clarified.

"Good luck!" Don replied. "We can't even see them."

"It's a big target," Commander Wilde replied.

"And if they are hiding over the North side of the island like Gibson said—"

"We don't know that."

"But we *have* detected anomalous temperature readings there. It makes sense. The only reason no one has opened fire on them yet is that they've been afraid it wouldn't do anything—and scared of reprisals. But now that we know what they're planning, and containment is breached, what do we have to lose? Hell, if I had a line to Washington, I'd tell them, too. For all we know, it's going to take a joint effort to bring those fuckers down."

Nuclear weapons... Beth frowned and bit her lower lip. That sounded like a dangerous plan to her. What about fallout?

Up ahead the road forked, but the left side looked like a path for horses. "Go left!" Don called down.

"You sure?" the commander asked.

"Yes!"

Commander Wilde turned left, spitting dirt and gravel, and Beth slammed into her door.

"We took the right side on the way up," Don explained. "It's the only path my grandmother knows! If anyone's on their way to cut us off, they'll be waiting down there."

Commander Wilde had to hit the brakes to stop them from careening out of control into the trees. Leaves and branches scraping the sides of the Humvee were a constant roar in Beth's ears.

"Where's this road come out?" Ashley asked from the back in a tense voice.

Beth was relieved to hear from her.

"On the outskirts of Lihue," Don said. "It takes us around Route 50, which should help us avoid any roadblocks that might be set up on the highway."

"That's a vague answer," Ashley said.

"What?" Don shouted back. "I can't hear you!"

Beth relayed what Ashley had said.

"We'll come out at the end of Route 50, right next to the Fire Prevention Bureau. From there it's a straight shot down Rice Street to the harbor."

"Good!" Ashley replied just as they flew through another pothole. "Because I'm not sure how much more of this I can take."

It took almost forty minutes to reach the end of the winding dirt trail, but as it left the mountains, it joined a wider, less bumpy dirt road that wound through the sugar plantations outside Lihue.

As they came within sight of the town, Beth saw a mysterious orange glow on the horizon. Power still hadn't returned to the island, as evidenced by the lack of light streaming from the windows of farmhouses and rural homes that they drove past.

"The town's on fire," Commander Wilde explained as they reached the end of the dirt road. A frozen, messy knot of traffic blocked the paved street in front of them, but those cars weren't moving, and most of their lights were off. A few with their headlights on were abandoned, their doors standing open and hazard lights blinking. People walked around aimlessly, staring up at the distant, muted flashes of explosions in the sky.

"Shit," Commander Wilde muttered. "We can't get through this."

"Hang on, I think I see a path," Don said. "But we'll have to push through."

"Push through?" Beth asked.

"There, between the Black Corolla and the Silver Hilux!" Don said.

The commander slowly joined the road, aiming for a gap between two vehicles. It wasn't nearly wide enough for them to get by, but he just kept going.

"Slow down!" Beth screamed.

They hit, and she slammed into her seatbelt. Glass shattered, tires squealed, and then they punched through. One lane of Rice Street looked clear as far as Beth could see, with vehicles pushed or driven up onto the sidewalk to get them out of the way.

"Looks like someone cleared a path for

emergency traffic," Wilde said. "Lucky us." They drove around a corner, and then he added, "We've got another obstacle up ahead."

He slowed down and Beth saw an overturned pickup lying in the road. They rolled to a stop in front of it.

"Looks like there's space on the sidewalk to go around," Don called down from the roof.

"Yeah... maybe," Commander Wilde agreed. "We can always nudge it a bit if not."

Beth watched as he drove up onto the sidewalk to go around the pickup. Going over the curb rocked the vehicle from side to side and Ashley moaned. Commander Wilde slowed to a crawl as they approached the gap between the overturned truck and the adjacent buildings.

Beth peered out her window into dark, broken storefronts. She made out several huddled, hazy shapes inside of a coffee shop. *People hiding from the conflict?* she wondered.

"It's gonna be close," Don said.

"Uhh... guys!" Beth said, her voice rising precipitously as the shadows came creeping toward the moonlit sidewalk. A second later they resolved into pale, four-legged things with four arms and four glinting black eyes.

"What?" Commander Wilde snapped.

"Crawlers!" Beth cried.

CHAPTER 59

Three Crawlers leapt through the broken windows of the coffee shop. Beth screamed and scrambled to recover her pistol from between her seat and the storage compartment. A Crawler slammed into Beth's window, starring it with cracks. She tried to shoot it through the glass, but the trigger wouldn't budge. The safety was still on.

"Shit!" Beth screamed.

A few rounds thumped out from the turret on the roof, but then Don cried out in pain and fell inside the vehicle.

A third Crawler landed on the hood and took a swipe at Commander Wilde, even as he brought his rifle to bear. Bullets rattled out, striking the alien in multiple places and drawing agonized screams from its lips.

Don leaned over the passenger's seat to get his rifle from where he'd left it on the floor, but two long, translucent arms reached in and forced him back. Another pair of arms shot through the broken window on the other side to get at Commander Wilde. He screamed and fired a steady stream of bullets at the Crawler. Then the one on the roof reached down the hatch and raked claws over Don's side. He cried out, and Beth flicked off the safety on her gun. She pulled the trigger again and again, firing at point blank range. The monster squealed but didn't retreat. Commander Wilde twisted around to look just in time for a flailing arm to slice his throat open.

Blood bubbled down his neck and out between his lips. Beth screamed, firing again and again, aiming for the head. At last, the Crawler subsided with a sigh, kicking her spasmodically in the thigh as it did so. Beth pressed her gun against the side of its head and shot it once more for good measure. Don struggled to rise under yet another alien corpse and grabbed the commander's rifle. He opened fire just as the Crawler on the hood came through. A short burst rattled through the monster's head and it fell off the Humvee with a loud *thump.*

"Fuck!" Don screamed as he crawled the rest of the way out from under the dead alien and climbed into the passenger's seat. "How many were there?" he asked, eyes darting in the sudden silence.

"I..." Beth cast back, thinking fast. "Three."

"We only killed two. There's another one out there somewhere."

Beth stared hard out the windows, blinking wide eyes into the night, but the missing Crawler didn't return.

"Must have run off," Don concluded. Glancing at Commander Wilde's dead eyes, he shook his head and then reached down to retrieve his rifle. He passed it back to Beth. "Here."

"What am I supposed to do with that?" she asked.

"What do you think? Take it! Two hands. It's already loaded and set to single-fire, so you shouldn't have a problem controlling it. All you have to do is turn off the safety when you're ready to fire. Got it?"

Beth grabbed the rifle in shaking hands. It felt heavy. "I think so," she said.

"Good. Because I need someone to cover me while I drive."

With that, Don leaned over the commander's lap, opened his door, and pushed him out. He fell with a sickening *thud.*

"You can't just dump him like garbage!" Beth said.

"If you want to stick around for the service you're going to have to join him in the casket. That fucker is still out there somewhere." Don pulled the door shut and hopped into the driver's seat. Beth leaned over to open the far door and push the dead alien out. It was surprisingly heavy, but she managed to shove it off the seat.

"Close the door!" Don snapped.

Beth did, and the Humvee jack-rabbited forward as Don hit the gas. They scraped through the gap between the coffee shop and the overturned truck, knocking off their right side mirror in the process.

"Open road," Don crowed as they emerged on the other side with no more obstacles in sight. "I wonder where all the damn Chinese went?"

Beth was too distracted to offer a reply. She was busy staring over the back seat into an empty cargo compartment. "Don..."

"Yeah?"

"Ashley's gone."

* * *

Don slammed on the brakes, and Beth's seatbelt dug into her chest. "What do you mean gone?" he asked, twisting around to look.

"I mean she's gone!"

"A Crawler pulled her out and you didn't notice?" he demanded.

"No, I..." Beth trailed off, shaking her head. With all the commotion she couldn't remember. "I don't know!"

"Shit," Don muttered. "She's probably dead. Either way, we can't afford to go back and look."

Beth lowered her window and stuck her head outside just as Don accelerated once more. Someone was limping after them, waving their arms in the air and screaming for them to stop.

"I see her!" Beth said. "Stop the truck!"

Don hit the brakes, and the tires squealed. "Where?" Don asked.

"Behind us," Beth replied as she unbuckled and yanked her door open.

"Beth, wait!"

She jumped out and ran, making sure to keep her rifle out of line with Ashley. "Come on!" Beth shouted to her. "We've got to go!" A rumbling whir of tires chased after her, rising swiftly in pitch as the Humvee reversed up the street. Beth reached Ashley's side to find her sobbing.

"It just reached in and dragged me out. And then it ran away!" Ashley looked around quickly, hugging and rubbing her shoulders. "Did you kill them all?"

"No. One escaped," Beth replied just as Don pulled alongside them.

"Beth, look out!" he cried.

She whirled around just in time to see a Crawler leaping down on her from a second-floor window. She whipped the rifle up and tried to pull the trigger, but the safety was still on.

The Crawler landed hard on top of Beth's chest, knocking the wind out of her and pinning her to the ground. Arms folded out, and claws flashed down.

A thumping roar began, and the monster flew apart, splattering Beth with a wash of hot, foul-smelling blood. Some of it got in her mouth. Leaping off the street, she repeatedly spat to clear the bitter, gamy taste of it. The Crawler lay in smoking pieces all around her, but the bulk of it was still moving, dragging itself away with its two remaining arms. Don stood in the gun turret on top of the Humvee, trying to angle the gun down far enough to shoot it, but it remained out of his line of fire.

Beth checked the side of her rifle, found the safety, flicked it off, and pulled the trigger. She fired one shot into the Crawler's backside, then pulled the trigger five times more, aiming for its head. Three shots missed, kicking up flecks of asphalt from the road, but two bullets tore straight through the creature's left ear. It reached forward one last time, but both arms froze halfway through the motion, and the Crawler lay still.

"It's okay," Beth said. "That was the last one. They're all dead now."

"Well, we're not out of the shit yet," Don

added. "Get in." He began to duck back inside, then hesitated. "Actually... maybe we should take that thing with us."

"What?" Beth shook her head incredulously. "Why?"

"Because we need an excuse to get the Chinos to take us into custody and listen to what we have to say. If we come bringing an alien corpse as a gift, they might be more willing to listen."

"A *gift?*" Ashley asked. She sounded equally horrified.

"Just trust me." Don ducked down, and Beth heard his door open. Walking around the front of the Humvee, he grabbed the alien by one of its reaching arms and dragged it over to the cargo compartment. Beth stood off at a safe distance, looking on with a frown. "No need to lend a hand or anything," Don quipped as he bent down to scoop the monster up and drape it over his shoulder. He stood up with a grunt. "Heavier than they look." Alien blood dripped from the Crawler's missing leg with a steady splattering sound.

Ashley looked on with a sneer of disgust, as if she couldn't believe he would consider taking the dead alien with them. "Maybe you could help me open the back?" Don asked.

Beth lurched into motion, felt around for the release mechanism in the dark, and struggled to open the bulky hatch. Don heaved the alien corpse off his shoulder and into the back. The vehicle sank visibly under the alien's weight.

And then the impossible happened: all of the Crawlers legs and arms sprang to life, scrabbling furiously in the back. A piteous wail began, and its head came around, glaring at them with three out of four eyes.

"Son of an alien whore!" Don screamed. He grabbed Beth's rifle and raised it to his shoulder.

"No!" Ashley cried. She lunged to reach Don but was too late.

He shot the Crawler in one of its big black eyes. It deflated like a balloon and lay still. Ashley punched him in the arm. "Ow! What the hell, Ash?" he asked, rounding on her.

Both he and Beth stared incredulously at her.

Ashley's anger faded to chagrin; she looked sheepish now. "We could have sedated it. That was the last living specimen!"

Don snorted. "Don't worry. I'm sure a shit-ton of others will be here soon." He passed the rifle back to Beth, flicking the safety on as he did so, and then slammed the hatch. "Let's go," he said.

Beth and Ashley ran around the back and yanked the rear doors open. They jumped in beside Beth's dad, but barely had time to shut the doors before Don hit the gas and they were thrown back against their seats.

"You must be feeling better..." Beth said slowly. Ashley was sitting up and wide awake as if she'd miraculously recovered from the bullet that had torn through her lung mere hours ago.

"Just the adrenaline keeping me going, I think," Ashley said with a tight smile.

Beth's dad moaned and stirred, drawing their attention to him.

Ashley casually reached over and grabbed Beth's pistol from where Beth had stowed it between her seat and the storage compartment.

"What—" Beth cut herself off as Ashley's blue eyes flashed and a cold smile curved her lips. The pistol swung into line with her chest, and before she could react, it went off with a deafening bang. A blinding pain tore through Beth's shoulder. She screamed, and her rifle fell from nerveless fingers.

CHAPTER 60

The first thing Corporal Gibson noticed when the helmet came off his head was the sound of aliens trilling in loud, mournful tones. Private Dekker jabbed him in the back with the barrel of one of the rifles, but his attention was elsewhere. One of the control stations not far from theirs was dark, and the Hydra seated there had slumped over it, all four heads and sets of arms draping over the console like an octopus's tentacles. Hydras around it were getting up from their stations and setting their glossy black helmets aside. Gibson sat on the floor, held there by the prodding barrel of Dekker's rifle, the knife in his boot within easy reach.

"What happened?" Gibson asked casually.

Dekker glanced down at him, then back to the motionless Hydra. "They killed all of the Seeders. Their director didn't have time to disconnect before the psychic shock killed him, too." Dekker's head turned as another Hydra walked by him. That was it. Gibson drew his knife and twisted out from under Dekker's rifle in the same instant. Dekker pulled the trigger, and bullets skipped off the deck to ricochet around the room. One of the Hydras roared in pain just as Gibson jumped up and sliced Dekker's throat open. His eyes bulged as a red river gushed out. Dekker's lips parted in shock. A flash of guilt tore through Gibson, but there was no time for it.

He caught Dekker before he fell, stole one of the two SCAR rifles. Dropping to one knee, he whirled around and opened fire on the nearest Hydra. Eight arms and four heads flailed as its body shivered with impacts. The alien crumpled to the floor, streaming colorless blood. More Hydras turned, rounding on him with wide eyes and gaping mouths. Everything seemed to slow right down, and Gibson saw them all turning to flee as if in slow motion. He rose to his feet and sprayed the room with bullets. Aliens fell in waves. The magazine emptied out in seconds, but Gibson ejected it and yanked another one off Dekker's belt to reload and keep the mayhem going. Some kind of alarm sounded in the room, blaring out with deafening force, but Gibson's ears were already numb from the rattling reports of the SCAR.

Within just a few minutes, he'd burned through three full magazines, and there were no

Hydras left standing. Most of them had gotten away, but he had to have killed at least sixty, several of which were moaning and twitching as they bled out on the floor. Gibson took that brief reprieve to steal the other rifle from Dekker's bloody body, along with both ammo belts, the packs of C4, and the bandoleer of grenades.

Now dripping with firepower, Gibson strolled down the aisles in the control room with a rifle in each hand, stepping over splayed alien bodies. He came to one Hydra that was paralyzed except for one of its four heads, which was raised and swaying like a Cobra to music.

He aimed his rifle at it. Its silvery eyes widened, and it made a trilling noise deep inside its throat. Two arms reached out with palms raised, as if in surrender, but Gibson wasn't in the mood to take prisoners. He pulled the trigger, and the head slammed into the control console behind it, driven backward by the momentum of the point-blank rifle shot.

"Enslave that," Gibson spat.

Looking around quickly for threats, Gibson realized that the control room was abandoned. He wondered if that meant the people the Hydras had been controlling were snapping out of it. Another pang of guilt tore through him as he realized that he might not have needed to kill Dekker. Clamping down on those feelings, Gibson cast about quickly, looking for the nearest exit. He was trapped on an alien ship of unimaginable size, and the chances were good that the Hydras had locked him in the control room by now. Gibson frowned, his heart pounding and mind racing as he tried to think of a way out of this. But he hadn't boarded that lander with Dekker thinking it would be a two-way trip. The better question was how could he deal a crippling blow to the Hydras before they found a way to kill him.

Gibson spied the nearest exit—a pair of massive, glossy black doors with gleaming silver inlay. He ran to them and looked about quickly for some kind of control panel. Finding a black screen beside the doors, he tried touching it. A blue outline flashed on the display—a small palm and four skinny alien fingers. Glancing back at the nearest dead Hydra, Gibson smiled grimly and stalked toward it. Setting the two rifles down, he drew the combat knife from Dekker's ammo belt and set to work.

CHAPTER 61

Beth watched through a blurry stream of tears as Ashley swept the pistol away from her to the back of Don's head. There were no headrests on either of the front seats—nothing to shield him.

Don twisted around to face the weapon, his hands leaving the steering wheel to grab it. His mouth moved, but no sound reached Beth's ringing ears. She cringed in anticipation of the gunshot that would end Don's life, but it never came. A look of confusion crossed Ashley's face, and her aim faltered. Then she winced and clapped a hand to her injured side, as if only then noticing that she'd been shot. Wasting no time, Don snatched the gun away from her and grabbed the wheel to veer away from a convenience store, seconds before they would have plowed through it.

"What the fuck!" Don screamed in a muffled voice. He slammed on the brakes and Ashley flew into his seat, knocking her head on his shoulder.

Don shrugged her off and whirled around to point the gun at her.

"Get out," he demanded in a shaking voice.

"Don, it's me, Ashley," she replied, shaking her head. "I..." she looked around with wide, frightened eyes. Her gaze met Beth's, and she shook her head. "That wasn't me! I didn't shoot her! Until just a second ago they were in control."

"You're infected?" Beth croaked.

Ashley nodded slowly. "I must be."

"Since when? I thought you were immune," Don replied.

"We just assumed that because the rest of the quarantine center was compromised and my samples were clear, but I took off my helmet on the way over to the Koa Kai so that I could make a call to the mainland. Soon after that, I lost control of my body." Ashley's lower lip trembled, and tears sprang to her eyes. "I could see everything going on around me, but I couldn't do anything! I was trapped in my own mind. I kept trying to warn you, but none of you could hear me!"

"Sounds pretty damn convenient to me," Don snorted.

"It's the truth!"

"We have to go," Beth gritted out, trying to ignore the fire still pulsing through her wounded shoulder.

"Right," Don sighed.

"Look, if you don't trust me, then sedate me like him," Ashley said, pointing to Bill. "It's probably safer, anyway. I don't know if whatever was controlling me will come back and take over again."

Don's eyes and aim never left Ashley, but he leaned over, reaching blindly for Ashley's bag of medical supplies on the floor in front of the passenger's seat. Hoisting it up, he dug around, glancing briefly into the bag to find what he was looking for. Apparently finding it, he struggled to manage the gun, a vial of clear fluid, and a hypodermic needle at the same time.

"Beth, I need you to watch her for a sec."

Blinking tears, she nodded. Beth let go of the bullet wound in her shoulder, blinking stars from her eyes and shaking her head to clear it. Grabbing the fallen rifle with her uninjured arm, she strained to balance the weapon in her lap and aim it at Ashley. Don lowered his guard and quickly worked to fill the syringe. When he was done, Ashley held out her arm for him to inject it. Beth took that as a sign that she was telling the truth. Her gaze dipped to Bill, wondering if he would also be back to himself when he woke up.

Ashley sighed and curled up against her door. Don watched her for a long minute before nodding and turning back around. "Keep an eye on them," he said.

Beth nodded absently, but she was fading fast. Her eyelids drooped, and her wounded arm felt numb.

"Beth? Shit—Beth!"

Her eyelids closed, and she slipped into a blessed well of darkness.

CHAPTER 62

Bill woke up lying on a hard metal surface in the back of a Humvee, hearing people shouting at each other. He lay there listening to the voices. One of them was familiar and speaking in English—a man.

The other voices spoke Mandarin. Bill understood some of it from classes he'd taken back in LA, but the sounds were too faint, and he couldn't make out the words.

Burning with curiosity, Bill wished whatever alien entity was controlling his body would sit up and take a look around—at least let him see what was happening! But long minutes passed, and he continued to lie there as if paralyzed. Bill inwardly groaned—

And his lips twitched.

He tried to move his fingers, and his wrists and hands exploded with pins and needles. He realized his hands were tied behind his back, bound at the wrists. He flexed both of them into fists several times to get the circulation back, and also to reassure himself that he wasn't dreaming—that he really could move again.

Elation soared, and Bill sucked in a deep breath. He couldn't believe it. He had become so used to being a prisoner in his own body that he'd forgotten what it was like to be able to move and feel. He released his fists and wiggled his fingers. Such a simple act—thoughts translated to motion—something he'd taken for granted his entire life. What had happened to the alien entity controlling him? Had someone finally blown them out of the sky?

Bill hoped to God that was true. He tried to twist around and sit up, but a heavy weight held him down. Managing to crane his neck to look, he saw two women slumped over him, both of them familiar. One of them was Doctor Carter, wearing the tattered, bloody remains of a hazmat suit. The other was Beth. The entire right side of her shirt had been torn open, replaced by blood-soaked bandages. Adrenaline sparked through Bill's veins. "Beth!" he screamed.

She groaned softly, and her eyelids fluttered. "Dad?"

"You're okay! What happened?"

Her eyes narrowed to slits. "Is it really you?"

"It's me. I can barely believe it myself. They let

me go," he said.

Beth's eyes flew wide; she threw her good arm around his neck and began sobbing beside his ear. "Do you mind cutting me loose?" he asked.

"Right! Of course..." Beth looked around quickly. Her eyes found Ashley's bag on the passenger's seat and she reached over the back for it. Pulling the bag down into her lap, she dug through it for a moment before withdrawing a gleaming silver scalpel.

"Careful with that," Bill said.

"Don't worry," Beth replied. She sliced his hands free and then leaned back to do the same with his ankles. Bill sprang up just in time to see a pair of armed men in black ski masks and blue-gray camo uniforms grabbing a familiar man in a baggy Hawaiian shirt. They roughly forced him to his knees, and one of them placed a rifle to the side of his head.

"Shit," Bill said. Not thinking twice, he launched himself over the driver's seat to the open door of the Humvee.

He fell out on the ground and twisted his wrist painfully in the process. "Don't shoot!" Bill screamed. The men holding Don—plus a dozen more—all turned to look at him in the same instant. One of the nearer ones shouted something in Mandarin and gestured to Bill with his rifle.

Don's eyes met Bill's with a dismayed look, and he gave his head a slight shake. Bill scrambled to his feet, and the advancing soldiers froze. Their rifles snapped up, and they shouted at him in Mandarin. Bill held his hands up and answered back in their language, mentally translating what he wanted to say — *"We friend. Have important thing to tell. Do not kill!"*

Close enough.

The Chinese soldiers appeared to hesitate and confer amongst themselves, taken aback by the fact that he knew their language. *And my ex-wife thought taking Mandarin was a waste of time.*

Bill smiled reassuringly at them and repeated, *"We friend!"*

CHAPTER 63

Bill explained in his rudimentary Mandarin that they were defectors with valuable information, but that they needed a translator to explain in greater detail.

After that, the Chinese reluctantly pulled Don to his feet. Two of them grabbed Bill, and another two went to the Humvee. They returned shoving Beth along between them.

"Be careful!" Bill said in Mandarin. *"She hurt!"* But the soldiers ignored him. They marched the three of them through the harbor and down the docks to a transport ship that was at least a hundred feet long, all matte gray angles and utilitarian design.

A dozen PRC marines joined them in a troop bay at the back of the ship. Two of them carried Ashley in and dumped her on the deck like garbage, and another two arrived carrying the dead Crawler between them. They dropped it beside Ashley. Bill, Don, and Beth were forced to sit on a hard bench along one side of the ship while enemy marines aimed rifles at them from all sides.

Then a deep thrumming started up, and the ship moved off. Don caught Bill's eye and nodded to him. "Good to have you back," he said through a smirk. "Should I call you Gibson or Bill?"

"What? Why would you call me Gibson?" Bill asked, shaking his head.

"Bill then," Don decided. "I didn't know you spoke Mandarin," he added.

"When I was going through my divorce, I needed something to take my mind off things, so I started taking Mandarin classes."

"Lucky us," Don replied. "Why Mandarin?"

Bill noted the suspicion in Don's voice, and he realized why. "Relax. It really is me. I took Mandarin because an old buddy of mine owned a hotel in Shanghai. When he heard I was looking for a break from LA, he offered to make me joint-owner with him in exchange for an investment."

"So you went to all the trouble of learning the language but decided to come to Kauai instead?"

"He went bankrupt before I could sell my business and finalize my divorce. I guess there was a reason he needed investors."

Don looked to Beth with eyebrows raised. "Any of that true, kid?"

She was leaning against the metal side of the

ship, her eyes shut, and skin pale. "Yeah," she said in a thready whisper.

A sharp pang of concern lanced through Bill, and he shot to his feet. "Beth—"

He took one step toward her before a marine jumped up and aimed a rifle at his chest. "Sit down," the man said in halting English. "We be there soon."

"My daughter is hurt," Bill replied.

"Sit!" the marine bellowed, and shook his rifle for emphasis.

Bill sat reluctantly, watching Beth with wide eyes, his hands restlessly clenching and unclenching with the impotent desire to help her.

"Well, shit," Don muttered.

"What?" Bill asked.

He shook his head. "If you're you, then my nana is probably back to herself, too, and I've got her locked in my basement like an animal."

Bill frowned. "She has food, right?"

Don shrugged, looking at his hands. "Yeah."

"Then don't worry about it. We'll go back for her."

"If we can," Don replied. "Seems to me like we're prisoners right now."

"Yeah..." Bill trailed off. "What exactly were you hoping to accomplish by getting us captured?"

Don arched an eyebrow at him. "Ideally?

Convince the Chinese to nuke the bastards out of the sky while we still can."

"What makes you think that will work?" Bill asked. "We don't even know where they are anymore."

"We have a clue. Commander Wilde mentioned that the air over the water on the North side of the island is suspiciously cold. I'm betting we're not the only ones who have noticed."

Bill shook his head. "And if they shoot down the missiles before they arrive?"

"No weapons, remember?" Don said.

"How do you know they don't have weapons?" Bill asked.

Don waved a hand at him. "Long story. Wishful thinking, maybe, but we have to risk it. Besides, if that was a lie and they really are packing heat up there, then we're fucked. At least if we fire the first shot, we'll go out with a bang. Their way looks to be a whole lot less pleasant—making us slaves. I'm guessing you know something about that."

Bill winced and nodded slowly. He'd been locked away inside his own body for three months. Compared to that, even a wash of nuclear fire sounded better.

* * *

Gibson grabbed the severed alien hand off his

belt and pressed it to yet another door scanner. A chime sounded, and the doors slid open. He ran down the deserted, gleaming corridor, just as he'd run down the last three, searching for something, anything, that might be critical to the operation of the ship—an engine room, a power generator... a big red self-destruct button. Gibson smirked and shook his head at the thought. If only it were that simple. The corridor went on for miles, winding through the ship past countless doors. He kept glancing at those doors, trying to decide which one he should bother trying to open, but they all looked the same.

Out of breath and seeing stars, Gibson slowed from a run to a fast walk. It didn't help that he was carrying at least a hundred pounds of gear.

He walked on for another fifteen minutes, heading for a distant set of doors, hoping to find something useful on the other side. Using the floppy white alien hand tucking into his belt, he opened that door, too—

And saw more of the same. Gibson let out a frustrated sigh and leaned hard against the bulkhead. How long would it take to walk from one end of Texas to the other? This was taking too long. It was a pity he didn't know how to use those mass transit capsules.

As he slumped against the bulkhead, a door

opened about two hundred feet away, and a pair of Hydras crept out, their heads turning every which way in the dim silver lighting.

Gibson brought one of his rifles up to his shoulder and aimed down the sights at them. He popped off a shot, and one of the two collapsed with a shriek. The other one darted back into the room it had come from, and Gibson heard the door slam shut.

He gave a predatory smile as he strode down the corridor to the wounded alien. It was kneeling and pounding on the door for the other one to open up.

"On your feet!" Gibson snapped.

The Hydra stopped hammering on the door and looked at him, all four sets of eyes wide and blinking.

"Shit, you don't understand me, do you?"

More blinking. Four sets of hands went up in surrender, and a guttural trill whispered from one set of lips.

Gibson frowned, his plan evaporating in a puff of smoke. There had to be some way to communicate his intentions. He needed a guide. Someone to take him to the sensitive parts of the ship.

Gibson stepped back, making sure he was out of reach, then shifted to a one-handed grip on the rifle and gestured with his left hand. He pointed to the alien, then down to the distantly-vanishing end of the corridor. "You lead," he said. "I need to speak to your leaders."

The wounded Hydra growled something that sounded like a question, and all four of its heads canted curiously to one side—all four sets of eyes were staring at the dead alien hands tucked into Gibson's belt.

Gibson gave the Hydra a cold smile and tried miming his intentions to the creature again, but he quickly gave up. "Just get up and start walking!" he yelled, shaking his rifle to indicate the far end of the corridor.

The Hydra made a strangled sound and then got up and began walking—limping—in the direction he'd indicated.

"Faster!" Gibson roared, and it picked up the pace—probably spurred on by fear rather than because it had actually understood him. Gibson trailed along behind the alien, frowning hard. They were still barely managing a stroll. At this pace he'd die of dehydration before he found anything. Gibson was just about to put a bullet through the Hydra's head—*heads*—when it darted sideways to a particular set of doors and pasted two hands to the sensor to open them. A familiar transparent capsule with rows of seats appeared. Gibson grinned and jabbed the alien in the back with his rifle. "Smart choice," he said. "Now let's see if you can pick the right destination to make me happy."

CHAPTER 64

Chinese marines shoved and prodded Bill, Beth, and Don down a bouncing metal gangway to an open door in one of the lower decks of a waiting Chinese aircraft carrier. Considering how few aircraft carriers the Chinese Navy had, Bill reasoned that this one had to be their flagship. That was a good sign. If he could get to speak to the admiral, there was a good chance that he wouldn't even need a translator. Anyone that highly placed in the Chinese Navy probably spoke English.

Glancing behind him, Bill saw a pair of marines carrying Ashley between them. She was still sedated according to Don, but Bill didn't like the pale, waxy color of her skin. Don had also mentioned that she'd taken a rifle round to her chest and suffered a collapsed lung.

As soon as they crossed the threshold and boarded the carrier, more blue-clad marines took hold of them and marched them through a narrow corridor.

Bill jerked a thumb over his shoulder to indicate Ashley. *"The woman need help,"* he tried to say—and earned himself a sharp jab from a rifle barrel. Moments later they emerged in a cavernous space with jet fighters on vehicle elevators—the hangar. Bill glanced behind him once more and noticed that Ashley was gone. A sharp spear of dread shot through him, but he calmed himself, thinking the marines had probably noticed her condition and decided to take her to their Med Bay. The remaining marines guided them along a winding path to an elevator platform with yellow metal railings for walls. One of them punched a simple up arrow on a dangling control box, and the platform lurched upward.

Beth swayed on her feet between the two marines holding her, and her eyes were half-lidded. She looked like she might faint.

"She needs to see a doctor!" Bill shouted in English to be heard over the sound of the elevator and the commotion in the hangar below.

"No doctor. Talk to Admiral first. Then treat injury."

"Fuck you!" Bill replied.

A rifle snapped up to the marine's shoulder, and he winked at Bill over the sights. "Bang," he said.

His buddies broke into peals of laughter.

Hot rage burned through Bill, turning his hands into fists and his blood to ice.

"Easy," Don whispered.

Bill forced his feelings down. Nationality wasn't the problem. War was the perfect excuse for people to let out their inner monsters.

The platform stopped, and the enemy marines ushered them out and down another narrow metal corridor to a sealed door. One of them opened it, and they stepped into a gust of warm, salty-smelling night air. From there they went up a long flight of metal stairs to the flight deck, right behind the carrier's control tower. Just as they emerged from the top of the stairs, Bill heard a jet roaring and turned to see a fighter streak across the deck with a squeal of rubber tires.

"Keep walk," one of the Chinese said and jabbed him in the back with his rifle.

Bill bit his tongue to hold back an angry retort, allowing them to shove him along into another elevator. This one was far smaller, and it had proper walls. Only four marines crowded in with them, leaving the others to run up a nearby flight of stairs.

When the elevator stopped, two of the runners were waiting for them with rifles already aimed, but they didn't look winded. Maybe it was an entirely different pair. It was impossible to say with all of them wearing black ski masks.

"Keep walk!" the one standing behind Bill said, jabbing him with his rifle again.

"I'm walking!" Bill snapped.

Soon after leaving the elevator, they came to another metal door, but this one was open, and a pair of masked marines were guarding it. The three of them were ushered inside. From the broad windows and high vantage point, Bill guessed they were on the bridge. Heads turned as they were shoved inside. One of the officers shouted something in Mandarin that Bill roughly understood to mean, *"These are the Americans?"*

Before the marine could reply, the officer spoke directly to them. "I'm told you have important information for me, but you could not tell my men because they would not understand."

Bill's eyes tightened as a tall man came to stand in front of him with shoulders squared and hands clasped behind his back. He wore a white and black captain's hat with gold braiding.

"Are you the Admiral?" Bill asked.

"Yes, I am Admiral Shengli of the People's Liberation Army Navy. Speak."

* * *

The capsule slid to a stop and Gibson hurriedly untangled himself from the web-like restraints to aim his rifle at the wounded Hydra. "Get up!" he snapped. The alien did so, probably understanding his tone and body language more than his words. Gibson followed it through the open doors of the capsule into yet another corridor.

"This had better take me somewhere interesting," Gibson warned.

The corridor curved around in a slow loop, and they came to a pair of extra-wide doors. Gibson frowned, wondering what was on the other side. The Hydra limped up to the door scanner and placed two hands against it. Gibson took aim, just in case.

The doors rumbled open to reveal another cavernous room with dozens of Hydras standing and sitting at stations arrayed in tiers of concentric circles on a clear floor. The walls and ceiling were equally transparent, giving a seamless view of stars above, shadows below, and a dawning arc of sunlight in between. The wounded Hydra said something in a trembling growl, and dozens of heads turned to look. All movement in the room suddenly ceased, and several Hydras leapt to their feet.

Gibson gave a predatory smile and stepped into the alien bridge. "You did good, stinky," he said, nodding to his wounded guide. His nose still hadn't adapted to the dead-fish smell of the Hydras. "Who's in charge here?" Gibson demanded. Not that he expected a reply.

But to his surprise, one of the Hydras came walking down a flight of glass-like stairs at the highest tier of control stations. It produced a black disc from a compartment in its shiny silver uniform and held it out in one small palm; then it barked and trilled something at him. A split second later, a small, halting voice bubbled out from the device in the Hydra's palm.

"I am in charge," it said. "What do you want?"

Gibson blinked in shock. "You have a translator?"

The alien said something else. "Rulers must be able to speak to their subjects and be understood if they wish to be obeyed."

"Yeah... about that," Gibson said, shaking his head. "You're going to have to find another planet to subjugate."

More alien sounds rippled out, followed by, "We like this one."

Gibson waggled his rifle at the alien and grabbed the other weapon from where it dangled by its strap. He aimed each of them at one of the alien's heads. "And I like putting holes in your heads, so we're going to have to come up with a compromise."

Four sets of eyes blinked slowly at him. "What do you suggest?"

"Leave," Gibson said.

"Impossible. We have traveled too far. There are no other worlds like yours for many light years."

"Seems like we're at an impasse," Gibson said.

More growls sounded, followed by trills and guttural grunts. "Not exactly," was all the translator said.

Gibson frowned. "All that for two fucking words?" Suspicion raised the hairs on the back of his neck a split second before he whirled around to see a Crawler standing behind him on two legs. Glassy claws flashed out, gleaming in the gloom. Gibson pulled both triggers just as alien claws shredded through his flak jacket and drew fiery lines across his chest. As he fell, Gibson glimpsed more Crawlers peeling away from the dark, transparent walls of the chamber. Crawlers were translucent, all-but-invisible in the faint light, with nothing but the blackness of space shining down on them. Gibson realized his mistake as the Crawler who'd flayed his chest open pinned him to the floor: the Hydras had plenty of weapons— living ones.

Jagged glass-colored teeth yawned wide. Gibson struggled to free his arms, but the Crawler was too heavy. It hadn't thought to pin his legs, though. Gibson snapped them up to kick the

Crawler off. The monster squealed, and reared back on its hind legs, giving Gibson just the momentary reprieve that he needed to bring his rifles to bear. Bullets roared, and the Crawler shuddered with dozens of impacts before it fell over, twitching and jerking. Gibson sat up, to find another six Crawlers rearing back, just about to spring on top of him. There was only one thing to do.

Dropping both rifles, he grabbed a frag grenade in each hand, pulled the pins with his teeth, and tossed them over his shoulders.

The Crawlers sprang into the air, and he had just enough time to grab another two frags. This time he pulled the pins and let the handles spring out to strike the fuse while he held the grenades. Gibson was dimly aware of Hydras trilling and growling at one another in urgent voices just before the Crawlers fell upon him and tore into him with claws and teeth.

Agony raked Gibson on all sides, but he gritted his teeth and bore it, knowing it wouldn't last long. The explosion from the first two frags shook the deck and pelted him with debris, and the next one wiped away the raking claws and gnashing teeth with a blinding wave of heat.

CHAPTER 65

When Bill finished his explanation of events, Admiral Shengli regarded him with a dubious frown.

"The quarantine was a lie, perpetuated by your government in order to maintain control of extraterrestrial technology."

"No, sir, it wasn't," Bill replied.

The admiral spread his hands. "Where is your proof? You cannot possibly expect me to take your word for all of this. The only part of your story on which we both agree is that the aliens never left. They are right there." Admiral Shengli thrust a hand behind him to point out the windows at the night sky.

Bill's eyes followed that gesture, and he frowned. One second the moon was shining through those windows, sparkling on the water and the flight deck below, and the next it was gone.

A moment after that, Chinese officers began exclaiming excitedly amongst each other and pointing out the windows.

The admiral turned to look and strode quickly up to the windows.

"Guess they got tired of hiding," Don whispered.

"Why now?" Bill asked. And then, just as suddenly as it had appeared, the dark shadow in the sky was gone, and the moon came blazing through the windows once more. "Must have been a mistake..."

Admiral Shengli began snapping orders to his crew. Then he snapped his fingers and pointed to Bill, Don, and Beth, giving an order to the marines holding them. They reacted by manhandling them toward the exit.

"Hey," Don complained. "Where are they taking us!"

"You're going to the med bay," Admiral Shengli replied. "We will see if there are any alien cells in your blood."

"In his blood," Don clarified, jerking his head to Bill. "The girl and I are immune."

"You will all be tested," the admiral replied.

"And what happens when you find that we were telling the truth?" Don replied.

"Then we will discuss your call for a nuclear strike, but the decision is not mine to make, nor do we have such weapons aboard this fleet."

"You're wasting time," Don warned. "They know what we're trying to do. If they can do something to counter us, they will."

"All the more reason for caution. If we fire the first shot, the result could be the same as it was for your fleet. Immediate destruction."

Bill's brow furrowed. "We fired the first shot?"

"You did. A torpedo sank one of our submarines. We were not as timid when we fired back."

"Hang on," Don put in. "You're telling me we surprise attacked *you*, and all we used was one little torpedo? Who the hell would be that stupid?"

"My intelligence suggests that it was the captain of a ship that you called the *Port Royal.*"

"The captain of the Port Royal?" Bill asked.

"Shit," Don added. "Now it all makes sense."

"What makes sense?" Admiral Shengli asked.

Bill hurriedly explained: "After we came in contact with the aliens and US Marines rescued us from the island, we were taken to the *Port Royal* and quarantined there for an entire week. The captain and crew must have gotten infected during that time. They were part of the quarantine. Don't you get it? We didn't fire the first shot! The aliens controlling the Port Royal did!"

"That is a convenient explanation."

"But it makes sense," Don added. "Think

about it. Would any Naval officer with the rank of *Captain* ever be stupid enough to start World War III without a direct order to do so?"

A thoughtful frown crossed Shengli's face.

"Would any of your captains do that?" Don pressed.

"No, they would not. We will determine the truth of the matter in the med bay. If we find the evidence you say we will, I will do what I can to convince our paramount leader to do as you suggest." Admiral Shengli gestured to the marines once more and repeated his prior command. They went along more willingly this time, but the enemy shoved and dragged them along anyway. Bill glanced at his daughter as they rode the elevator down from the bridge. Her head was lolling, and her eyes barely open. At least now she could get proper treatment for her shoulder.

Bill tried to sigh, but his lungs wouldn't respond. That was when he noticed how numb he suddenly felt.

No! Let me go! He screamed, but not even a whisper escaped his lips.

CHAPTER 66

Beth drifted in and out of consciousness. In one of her waking moments, she noticed Ashley lying on a steel table with a blood bag hanging beside her and a tube sticking out of her chest. Beth was glad to see her finally getting proper medical care.

The enemy marines flanking Beth half carried and half dragged her to a matching metal table and forced her to lie down.

A Chinese doctor came along soon afterward and loomed over her. A female assistant joined him, and then they set to work. Her consciousness fading again, Beth only dimly felt needles poking her—first in her wrist, then around her wounded shoulder. At some point her father ran into view with two marines in hot pursuit. He spat in the doctor's face and screamed something about them not laying a hand on his daughter. Beth frowned. Her dad would never spit in anyone's face, no matter how angry he might be. The doctor wiped spittle from his face with a sneer. Marines grabbed her father and pushed him to his knees, shouting at him in Mandarin. Beth wanted to intervene, but she was too sleepy. *Maybe this is a dream...*

Beth's eyelids began sliding down, driven inexorably shut by more than blood loss and fatigue. They must have given her something to put her to sleep. On the heels of that, a dark thought chased her into oblivion: her dad wouldn't spit in anyone's face, but the aliens who'd been controlling him would. *They're back!* Beth thought urgently, fighting to wake up. Her eyelids inched open, and her heart began pounding feebly in her chest, but no amount of adrenaline could beat the drug-induced haze. Beth's mind blanked.

When she came to, she felt much better—rested, clear-headed, and warm. She noticed a blood bag hanging beside her. Scraps of memory trickled back, and Beth recalled the strangest dream. Her dad had spat in the doctor's face. Looking the other way, Beth saw him and Don both lying on tables like hers, tied down with strips of bandage as improvised restraints. Beth frowned at that, wondering what she had missed.

"Why are you tied up?"

"Because your dad tried to infect the doc," Don replied.

"I'm not contagious," her dad insisted.

"See?" Don replied. "An outright lie."

"Dad... you know they infected you. Why would you intentionally spread it to someone else?"

"Whatever they did to me, it's over now," he said. "I guess I thought that meant I'm cured," he said. Lifting his head up as the doctor walked by, her dad said something in Mandarin.

The doctor nodded and replied in English. "Apology accepted."

Beth watched him walk over to a microscope on the far side of the room. The doctor peered through the lenses for a moment, then withdrew and shook his head. "There is no sign of any alien cells. None of you are infected. Or perhaps it would be more accurate to say that none of you ever were. It is just as the admiral said. The quarantine was a lie designed to protect American interests."

"Bullshit!" Don roared, struggling to free his arms and legs from their bonds. "He's infected! Someone else needs to look at those samples!"

Beth felt a chill come over her. "How long have we been here?" she asked.

"Do I look like a watch?" Don snapped. "I don't know! Maybe an hour? Long enough for that alien shit to incubate, apparently."

The Chinese marines began murmuring

amongst themselves, to which the doctor replied in the same language. He smiled and talked in soothing tones.

"Where is the woman who was helping him?" Beth asked. "Dad didn't get her."

"The doc dismissed her before she could get a look at our blood samples!" Don said. Craning his neck to glare at the nearest marine, he added, "That's pretty fucking convenient don't you think? Get rid of any educated witnesses and leave the jarheads behind. Please tell me one of you took biology."

The marines murmured some more, while the doctor went on talking in his reassuring voice. After a second, one of the marines stepped forward. "I know little bit. What I looking for?"

"You're looking for cells that are smaller than normal red and white blood cells," Don said. "They have hazy edges and web-like structures inside of them at high zoom levels. Depending what stain you're using, the alien cells might appear blue. You get all that?"

The man nodded slowly. "Small cell. Look like web like from spider. Maybe blue."

"Good enough," Don grunted.

The marine started toward the microscope, but before he could reach it, the doctor stepped in front of him and shook his head, saying something in

Mandarin. The marine argued with him, shook his head, and pushed the doctor aside to get to the microscope.

Beth watched the doctor's eyes dart around for a minute before he gave up with a sigh and went walking back through the room. He brushed by one of the other marines on his way, just as the one at the microscope began exclaiming excitedly about something he'd found.

"Busted," Don crowed.

The doctor spun around, a silver object glinting in his hand. Then it was sticking out of the nearest marine's throat with blood spurting out around it—a scalpel. The man collapsed. Before any of the others could react, the doctor grabbed his sidearm and began shooting.

Beth's heart hammered in her chest as bullets struck one man after another—perfect head shots, right between the eyes. Three men fell in as many seconds, leaving just the one standing by the microscope, but he had his weapon drawn now, too.

Bang! Bang! He pulled the trigger before the doctor could, and a sudden ringing silence fell.

"At least now you know we were telling the truth," Don said with a sigh.

Beth battled to rise, hurriedly pulling out her IV line while the surviving marine got on his radio to report what had just happened. Before Beth could completely sit up, she heard an inhuman screech and saw Ashley become a blur as she launched herself off the table.

"Look out!" Beth cried.

But Ashley was too fast and too close. Just as the marine turned to face her, she stuck the needle from her IV straight through his eye, and he crumpled to the deck, his radio hissing with static.

"Fuck!" Don said, pounding his table in a desperate attempt to escape his bonds.

Ashley rounded on them with a cold smile, and Beth dived off her table for the nearest gun.

"I wouldn't try that if I were you," Ashley said as Beth's hand closed around the weapon the doctor had used to shoot the other three marines. She hid under and behind Don's table. "I'm a much better shot," Ashley went on. "Four heads and eight eyes—we have spatial awareness that you can only dream of."

"Four heads?" Don echoed. "So Billy-Gibson was telling the truth?"

"Of course," her dad put in. "The previous operator's mission was to buy time, and the truth is far more distracting than lies."

Beth gave no reply, irrationally hoping that Ashley didn't know where she was hiding.

"She's coming," Don warned.

Beth heard approaching footsteps and tightened her grip on the gun. She braced herself, trying to decide which side of the table to dart out from, but her right arm was in a sling and weak from a combination of anesthesia and torn muscles. She didn't stand a chance against Ashley with her offhand.

"Come out, come out, wherever you—"

More footsteps sounded in a stampeding rush, cutting Ashley off. Then came raised voices shouting in Mandarin.

"I surrender," Ashley said, and Beth heard her gun fall with a noisy clatter.

Beth peered around Don's examination table. Seeing that Ashley had her hands up, she stood up from behind Don's examination table. Marines began shouting at her as she did so, gesturing violently with their weapons.

"Beth! Drop the gun!" Don said.

She dropped it at her feet, and then one of the marines came and grabbed her roughly by her arms. The jostling disturbed her wounded shoulder, and she cried out in pain. Her dad didn't even comment. So much for his concern about them laying hands on her.

Another pair of marines took hold of Ashley. She smiled smugly at Beth as if she'd somehow won the standoff. Don and Bill were cut free and hauled off their tables, while more marines crowded in. Beth watched the enemy checking their dead for signs of life and shaking their heads.

"We have to tell them what happened," Beth said, nodding to Don.

"There are no witnesses besides the four of us," Don said quietly. "Who do you think they're going to believe?"

Just then the enemy marines began hauling them out. "Hey!" Beth tried. "It's the infection! They're trying to hide it! Someone check the microscope! You'll see!"

But none of the marines replied.

"Are you even listening to me?" Beth yelled, as the four of them were escorted from the med bay into the adjoining corridor. "They're going to get away with it!"

The man holding Beth snapped at her in Mandarin and jerked her injured arm roughly, bringing tears to her eyes.

"I don't think any of them speak English," Don said.

"Where are they taking us?" Beth asked, glancing around desperately.

"If I had to guess, probably a firing squad," Don replied. "Sorry kid. Looks like it's game over for us."

CHAPTER 67

The Chinese marines took them back up to the flight deck and marched them right up to the edge at the back of the ship. All four of them were made to stand with their backs to the water, with the wind buffeting them, and several dozen marines aiming their rifles at them from point-blank range. Long minutes passed like that. Beth fidgeted nervously and glanced over her shoulder at the spreading white wake far below. Dawn had lightened the sky and sea to a rosy hue, but that didn't make the distant surface of the ocean look any more inviting. Beth had a bad feeling that if they jumped from here, they wouldn't survive the fall.

Raised voices shouted something in unison, and Beth turned back to the fore to see a procession of Chinese officers marching their way from the direction of the control tower. When they came near, a familiar-looking man stepped forward. He was wearing a white and black captain's hat with gold braiding. She vaguely recalled that he was an admiral, but couldn't remember his name.

"It seems you betrayed us," the admiral said. Beth noticed Ashley and her father trading faint smiles.

"It wasn't us!" Beth said, shouting into the wind. But even as she said that, guilt tore through her for trying to bargain for her life at the expense of her father's.

"Admiral Shengli," Don began, "you need to send someone else to look at the samples in the med bay!"

Shengli, Beth thought. *That's his name.* "Please, Mr. Shengli," she said. "You have to believe us."

"Silence!" he snapped. Then he pointed to her and Don and said something in Mandarin to the men who'd brought them this far. All eight marines marched her and Don over to him, then dragged them aside to watch her father and Ashley standing alone at the back of the flight deck. Beth had a bad feeling about it.

"There's no need to examine the samples," the admiral explained. "We looked at the security footage from the med bay. Watching Doctor Chen murder my marines is convincing enough."

"What about the attack?" Don asked. "Their spaceship is still up there. Did you get to speak to your president?"

"I am not at liberty to discuss that," Admiral Shengli replied. He nodded to another officer standing beside him, and that man barked a command to the firing squad, who abruptly raised their rifles to eye level.

"Wait!" Beth said.

All eyes turned to her, and she hesitated, struggling to think of a way to save her dad's life. Before she could, a blinding flash of light tore through her peripheral vision. It was there and gone in an instant, but left her eyes dazzled. Blinking green spots from her eyes, Beth turned to look for the source of that flash just in time to see another one. She slammed her eyes shut and clapped a hand over her aching retinae. All around her people were screaming in Mandarin, but no gunshots sounded.

"I can't see!" Beth cried.

More flashing lights tore through her hands in quick succession, lighting them brightly from within and revealing the squiggly lines of her blood vessels.

"Don't look!" Don ordered as Beth sank to her knees, disoriented. "Just wait for it to be over." Firm arms wrapped around her shoulders, forcing her into a fetal position.

"For what to be over?" she cried, but she already knew the answer.

"The Chinese are nuking the hell out of them."

"But... it hasn't been that long since we were in the med bay. How is that even possible?"

"ICBMs, baby. They're hella fast," Don replied through the on-going commotion on the flight deck. The Chinese voices sounded farther away now, retreating fast.

Beth looked up between flashes of light to see that her dad and Ashley were gone. For a minute she feared that they'd fallen off the back of the carrier, or that she'd somehow missed the cracking reports of the rifles that had killed them, but then she spied her dad peeking out from behind a square white tank of fuel beside a nearby helicopter. He was waving her over.

"There they—" Another flash of light stabbed her eyes from the sky over Kauai. The flashes were smaller and more sporadic now, but they still brought tears to her eyes. Don got up slowly, shielding his eyes against the glare to peer into the sky.

"Shit," he said slowly. "It didn't work."

"What do you mean it didn't work?" Beth demanded.

"I mean it didn't..." Don trailed off in a gasp. "Mother of—!" Suddenly a massive shadow appeared over the island and in the sky—but it was torn in a ragged line down the center. As Beth watched, the smaller, nearer half of the ship angled down and its leading edge began to glow bright orange.

"They did it!" Don whooped. "Those damn Chinamen did it!"

"Guess you're going to have to call them something else now," Beth suggested.

Don arched an eyebrow at her. "Fuck it, I'd bow and kiss the admiral's boots if he hadn't already run away like a little sissy."

Her father was waving to them again. Beth pointed him out to Don. "I think my dad and Ashley are on our side now."

"I don't know..." Don said.

More nuclear explosions peppered the sky with blinding pricks of light. Beth watched with a giant grin, heedless of the damage they might cause to her eyes. A few moments later, streaks of fire began erupting from all sides of the crashing spaceship, falling like meteors.

"They're evacuating," Don said. "Speaking of which..."

Beth couldn't tear her eyes away from the sky. The nearest half of the alien ship was already a third of the way to the water and blazing brightly as it fell. The other half wasn't far behind, heading for the other side of Kauai.

"Shit, we're in trouble," Don said.

"What?" Beth turned from the sky with wide, blinking eyes full of the dancing green spots like you get from staring at the sun.

Don pointed to the crashing spaceship, but her eyes remained fixed on him. "That thing is the size of Texas, right?"

Beth nodded slowly. "Yeah, and we shot it down!"

"You don't get it, kid! When it hits the water, the wave it kicks up is going to be like nothing this world has ever seen."

Beth's eyes narrowed in sudden concern. She'd been dazed from the light show and riding high on their victory. "But we're on an aircraft carrier," Beth said, glancing quickly back to the crashing spaceship. It was halfway to the water now. Maybe another minute from impact. "We'll just ride over the wave, right?"

"Hell no. It's going to rip this entire fleet apart and wash clear over the islands from one side to the other. The west coast isn't going to have a much better time of it. The only chance we have is to get in the air, and fast." Don nodded to the helicopters and fuel tanks where her dad had hidden. Not waiting for her to snap out of it, he grabbed her by her good arm and dragged her in that direction. "Let's go!"

"You can fly?" Beth asked.

"I flew Blackhawks in Afghanistan." Don pulled the back door open. "Get in!"

"What about my dad? And Ashley?"

Don hesitated, but before he could make up his mind, the door on the other side of the helicopter slid open, and Bill's head popped in. His eyes widened when he saw them, and he pointed over their shoulders. "Look out!"

Beth spun around just in time to see several squads of Chinese marines sprinting across the flight deck to reach them.

"Get in!" Don yelled again, boosting Beth up from behind and then flying in after her. Bullets came *clinking* off the doors, while several more fractured the nearest window with cracks.

"Keep your heads down!" Don said as he crawled into the front of the helicopter to get to the controls. Her dad and Ashley dived in from the other side. Beth curled up below the seats beside the opposite door and clapped her hands to her ears. "Shut the doors!" Don screamed.

Bill pulled Beth's door shut amidst a hail of *clinking* bullets.

"Are you okay?" Beth asked, staring at him in shock.

Her dad patted himself down, then nodded. "Yeah. Lucky me."

A whirring roar of rotors started up, and

muffled voices came to their ears, shouting at them in Mandarin.

Beth's dad locked the door just as they began pounding on it.

"Hang on!" Don said, and then the helicopter leapt off the deck and listed sharply to one side. Ashley screamed, sliding toward the open door on her side.

"Ashley!" Beth cried, swatting blindly to reach Ashley's hand as it flailed past her head.

Bill twisted around, swiping for her other hand even as her legs went out the open door.

His hand closed around her wrist, and Beth grabbed on with both hands before Ashley's weight hit Bill, nearly dragging them out together.

Ashley dangled from the open door. "Pull me in!" she screamed.

Gritting his teeth and bracing with his legs on either side of the opening, Bill pulled her back in.

The helicopter wobbled from side to side as if it were a dog trying to shake off fleas.

"I thought you said you knew how to fly?" Beth screamed to be heard over the sound of the rotors, but she could barely make out her own voice. Her dad reached around and heaved the open door shut, then he passed dangling headsets to Beth and Ashley. He put on a third as he got up and climbed into the passenger's seat beside Don.

"Holy shit!" he screamed, his voice roaring through Beth's headset. Heedless of the Chinese marines still shooting at them from the deck of the carrier, Beth jumped off the floor to get a look at whatever her dad had just seen. The first half of the crashing ship was just now hitting the ocean on the far side of the island, veiled and sheathed in a cloud-like spray of water that stretched a hundred miles into the sky. The monstrous ship stood up at an impressive angle, like the tallest, sheerest mountain in the world. The island of Kauai lay before it, but the massive shipwreck dwarfed it. Just then, a rushing wall of white water swept over the island, skipping over the mountains. The island vanished in seconds, entirely swallowed by the spray.

"Fuck!" Don screamed.

CHAPTER 68

"Have you lost your mind?" Bill demanded. "Why are you flying so damn low?"

Don gritted his teeth and shook his head as they skimmed low over the water, heading *toward* the wave that had just swallowed Kauai. "I have to time it!" he replied. "Can't go too high or they'll shoot us down!"

"I think they've got bigger problems," Bill replied.

Don shot a wary glance at him, then back to the fore.

"It's me again, damn it."

"That's what you said the last time, so you can understand my confusion."

Bill scowled. "The aliens have bigger problems, too. Whoever was controlling me is probably busy fleeing for its life."

Don didn't reply. He was too focused on the task of piloting the helicopter. The wall of water and mist that had swallowed Kauai was spreading fast in all directions. It reached the farthest ship in the Chinese convoy—little more than a gray speck from this range—and Bill saw it fly up and tumble end over end.

"Don!" Bill urged.

"Almost..."

Another ship flipped end over end, cracking in half as it did so.

"Don!" Bill was just about to grab the stick away from him.

"Now!" Don said and pulled up hard on a lever next to his chair, and they angled sharply up into the sky.

Just as well Bill hadn't grabbed the stick. Apparently, that lever controlled their altitude, not the stick.

The ocean fell away at a dizzying rate, and Don gritted his teeth as they flew toward the rushing wall of mist, but then he turned them around and had them flying the other way, back toward the carrier they'd launched from. Bill peered through a window between his feet at the massive ship. It appeared no longer than his pinky finger now.

"How high are we?" Bill asked.

"One thousand feet and climbing!" Don said.

Just then the leading edge of the wave hit the back of the carrier. It tipped up and flipped over

— 447 —

from stern to bow, and then the mist surrounded them, pelting them with heavy raindrops and shaking the helicopter hard. It plunged, dropping for several seconds, and Bill heard his daughter scream. They were all weightless.

"Don!"

"I've got it!" he replied. A few seconds later they were free of the mist and watching massive ripples undulating across the open ocean at speeds they couldn't hope to match.

Bill let out a shaky sigh and slumped against his chair. "Shit!"

Don nodded slowly but gave no comment. Bill shared a moment of silence with him as he realized that their survival was dwarfed by the millions who were going to perish when those waves came to shore all around the world. Tens of thousands of Chinese sailors had just died, along with the entire population of Kauai. And yet, Bill allowed himself a moment of selfish joy as he twisted around to look at Beth and Ashley. Both of them scrambled to buckle in, looking pale and terrified, but otherwise good. Their lives might be a nit in the big picture, but they still mattered.

"I can't believe we made it," Beth said in a shaky voice.

"Me either," Ashley replied.

"Can it," Don snapped.

"What's wrong?" Bill asked.

"What *isn't* wrong? You have any fucking clue how many people just died? My nana among them. Fuck! I should have taken her with us!"

Bill swallowed thickly and nodded. "I'm sorry, Don. You couldn't have known. Maybe she made it. Your place was in the mountains..."

"And that wave swept right over them!"

Bill winced. "She's in a better place. They all are."

Don arched an eyebrow at him. "If they are, we're on our way to meet them."

"What are you talking about?" Beth asked.

Bill shook his head, not getting it either. "What aren't you telling us?"

"Isn't it obvious? We're in a helicopter in the middle of the Pacific. The only land in sight is the Hawaiian islands, but they're all about to be washed clean as a baby's backside. Not to mention, there are thousands of alien landers coming down all over them. We're smack in the middle of a real invasion. Oh, and here's the kicker, I don't know what kind of range this thing has before we run out of fuel—or which way to fly to reach the nearest island. In short, we're fucked, ladies and gentlemen."

CHAPTER 69

"Land!" Bill screamed. "That's land, isn't it?"

"Son of a gun," Don said, letting out a shaky breath.

"How much fuel do we have left?" Bill asked.

Don's eyes dipped to the gauges in front of him. "We're on empty, that's for sure."

"Are we going to make it?" Beth asked.

"I don't know! Shut up and let me concentrate!"

Bill bit down on a rebuke. Now wasn't the time to argue. Silence fell inside the helicopter but for the endless thumping of the rotors.

Long minutes passed, and the island came into better focus as they drew near.

"It's big..." Bill said. "That has to be Hawaii."

"Sure as shit is," Don replied. "We're a bunch of lucky SOBs." He pointed to the horizon. "Mauna Kea and Mauna Loa are both over four kilometers high. No way the waves went up that far. And that means we're not headed for desolate flood lands, after all."

"But is there anything up there?" Bill asked.

"Yeah. The Gemini Observatory," Don replied. "They'll have supplies. Hopefully enough to last. Maybe even a helicopter of their own and spare fuel."

Beth and Ashley began whooping for joy.

"Settle down!" Don said. "We still have to make it there and land this bucket in one piece. And you better just hope none of those aliens landed next to the observatory."

"They don't have weapons," Bill said.

"Neither do we," Don added.

"What about Crawlers?" Ashley asked in a small voice.

"They can't come out in daylight," Beth added.

"They might wait," Don said.

"Stop scaring her," Bill snapped.

Don flicked a scowl at him. "After everything we've lived through, you'd rather we let down our guard and get ripped apart while we sleep?"

Bill frowned. The island swept in beneath them—a scene of unimaginable destruction. The beaches were gone. The jungles, fields, and towns likewise—not a scrap of life remained. Dirty, water-filled ruins stretched as far as the eye could see.

"Maybe we should go down there and try to

help..." Ashley said.

"Help who?" Don asked. "They're all fucking dead. We've still got a chance to save ourselves. Let's not waste it."

It took another fifteen minutes to cross the island to the soaring peak of Mauna Kea. The top of the mountain was wrapped in clouds, and the ground, racing by close below was covered in brown grass and patches of snow—a good sign.

"Why are you flying so low?" Bill asked.

"Low?" Don quipped. "We're almost four thousand meters up!"

"You know what I mean!"

"The air's thin, and we're low on fuel. I'm trying not to push it," Don replied. "Hang on, we're almost there."

The seconds dragged at an agonizing pace, and then a silvery dome appeared at the tip of the mountain.

"Is that it?"

"Better be," Don said.

They buzzed straight over the observatory, low enough that Bill could see a group of people standing around outside in colorful jackets—red, blue, and yellow. A few cars were even parked up there. As they flew overhead, those people twisted around and pointed up at them.

"I don't see a helipad," Bill said.

"Don't need one," Don replied, swooping back around and careening toward a two-lane road. The rotors hiccuped and then went on churning. "Hang on!" Don said as the ground came up fast beneath them. He hit the throttle for one last gasp, and they swooped up suddenly just before their skids touched down with a hard *thunk*.

"Terra firma!" Don cried as he reached up and killed the engines. "Let's go meet our roommates."

CHAPTER 70

—Three Weeks Later—

Beth stood outside the observatory in her borrowed jacket, watching as a pair of helicopters came thumping toward them, straining in the thin air to reach their location.

Relief spread through her like melting ice—something she knew entirely too much about thanks to the frigid air at their altitude.

"You ready to go?" Beth's dad asked, walking up beside her.

"Are you kidding?" she asked, furrowing her brow at him.

He smiled tightly back and pulled her close. Don, Ashley, and the six scientists who'd been trapped at the observatory before they'd arrived stood off to one side, watching the helicopters fly in. By some miracle none of the aliens had found them up here, and there'd been enough food and water to keep them going until the USS Enterprise (of all things) could arrive and rescue them.

While they'd waited, Ashley had made good use of the observatory's independent electrical systems and satellite-based internet to make contact with her superiors in Atlanta. They were relieved to hear that there was a simple solution to the alien infection, and that it wasn't dangerous—if you didn't count the possible side effect of literally losing one's mind—but the aliens had yet to try and take control of either Ashley or Bill again, and both Beth and Don had concluded that they'd lost the ability to do so with their ship.

It had been surreal watching from a place of utter boredom as news reports on the Internet surfaced with images of the real aliens being captured all over the world—fiercely intelligent four-headed monsters with chalk-white skin, eight arms, eight eyes, two legs, and absolutely no weapons of any kind.

Beth smirked and shook her head as the two helicopters touched down beside their stolen Chinese one. Two fire teams of fully-armed US Marines jumped out and came running toward them. *They should have thought twice about invading us.*

But that triumphant thought was tinged with the terrible knowledge of just how many people had died when the Chinese had nuked the invaders out of their foolishly low orbit.

Beth's dad turned to her just before the Marines reached them. "You ready to go see mom?"

Beth nodded quickly and flashed a quick smile. Her mom had lived, having found herself on the outskirts of LA when the evacuation alert came—but millions more had perished, including Beth's stepdad and pretty much everyone she'd ever known in LA. Her mom had been devastated. Beth called her every day on Skype, but there was only so much cheering up she could do through a computer screen.

The Marines arrived in a rush of boots and questions. They asked if she was injured or in need of aid, she shook her head and pointed to Ashley. They'd recovered fairly well over the past three weeks thanks to Don's EMT training, but there was only so much he could do, and a collapsed lung was a serious injury.

Don was already helping a pair of Marines load Ashley onto a stretcher.

"We're okay, Sergeant," Bill said. "Just get us out of here."

"Can do, sir. This way!"

Beth hurried along behind them, running toward the helicopters with the others and wiping happy-sad tears from the corners of her eyes. Don held Ashley's hand as he walked alongside her stretcher—something new and beautiful sewn together from the ashes and ruin. Don and Ashley had grown surprisingly close during their time together at the observatory. Beth couldn't help feeling a twinge of hope from that, like maybe someday she'd break through the haze of nightmares and panic attacks that haunted her to find something new and beautiful of her own.

Fresh tears streamed from Beth's eyes as she climbed into the helicopter behind Don. He glanced curiously at her as they settled into adjacent seats and buckled up.

"It's bittersweet," Beth explained, shouting to be heard over the roar of the rotors.

"Tell you a secret, kid?" Don yelled back.

"What?"

"It always is."

The End.

GET MY NEXT BOOK FOR FREE

Scott Standalones #2: Title To Be Determined
(Coming March 20th, 2019)

Get a FREE digital copy if you post an honest review of this book on Amazon and send it to me here:

https://files.jaspertscott.com/standalones2.htm

Thank you in advance for your feedback!

I read every review and use your comments to improve my work.

KEEP IN TOUCH

SUBSCRIBE to my Mailing List and get two FREE Books!

http://files.jaspertscott.com/mailinglist.html

Follow me on Twitter:

@JasperTscott

Look me up on Facebook:

Jasper T. Scott

Check out my website:

www.JasperTscott.com

Or send me an e-mail:

JasperTscott@gmail.com

OTHER BOOKS BY JASPER SCOTT

Suggested reading order

<u>**Scott Standalones**</u>
(Unrelated Standalone Novels)
Under Darkness (Book 1)
Book 2: Title To Be Determined
(Coming March 20th, 2019)

<u>**Rogue Star**</u>
Rogue Star: Frozen Earth
Rogue Star (Book 2): New Worlds

<u>**Broken Worlds**</u>
Broken Worlds: The Awakening (Book 1)
Broken Worlds: The Revenants (Book 2)
Broken Worlds: Civil War (Book 3)

<u>**New Frontiers Series (Loosely-tied, Standalone Prequels to Dark Space)**</u>
Excelsior (Book 1)
Mindscape (Book 2)
Exodus (Book 3)

Dark Space Series
Dark Space
Dark Space 2: The Invisible War
Dark Space 3: Origin
Dark Space 4: Revenge
Dark Space 5: Avilon
Dark Space 6: Armageddon

Dark Space Universe Series (Standalone Follow-up Trilogy to Dark Space)
Dark Space Universe (Book 1)
Dark Space Universe: The Enemy Within (Book 2)
Dark Space Universe: The Last Stand (Book 3)

ABOUT THE AUTHOR

Jasper Scott is a USA TODAY bestselling science fiction author, known for writing intricate plots with unexpected twists.

His books have been translated into Japanese and German and adapted for audio, with collectively over 750,000 copies sold.

Jasper was born and raised in Canada by South African parents, with a British cultural heritage on his mother's side and German on his father's, to which he has now added Latin culture with his wonderful wife.

After spending years living as a starving artist, he finally quit his various jobs to become a full-time writer. In his spare time he enjoys reading, cycling, traveling, going to the gym, and spending time with his family.

Made in the USA
Columbia, SC
16 March 2020